Show Biz Kids

Thanks for the support.

Show Biz Kids

Growing Up In Hollywood's Golden Age

Rick Karlin

To order additional copies of this book, contact:
Xlibris Corporation
1-888-795-4274
www.Xlibris.com
Orders@Xlibris.com
33554

Dedication

For Gregg and Adam whose constant love and support is cherished.

ACKNOWLEDGEMENTS

F or my friends and family, especially Gregg who have lived with the *Show Biz Kids* and offered suggestions, I appreciate your support and encouragement. I have deeply felt gratitude to Cindy Stern, whose friendship, insight and eagle eye was a tremendous help.

Although many events are inspired by historical events, the main characters in this book are purely fictional and do not depict any actual people.

1956

CHAPTER 1

Beverly Hills

As Angelina sat on the clown's lap posing for her picture, she felt something strange poking her between the legs. She knew that this was not the time to say something about it. The news photographers were there and her mother always wanted everything to look perfect for them. Angelina couldn't figure out why people from the papers needed to be at her birthday party. After all, it wasn't like her daddy was even there. Ever since he started on that new television show, he was the one the newspapermen always wanted.

It was Angelina's twelfth birthday and everything should have been perfect, but it wasn't. Daddy was away. Again. Since he'd gotten that stupid television show, he was never around anymore. She liked it better when he was on the radio, he was always home then. At least with him gone she wouldn't have to share him with that creepy Wilbur Wormly puppet of his.

"Hey Angie baby," said one of the photographers, "Lean a little closer to Koko, will ya?" As soon as she leaned in, Koko lifted up a Wilbur Wormly doll and made it kiss her on the cheek.

"My name's Angelina!" she snapped. She hated it when the news people acted like they knew her. If he knew her, he'd know that she hated to be called Angie, almost as much as she hated that damn puppet. But, like a good little girl, she leaned forward and smiled as she whispered to Koko. "Poke me with that needle dick of yours once more and I'll snap it off." Then she hopped off the startled clown's lap, smoothed the front of her blue and white pinafore, and headed over to the picnic table where her best friend Priscilla waited with the other kids for cake and ice cream.

"Yuk!" whispered Priscilla with a big fake smile on her lips. "I hate when the publicity department sends the press to kids' things." She popped a huge piece of chocolate cake in her mouth and said. "Did Koko get a woody again?"

Angelina got out of her seat and, still wearing a frozen smile, spun around, as if showing off her outfit, and said, "Did the pervert get a spot on the back of my dress?"

"Naw," laughed Priscilla. "I just recognized the look on your face. Do you think we should say something to your mother?"

Angelina almost passed the entire glass of punch through her nose. "God no!" she gasped, then realizing her mother was watching her, picked up a napkin and

daintily pressed it to her lips and surreptitiously mopped up a dribble of punch.
"She'd just make life unbearable. Besides, he's harmless. It's not like he would do
anything. Would you tell your mother?"

Priscilla seemed to ruminate on this for a while, then answered, "No, she'd
probably have to take a tranquilizer." This response made both girls break out in a
hysterical giggling fit.

On the other side of the spacious lawn, Ingrid Ferrara stared at her daughter.
She didn't like her to laugh too loud; it wasn't ladylike. That Priscilla Best child was
not a good influence. But then, how could she be, with a washed up drunk for a
mother? Ingrid supposed she should pity the girl. Her parents, Eddie Best and Rosie
Campbell, were both so troubled, and while that wasn't exactly a rarity in Hollywood,
it still couldn't be easy on the child. Especially if the rumors going around town
about her father were true. Ingrid shivered at the thought.

"Darling, did you get a chill" slurred Rosie Campbell.

"Just a slight one," Ingrid smiled back, wondering how the woman got so drunk
this early in the day. "Nothing to worry about."

"Someone must have walked over your grave," nodded Rosie.

"I beg your pardon?"

"It's an old superstition," replied Rosie. "If you shiver it means someone has
just walked on your grave."

"Better than having one foot in it, though, isn't it?" smirked Ingrid as she got
up to leave. "Excuse me a moment, I must see to the birthday cake."

"What did she mean by that?" asked Rosie, turning to one of the numerous fey
boys she always kept around her as her assistants.

"Nothing for you to worry about Rosie," hissed the young man. "Just another
catty comment from the ice princess. But, as Doris Day's new song goes, 'que sera,
sera'."

"I was supposed to record that, you know, darling," Rosie murmured and the
young man instantly regretted bringing up the title of the hit tune.

"Yes, dear, I know," he soothed. "And you would have done it much better,
with more of an edge. She does it so sweetly, you could contract diabetes." Seeing
that he got a smile out of her, he felt better. He motioned another young man over,
"Go get Mama another of her special lemonades, darling," he said to one of Rosie's
numerous sycophants.

CHAPTER 2

Jenny Mason looked at the big girls at the end of the table. They looked so beautiful. She knew Angelina was the dark haired one with the round face, and Priscilla was the tall skinny one. She knew that their daddies worked with her daddy sometimes. Even Priscilla's mommy worked once in a while, but only when she could stand up. She had heard her daddy tell someone that. Angelina's mommy didn't work, but even she was different from Jenny's mommy. Jenny's mommy was sick a lot. She and her brother Jonny would go and see Mommy when she was sick, sometimes. But not for too long, and they couldn't talk too much.

She liked it better when Mommy was feeling good, like she was today. When Mommy felt good, she would sing and laugh. Jenny looked over at her mother. As soon as she turned her head to look, her brother Jonny did the same thing. They did a lot of things at the same time. People said twins do that a lot. People said a lot of things about twins that Jenny didn't understand. Like how boys were usually so different from girls. But Jonny wasn't different; he was just like her. Before they made him cut his hair, no one could tell them apart. The only way they were different was that Jonny didn't like to talk. Jenny usually talked for both of them.

Mommy was sitting next to Daddy on a big chair. All the grown-ups were laughing, even Daddy was laughing. Jonny turned to look at Jenny and they both smiled. They liked it when Daddy laughed. He didn't smile much when Mommy was sick. Priscilla's daddy was taking Mommy's glass and going over by the man that looked like the man on television who sang a song about hound dogs. The man was shaking a big metal thing and pouring out drinks. Priscilla's daddy reached over and pinched the man's hiney. Jenny and Jonny started to laugh. Priscilla saw them laugh and looked over. She didn't laugh when she saw her daddy with his hand on the man's hiney. Jenny didn't understand why. It looked funny.

When Jonny saw her smile, he took his napkin and put it on his head like a hat. That made Jenny smile even wider. Then he made his "movie star face". He pushed his lips way out like he was going to kiss someone and he opened his eyes real wide. That always made Jenny laugh. Angelina laughed. Even Priscilla laughed, but not with her eyes.

CHAPTER 3

New York City

A t that very moment, on the other side of the country, in a smoky Greenwich Village nightclub, two couples were having dinner and sharing a bottle of wine. Nothing that unusual about such a scene, except that one couple was white and one was Negro. They were just two couples who were the best of friends. They didn't think about it much in New York City . . . in Greenwich Village . . . in this particular supper club. They knew their territory. This place was like home to them, one of the few places where everyone was welcome, regardless of their skin color. It was where they all had met.

Frankie Kaye, a stand-up comic, got his first paying gig at this very club five years earlier. He and Sonny Lewis, the club's headline singer, hit it off right away. They hung out together. Hell, Sonny had even taken Frankie in when Frankie got evicted from his old apartment, before Frankie married Rochelle. Now, both of them were doing all right for themselves. Both were married. Sonny's wife Lavinia had been a secretary at the office for Sonny's record label until she got pregnant a year ago. The families were joined together by friendship and business.

Sonny's record label! The guys could hardly believe it, his first shot at stardom and he made it. His first record, *You're A Part of Me* had gone gold, and then was followed by three more, including a cover of *On the Street Where You Live* from "My Fair Lady". Now, he didn't have to perform in basement dives like this one, even if they still liked coming here, it was a dive and they all knew it.

Sonny was working his way up to major venues, and good friend that he was; he was taking Frankie with him as his opening act. It worked out well; Frankie softened up the uptight white folks by making jokes about their friendship. It was a bit harder for Frankie when they played all-Negro shows. The audience was always a little cold at first, but they soon warmed up to him. They could sense that he didn't have a prejudiced bone in his body, that he was a blue-eyed brother.

The newfound success was even better now that Sonny was close to signing a television contract. Frankie was Sonny's manager, as well as his opening act, and Sonny always thought that it was the best arrangement they ever made. Frankie was the one who sold the idea to the television executives. He convinced them white folks would welcome a Negro singer into their homes, if he were presented the right way. Frankie had made it sound like the most natural thing in the world, even if he himself wasn't certain it would work.

Tonight they were celebrating their new homes. Buoyed by the new contract, each couple had signed long term leases on side by side apartments in the same building. It was one of those old townhouses that had been divided up into smaller apartments after the war. A pair of massive doors separated their apartments. They managed to unlock it so they could visit back and forth easily, but still have privacy. It was perfect and just a few blocks away from the club where it all started.

Of course, it was only in Greenwich Village that Negroes and whites could even think of living in the same building. The Kayes and Lewises weren't unaware of the realities of life, "on the outside", as they put it. But they seldom said the words aloud. Both couples were aware of the pain it caused, so they avoided the subject and focused on their good luck . . . and friendship.

CHAPTER 4

Beverly Hills

I ngrid Ferrara was angry. The servants could tell by her clipped tones, so they all stayed in the kitchen, dreading a summons by the lady of the house. There was no need for any of them to leave the kitchen; the lady was in her boudoir relaxing after the party.

Angelina was at the pool with her swimming instructor. No break from her lessons just because it was her birthday. Mrs. Ferrara was a tough taskmistress; she expected only the best from her husband, herself and little Angelina. Just as she expected only the best from her staff.

She was as responsible for her husband's success as he was, and everyone knew it. Angelo Ferrara was a ventriloquist of moderate talent. He made no attempt to keep his lips from moving. But, he had a twinkle in his eyes that delighted both adults and children. His "sidekick", Wilbur Wormly, was beloved by everyone in the country. But it wasn't always that way.

Angelo Ferrara came to America as a young boy. He was painfully shy and refused to speak English; afraid that other kids in his Lower East Side neighborhood would ridicule him. To help him learn English his parents bought him a ventriloquist's dummy. The plan worked. Eventually, Angelo began to entertain at neighborhood festivals. From there he moved on to Vaudeville, working the "B" circuit. One day, the trunk containing his dummy was shipped out to the wrong city. With just a few minutes to prepare before his spot, he sewed a couple of buttons on a sock for eyes, used a ripped g-string, given to him by one of the chorus girls, for a tongue and went on stage with his new partner, Wilbur Wormly.

His act didn't work as well with a sock puppet and the audience began to heckle him. It was Angelo's worst nightmare, but suddenly, Wilbur began to snap comebacks to the hecklers. Soon Angelo was ad-libbing an entirely new act and the audience ate it up. It wasn't long before Angelo and Wilbur headlined at the better clubs. A few years later, Angelo and Wilbur had their own radio show.

To spice things up, the advertisers asked Angelo if Wilbur would do commercials with their spokesperson, Ingrid Swenson. A former Miss Sweden, Ingrid was featured in all of Lucky Soap's print ads. Ingrid was a smart woman, aware of her limitations as well as her talents. She knew that she was no actress and appealed to Angelo for his help. Angelo tried to explain to the sponsors that, while Ingrid's peaches and cream complexion might sell soap in magazines, her heavy accent made radio work difficult at best. But the advertisers were adamant, Ingrid was in the commercials, or they were out.

The two performers got together and hatched a plan. They would make fun of Ingrid's accent and mistakes in English. They would even accentuate them. Angelo suggested that Wilbur should have a crush on Ingrid. It wouldn't be the first time Wilbur spoke what Angelo felt. The commercials were a big success, and Ingrid became an integral part of the show, and Angelo's life.

After a brief courtship, she made more and more decisions about the act, which was fine with Angelo. It was Ingrid who first predicted the death of radio and negotiated with the television networks for Angelo. Everyone insisted that she was a fool, that television was a fad, but Ingrid's instincts had been good. As one of the first big names to move from radio to the new medium, Angelo had an established show when everyone else was scrambling to find a place in the schedule. The advertisers were loyal and with good reason; Angelo had the most viewers, even that upstart Milton Berle played second fiddle to Angelo and Wilbur.

Ingrid knew Berle might prove problematic, but there were plenty of viewers to go around. Ingrid was a pragmatist, without the slightest shred of ego. When the show moved to television, she insisted that a new actress take on the femme fatale role. Ingrid had enjoyed the spotlight and used her beauty to help her escape the harsh farm life in Sweden, but knew that she was growing too old to get away with the sexpot role on television. Her sultry, accented voice was perfect for radio, but television cameras would show every wrinkle she got from the hours she spent in the southern California sun. Ingrid had no regrets about her new role behind the scenes. Angelo took the bows, but she called the shots.

Ingrid knew that part of running the show was publicity, but to her chagrin, she didn't have a say in that area. The studio arranged the publicity, while Ingrid tried to arrange a balance for Angelo between his career and his home life. That's what Ingrid was arguing with Angelo about at that very moment. That was the reason why the staff huddled in the kitchen.

"Damn it, Angelo," she yelled into the phone. "Today is Angelina's birthday. You should have been here. The show is on a break now; you could have scheduled your publicity junket a week later."

The angrier she got, the calmer her became. "Ingrid darling," he answered soothingly, "I wish that were true, but Marshall Field's had a new store opening this week and they're kicking off the new Wilbur Wormly doll. I couldn't miss that. I explained that all to Angelina, I even told her I'd bring her back a doll."

As always, his calmness spread across the telephone wires and into her body. By the end of the conversation, she had accepted his explanation. It helped that she knew he was a loving father. She often wished that she could be as close to Angelina as he was, they had that special bond that only fathers and daughters could enjoy. Fathers and daughters, mothers and sons. A bond without any kind of competition allowed for a special closeness. She had hoped to have a son, but after Angelina, the doctor told her she couldn't have any more children.

With a sigh, she undid her robe and took a swimsuit out of a drawer in her dressing closet. She'd join Angelina in the pool for the last few minutes of her swimming lesson. Mrs. Ferrara was a firm believer about the benefits of exercise. She was specific in her instructions that Angelina never miss a lesson, and with swimming, gymnastics, ballet, tennis, and horseback riding, there was always a lesson to be taken or a skill to practice.

As Ingrid headed out to the pool, she poked her head into the kitchen to give the cook instructions for dinner. "Nothing too heavy for dinner tonight, Alice. It will just be Angelina and me. She had enough at lunch to last a whole day. Just a light salad and some broiled fish, no bread, no potatoes and only fruit for dessert." She smiled. "And thank you all for the wonderful job you did for Angelina's party," she added as she let the door swing shut behind her. The staff breathed a collective sigh of relief.

CHAPTER 5

Hollywood Hills

Helen Mason returned from the birthday party and immediately retired to her bedroom. Justin knew better than to disturb his wife, so he helped Jenny and Jonny change out of their party clothes. Soon the twins were standing before him in their play outfits. He tried to get Jenny to wear something a little more feminine, but she insisted on the same blue jeans and striped polo style shirt as her brother. "Daddy," she said as she tilted her head to the side and smiled, "Jonny and I are building a tree house in the yard. I can't wear a skirt and blouse for that."

As usual, she charmed her father into agreement. Secretly, Justin was glad. He hated taking the kids to those Hollywood birthday parties. He tried to raise them just as he had been growing up in Kansas. He knew how ridiculous these Hollywood events could be. The only reason he agreed to take the kids to this at all was because he was pretty certain Ingrid Ferrara wouldn't let things get out of hand, and he was right. No merry-go-rounds, no pony rides, just good old Koko the Clown. It wouldn't be a Hollywood party without Koko. The kids all loved him, and he loved them.

Besides that, he needed to get some good publicity. His last movie had bombed. Why he had let his agent talk him into that big budget interpretation of the story of Noah was beyond him. "Don't blame your agent," Justin muttered to himself as he placed the children's clothing into the hamper. "You know damn well you took that role for the money." He had needed to pay for Helen's last visit to the "rest home". It set him back about $10,000 for the month, but it seemed to be worth it. Helen was happier than she had been in years. Why, she had even asked to go to the party today, and she hadn't done that since the twins were babies.

Justin thought back to the early days, when he and Helen lived in a cold-water flat at the edge of Harlem. He was just starting out on Broadway, getting small roles in big shows and bigger roles in smaller shows. Helen was designing costumes. Their joy continued when they first came to Hollywood, after he'd been discovered in one of Caleb Edward's plays. He then came out to California to star in the movie version.

Helen worked in MGM's costume department until ten years ago when she discovered she was expecting twins. It wasn't a difficult pregnancy, but problems arose soon after the babies were born. Helen got depressed and didn't seem able to recover. Justin even had to hire a nanny to take care of the babies. Helen stayed in bed with the drapes drawn; it went on like that for months. Then one day, Helen came out of her room, fired the nanny and everything seemed fine. For a while.

A few months later she sank into an even deeper depression. The pattern seemed to repeat continually, and each time Helen's periods of happiness were shorter than the time before. Justin held onto the hope, against all evidence, that it was all over now. Helen seemed to be recovering. The last couple of weeks she'd been like her old self. Well, not exactly like her old self, but a lot better. Why, she'd even had a long conversation with Ingrid Ferrara. And he saw her laughing with that nancyboy that Rosie always brought with her. So what if she had a headache, it was a pretty full day for everyone, and Helen certainly wasn't used to all that sun.

He walked over and looked out the window at Jonny working on the tree house. He looked so cute with that hammer. Justin made a mental note to have the gardener check the structure when they were finished to make certain that it was sturdy enough to support both kids. It wouldn't do any good to have the kids up there and . . . his reverie was interrupted by a bloodcurdling scream from Helen's room. He ran down the hall and saw Jenny standing in the doorway crying. As he got closer, he realized it was Jonny, not Jenny. He looked down at the floor and saw Helen; she had slashed her wrists. There was blood spattered all over the deep pile white carpeting.

Justin ran to the phone and called the operator, "Send an ambulance to 9000 Sunset Boulevard in Beverly Hills, there's been a horrible accident." He then turned to Jonny, "Go in the bathroom and get a couple of towels, then go down in the kitchen and wait for me. Mommy's going to be all right. She probably just cut herself by accident," he said, knowing that Jonny didn't believe him for a second.

Jonny didn't hesitate. Like most children of dysfunctional parents, he was remarkably adept at handling a crisis. He brought two red hand towels, ones that wouldn't show the stains as much. He rolled them into tubes and applied one to his mother's arm and handed the other to his father, to do the same. They applied pressure until the ambulance came. As his mother was being loaded onto the ambulance, Jonny went to his room, changed into his pajamas and went to sleep immediately.

CHAPTER 6

New York City, Greenwich Village

Rochelle and Frankie entered their apartment at the same time that Lavinia and Sonny entered their side of the flat. The walls of the old building were solid, but they could hear when the babysitter left. Soon thereafter there was a rap on the doors that separated their apartments. The doors were so heavy that it took Sonny and Frankie, each pulling from their side, to slide each door into its pocket in the wall. The dining rooms, or what had been converted to dining rooms in each apartment, were almost mirror images. The Lewis' side was actually a little larger, but not by much. As was typical in older buildings, the rooms were plentiful, but small.

"I don't know why we don't leave it open," said Rochelle. "It's not like any of us is that worried about our privacy."

"Touring together got me over that real quick," laughed Lavinia from the bathroom in their side of the building, as she took off her make-up. She had already changed from her cocktail dress into a robe and slippers.

Sonny entered the room from their kitchen, "I wonder why they had this door between these rooms in the first place?" he asked. "It's kind of weird. Each room on its own is really too small for a dining room, but with the doors open, it's a nice size."

"These were probably twin parlors," Frankie stated. "I've been reading up on buildings from this era. One of the parlors was usually a formal one for company. The second, back one, was usually for the family. Our bathroom was probably for servants, in fact most of the back part of the apartment was probably the servants' quarters."

"Oooh, baby," said Sonny. "Maybe I should have moved into that one instead of you, Frankie. Then I would be in my rightful place."

"Well you are the one holding the tray," Frankie shot back.

"Stop it, guys," Rochelle snapped, a bit too quickly. "You know I don't like when you do that offstage. We don't need that in our everyday lives. It's bad enough you have to do it when you perform."

Lavinia brought a cup of tea to Rochelle. "Something tells me you saw something at the club that we didn't. Was somebody giving us a dirty look?"

Rochelle took the teacup from Lavinia and passed her friend the sugar bowl. "You know me too well. There was a suburban couple giving us dirty looks all night long. I don't know how you three can be oblivious to it."

"Not oblivious," said Sonny, his speaking voice as soothing as when he sang. "We've just blocked it out for so many years that it's become second nature. Don't let it get to you."

"Yeah," added Frankie sipping his tea. "Things are changing, little by little. Sonny's television show is the biggest indication of that. It just takes time, that's all."

Rochelle sighed, "I guess you're right. All I know is that I truly love all of you. And, I don't care how rich or famous you guys get; my favorite time will always be when we all sit down to tea at the end of the day."

"One day at a time," laughed Sonny. "We're not rich yet."

"We will be tomorrow when you sign that contract," smiled Lavinia. "Rochelle, how about if we celebrate by shopping for new curtains for this room tomorrow?"

"Uh-oh," said Frankie. "We don't even have the money yet and they're spending it. I don't know about the rest of you, but I'm worn out. I'm heading to bed."

"Lavinia, sounds like a plot stop us from making plans," Rochelle responded. "How about if we look at some furniture for the nursery?"

"I don't think we need anything else for Francie's room," Lavinia answered with a puzzled look. "What were you thinking about getting?"

"It's not for Francie's room," Rochelle said with a smile spreading across her face. "I was going to tell you all at dinner, but we got so wrapped up in discussing the television show, I never had a chance. I'm pregnant."

Sonny and Lavinia jumped to their feet and began a round of hugs, congratulations and questions. Frankie just stared at her.

1960

CHAPTER 7

Santa Barbara, California

For years Camp Ori-Pahs had been the place for Hollywood's elite to send their children for the summer. Not only were the camp's owners Shirl and Jerry Shapiro great with kids, they were also discreet. Any problems that might arise were never leaked to the press. Shirl and Jerry also knew how to work the publicity game to the benefit of their star parents. Today was one of those days. There were always two parent weekends scheduled during the summer. The first, in late July, was a private one. Only parents of the campers and their significant others were allowed. It was a chance for everyone to let their guard down and act like real families, warts and all. This was a new experience for some of the participants, and one in which many of the parents felt uncomfortable, but the kids loved it. They didn't have to "act" for the news media.

Today's event was the second family day of the summer, the one to which the media was invited. To say things were a little tense was an understatement, but Shirl and Jerry handled it all with ease. They ushered the photographers and reporters with the same finesse they used on the parents. The Shapiros were sly; not one reporter felt as if they were being led on a leash, which of course, they were.

If any of the campers or their families seemed to be having a problem, a disagreement, argument, or a temper tantrum (parent or child), they were shown to Shirl and Jerry's private domain to work things out, away from prying eyes. Over the years, the Shapiros had managed to keep all scandals and bad publicity hush hush. One of the reasons they were able to do this so well was that they never hired outsiders to work at the camp. From the cook to the cleaning staff, all employees were relatives of the Shapiros.

All the kids working as counselors came from the homes of Hollywood's elite. None of them needed to work for the money, but they enjoyed the feeling of independence the job provided. More importantly, it gave the teens and their parents a break from the pressures of Hollywood. Their parents had a feeling that they were instilling their children's lives with some semblance of normalcy, and in a strange way, it was true. This was one place where they could do the things other kids took for granted. They worked as counselors, without having other kids jealous of them because their parents were famous. At Camp Ori-Pahs everyone's parents were stars or show business insiders.

Angelina Ferrara and Priscilla Best were senior counselors, 16 and 15 years old, respectively, and they usually loved their jobs. Right now, they were dealing with a situation. Jenny Mason was having a tantrum because her father had shown up with his new wife. Jenny hated Ani Mason. Ani had been her mother's nurse and personal assistant until her mother committed suicide. After that, she helped Justin Mason care for Jenny and Jonny. Eventually she graduated from au pair to Justin's wife and that's when the problems with Jenny began.

When Jenny entered her teens, she became rebellious, fighting Justin and Ani at every turn. Justin and Ani had not been prepared for this. Jenny and Jonny had both adored Ani before their mother's death and seemed to bond with her afterwards. It was only after the marriage that Jenny began to show resentment. She actually did everything possible to make life difficult for the newlyweds. If it weren't for Jonny's devotion to his new stepmother, and Ani's love for both of the children, the marriage might not have lasted through the initial few weeks. That was part of the reason Jenny and Jonny had been sent to camp. Justin thought that some time away would give Jenny a chance to come to terms with the new relationship. Ani wasn't so certain but deferred to her husband's wishes in this case.

At first, it seemed to be a good decision. Jenny's letters home began to show an acceptance that pleased the couple. Jonny didn't talk about the situation much, but when questioned, indicated that Jenny was mellowing. During the private parent's weekend in July, Jenny was distant, but polite. That was why this morning's scene took everyone by surprise.

At the first sign of commotion, Shirl and Jerry had ushered the visiting press into the dining hall for breakfast while Priscilla and Angie took Jenny aside. They were waiting for Ani and Justin Mason to meet them after taking some pictures with Jonny in the mess hall. Justin didn't work for the year following Helen's suicide as he recovered. Many said his career was dead. This was his chance to reenter the industry at the top. He needed everything to work out beautifully. Justin was back in the spotlight. He had just signed an option on the new book Growing Up Absurd. It was to be his first time producing and directing, rather than just starring in a movie. He didn't need any negative publicity right now; he needed a stable home life to attract backers.

Ani had been the best thing to happen to Justin. She had taken over after Helen's death, managing the day-to-day affairs of the house and helping with the children. Jonny adored her, and she filled a void in the lives of both of the men in the Mason household. Jenny had also adored Ani until Justin had begun to show an emotional attachment to the attractive brunette. Then Jenny had turned nasty. Perhaps she felt Justin was betraying her late mother. Justin worried about that, too. Was he replacing Helen too quickly? But the truth was, Helen had left him years before her suicide. She never recovered from her postpartum depression, and, as much as he loved her, he couldn't get close to her again. She wouldn't let him.

It was more than a year after Helen's death when Justin realized that he had fallen in love with Ani. It took him a month to bring up the courage to tell her, afraid that if she didn't feel the same, he, and more importantly, the children, would lose her. Luckily, Ani shared his feelings. They decided to keep it from the children until just before they married. Maybe that was a mistake; maybe they should have given the children more time. Jonny seemed fine with the new family make up, but Jenny was having a harder time adapting.

Jenny was sitting on the sofa in the Shapiro's cabin fuming. If this were a cartoon, smoke would be streaming from her ears, thought Priscilla. The image made her giggle, as she popped a piece of chocolate in her mouth.

"What's so funny?" barked Jenny.

"I'm sorry," responded Priscilla, she then explained the visual image to Jenny, who halfway smiled despite her anger. "Jenny, why the big scene out there? I thought you liked Ani." She offered the girl a piece of her candy.

"She's not my mother! I don't like it when she acts like my mother," Jenny responded through clenched teeth.

"I don't think she's trying to," added Angelina. "She's just trying to be a good wife for your father. What did she do that was so terrible?"

"I don't like when she tries to dress me up in frilly, girly things. This is summer camp. I didn't want to wear this dress," Jenny pulled the bow out of her hair defiantly. "She's always trying to change things."

Just then, Justin and Ani entered the cabin. Justin sat down next to his daughter; he took her hand and started to lecture her on her behavior. Ani stood behind them and saw Jenny's back become ramrod straight in rebellion. Justin wasn't getting through to her. Normally, she would have ceded to his decision, but she saw that this discussion was going to get them nowhere. She smiled at Angelina and Priscilla and motioned for them to leave. They did so happily, not knowing quite what to do.

"Justin," she said, as she settled on the sofa. "I think I'm the one who made a mistake. This outfit is inappropriate for camp. I'm sorry Jenny, you're right. I was just trying to help you look pretty for the photographers. Please forgive me."

"No, Ani," said Justin. "Jenny was wrong to behave like that."

"Justin," said Ani, eyeing him over Jenny's head, "Jenny is old enough to select her own clothes. Maybe she could have reacted better, but we're all under stress because of the press being here." She looked at Jenny. "I'm sorry dear, but I'm still new at this. Will you forgive me?"

Jenny looked at Ani's pleading eyes and knew that this wasn't just a ploy. Ani was truly sorry that they weren't getting along. "I guess so. Maybe I shouldn't have made such a fuss. It is a pretty dress."

Justin looked at his daughter in amazement. Usually she was so stubborn that she couldn't be budged, and here Ani had gotten her to admit that maybe her behavior was wrong. He shook his head in disbelief, "I have to admit we were surprised," he said. "After all those letters telling us how much you were looking forward to seeing us again."

"What letters?" asked Jenny, looking from her father to Ani.

CHAPTER 8

Priscilla and Angelina walked through the woods on their way back to the mess hall. Priscilla was really downing the chocolates, she was a little nervous, her mother and father were at the camp, and of course, her mother was already drunk.

"I envy you," said Priscilla. "Your parents aren't coming, you lucky dog." Angelina smiled and let her best friend vent her frustration. "Of course, even if they did, it wouldn't be so humiliating. Your mother never does anything to embarrass you. Want a chocolate?"

Angelina shook her head and her smile faded a bit. "Well, I suppose you're right. She never does or says anything in public. But my father's another story. Every time the press is around I have to pose with that damn puppet." Just then she caught sight of something out of the corner of her eye. "Did you see that?" she asked Priscilla.

"What?"

"I thought I saw someone go into the shed behind the Shapiro's cabin." Angelina explained. "Maybe we'd better take a look."

"Anything to avoid the inevitable," sighed Priscilla. "The news people don't even know about this area, so it must be one of the kids." They headed towards the whitewashed building. As they neared, they could hear muffled voices. They peered through the dusty windows of the storage building and saw the Shapiro's nephew, Sid, taking a couple of cot mattresses off of a shelf.

"It's only Sid," whispered Angelina. "He's probably getting some supplies. Let's go."

"Only Sid!?!?!" said Priscilla in amazement, she had a crush on the handsome 20 year old lifeguard/handyman. She peeked in the window. "You didn't say he was practically naked!"

"He's not naked; he's got on a pair of khaki shorts. He probably just took off his shirt so he wouldn't get it dirty. You've seen him in less at the lake," she responded impatiently. She didn't understand Priscilla's attitude toward boys. She talked like a tramp, but never gave any of the boys the time of day. Still, the boys followed her around like puppy dogs. Angelina wished they looked at her the way they looked at Priscilla. But Priscilla's long legs and slim body made her look like a woman. Angelina's soft roundness made her look like a kid. No matter how many chocolates Priscilla ate, or how often Angelina refused them, she knew their body types would never switch. She often wished she took after her mother's Nordic physique instead of her father's Italian peasant build. "C'mon, let's go."

"But this is so terribly, oh I don't know, surreptitious!" snickered Priscilla, proud of her expansive vocabulary. "Oh my Gawd!!! He's taking off his pants," she said wolfing down four pieces of chocolate at once. "Look at that boner sticking out from his underwear!"

Angelina, who had been walking down the path, turned around and started back, then stopped. "Oh no you don't," she chided. "You're not fooling me." But, something about Priscilla's labored breathing convinced her that this was no joke.

"Shit, he's taken his thing out and he's playing with it," Priscilla whispered.

"What thing?" she started to say, then realized what her friend meant. "I don't believe it."

Angelina peeked in the window and sure enough there was Sid in all his muscle-bound glory laying back on one of the mattresses stroking his throbbing member. "Wow, it seems big," whispered Angelina. "I never saw one before!"

Priscilla looked at her, "You're kidding, right?"

Angelina just stared back. This was the first indication she had that Priscilla wasn't a virgin like she was. "No, have you?"

"Once or twice," responded Priscilla, trying to sound blase' but not succeeding. "But never one so big. It's huge. It must be a foot long."

Then they heard Sid's voice, "Well, are you gonna do me or not?" The girls looked back into the window Sid was standing up now, his hands on his hips, his joystick bouncing up and down in front of him. "I'm all excited now, so get to it."

Suddenly, another figure stepped out from the shadows and knelt before Sid. It wasn't until the guy had his lips wrapped around Sid's cock that the girls realized that it was Priscilla's father. They stared in amazement as Eddie Best gave Sid a blowjob to end all blowjobs. The girls were frozen; transfixed as if watching a car accident, so it was no surprise that they didn't hear the footsteps behind them.

CHAPTER 9

J onny Mason hung his head sheepishly. When Jenny expressed amazement at the news about her letters from camp, it didn't take long for everyone to figure out that Jonny had written them. "I just wanted everyone to get along," Jonny admitted. "Jenny was so angry all the time it made me sad. And I knew that Daddy wasn't happy either."

Justin Mason took the boy's chin in his hand and lifted his face. "Jonny, we appreciate why you did this, but it's wrong. Do you understand that?" Without realizing it Justin had dropped his voice into his Academy Award winning baritone.

Jonny trembled at the sound of his father's voice; He was easily upset by any show of anger or disapproval. He was so nervous that he could feel urine seeping into his underpants. It was only by focusing all of his attention to his urethral muscle that he was able to stop the dribble before it became a flow.

Jenny, sensing her brother's nervousness, piped in, "Daddy, I think Jonny did the right thing. After all," she said cocking her head to the side and smiling broadly, "Everything's turned out all right. Hasn't it, Ani?"

Ani smiled at the young girl, fully aware that she was manipulating the situation. "Yes, I guess so. Don't you think so Justin?"

Justin moved his hand from his son's chin to the top of his head and tousled his hair. "I guess so. How about if we all head over to the mess hall for breakfast? I'm starved." Jenny reached for her father's hand and led the way.

Jonny looked up at Ani gratefully and tenuously put out his hand. Ani smiled broadly and took it, letting him escort her to the mess hall as grandly as if they had been walking down the aisle at the Academy Awards.

CHAPTER 10

Central Georgia

Frankie and Sonny loaded the last of the suitcases into the trunk of the rental car. They were feeling light-hearted after finishing a successful run at the Eden Roc, but the south's sweltering summer sun made them happy that the car was air-conditioned. They could have flown home, or taken the train, but both men were grateful for a little down time. The drive to New York would allow them to relax a bit before beginning a night club engagement at the Gotham Club.

As they hit the road, Lavinia and Rochelle settled into the back of the luxurious Cadillac with five year old Francie sleeping on Lavinia's lap, and Richie in his favorite place, on the pull down arm rest between them. Rochelle was busy crocheting a new dress for her goddaughter. Lavinia was sorting through the contracts for their next gig and reviewing the books from the last engagement. Lavinia's head for figures proved to be quite an asset. As the partners' career took off, she became their de facto business manager, and the financial brains in their extended family.

"You guys did quite well. The profits from that gig generated more income than you did in your entire first year," she laughed.

Frankie looked over his shoulder and winked, "That's because we have a sharp business manager."

"I can't believe that you got the management to pay the rent for that beautiful house for the month," chirped Rochelle as she counted her stitches. "It was so much better than staying at the hotel."

"I don't think they minded. It was better than having a four and five year old on the property, and it avoided a whole lot of issues for them," Sonny chuckled.

"More privacy, too," laughed Frankie. "Wow, we're making great time. Georgia's northern border is only 60 miles away. Let me know when you want me to take over the driving Sonny, I'm going to catch a few winks," he said, as he slouched down and pulled his straw hat over his eyes.

Sonny was about to answer when a loud explosion silenced him. The car began to swerve and Sonny was only able to guide it to the side of the road by sheer luck. They all got out of the car, Lavinia clutching the crying Francie, Rochelle holding Richie's trembling hand.

"I suppose we're lucky, we could have easily gone into oncoming traffic," stammered Sonny, shaken by the accident.

"What traffic?" asked Frankie, "We're in the middle of nowhere." It was then that he noticed Sonny staring at the side of the road. He saw two men carrying shotguns.

"Well, looky here," said one of them, "We got us a zebra-mobile. It's black and white." He laughed uproariously at his own joke.

"What are you folks doin' here?" asked the second suspiciously.

Frankie went into full charm mode automatically, "Hi guys. I'm real glad to see you. Sonny here was driving, and we got a blow-out. Is there a service station anywhere near here? We're going to New York and we're in a real hurry. There's twenty bucks in it if you can help us out," he said, pulling the cash from his wallet.

"Why don't you have the boy change the tire?" asked the shorter of the two.

Frankie took one look at the seething Sonny and rushed ahead, "Well, it's not our car, and I'm not sure either of us could figure it out."

"City folks shouldn't be driving the back roads if'n you don't know how to fix a flat," said the taller one, as he glanced sideways at his cohort.

"You're probably right," Frankie said. "But, Sonny and I are in show business, and we don't know anything about cars."

"Show business?!?!" the bumpkins asked.

"Yeah, this is Sonny Lewis, the singer," answered Frankie. "Have you heard of him?"

"Sure have," one said spitting on the ground. "My wife said that if he wasn't a nig . . . colored man, she'd marry him, he sounds so good."

"Well isn't that nice," charmed Frankie as he swallowed his bile. "You look as if you know a thing or two about automobiles."

"I ain't met a car I couldn't fix," said the taller one, smiling and showing an expanse of gums. "Twenty bucks you say?"

"I'll make it fifty and an autographed record from Sonny, if you can get us back on the road in 15 minutes," smiled Frankie, reaching back into his wallet.

Rochelle felt uncomfortable, exposed, standing next to the men. "Lavinia," she stammered, "Let's take the kids and sit in the shade under that tree. Sonny, can you please bring the kids' toys over here?"

The women sat on the side of the road while the two locals changed the tire with a speed that was truly amazing. Sonny came over and helped Lavinia and Rochelle pack up the kids' things when the men were done. They settled into their original positions as Frankie charmed the locals and thanked them. It seemed to take forever before the two men ambled back into the woods, clutching Sonny's record like it was pure gold.

Frankie got in the car and let out a sigh of relief, "Well, I'm glad that's over" he said as Sonny started the car. "I thought it was going to get ugly for a minute."

"It would have if you weren't here," said Lavinia as she opened the ledger book and added $50 to the expense listings. "Those two might just as well have had on their sheets."

Sonny started the car, barely able to repress the anger he felt. The only reason he didn't scream was because he didn't want to upset the kids. They drove along for hours; the only sound breaking the tense silence was the tapping of Rochelle's crochet hook against the car door.

CHAPTER 11

Santa Barbara, Camp Ori-Pahs

"There you are darling!" chirped Rosie Campbell as she carefully negotiated the gravel path. She had on black Capri pants and an oversized white blouse, her short curly hair swept off her face with a red chiffon scarf. She looked like a movie star even in such a simple outfit; it was the result of all those years at the studio as a child. She radiated an aura that was unmistakable. If she were wrapped in a horse blanket from head to toe, you'd still know it was Rosie Campbell. Even though she was wearing flats, she walked carefully, her sense of balance deteriorated after years of alcohol abuse.

Priscilla spun around, away from the window of the Shapiro's cabin at the sound of her mother's voice. Angelina reacted a moment or two later. Rosie gave no indication of realizing that something was wrong in the split second that Priscilla took to compose herself.

"I was looking for you," Rosie continued. "Your father and I have some interesting news. Have you seen him yet, dear?"

"No!" Priscilla responded. "Let's go see if he's up at the camp waiting for us." She started to lead her mother back up the path with Angelina. "Joey, c'mon," she called to her mother's fey assistant as he began to peer into the window of the shed. His eyes widened for a split second and then he hurried away from the window, helping the girls hustle Rosie up the hill.

"I've got the most wonderful news," Rosie said as she slipped her arm around her daughter. "I'm going to New York this fall and you're coming with me."

"New York?" queried Priscilla, "For how long?"

"Hopefully for months and months," laughed Rosie. "I've been asked to take the lead in a Broadway musical and I said yes."

"Broadway?" echoed Priscilla, still stunned.

"Yes," giggled Rosie like a schoolgirl. "They figured if Ethel Merman can still pull them in with something like 'Gypsy', then I can do even better. We'll open right after the holidays. Since they don't seem interested in making musicals here in Hollywood, I thought, 'Why not?' I haven't even gotten to the best part," smiled Rosie. "Oh, Joey, I'm too excited. You tell her."

Joey relished being the center of attention and waited a full five seconds before continuing, "Your mother's going to star, and you can have a part in the chorus. She's even arranged a tutor, so you won't miss any school. Isn't your mother the greatest, you lucky girl?!?!"

"The greatest," echoed Priscilla. "Yeah, the best."

CHAPTER 12

Beverly Hills-a few weeks later

Priscilla and Rosie came home from shopping in preparation for their trip to New York. Priscilla carried an armload of packages, as did one of Rosie's boys. Rosie carried a small shopping bag and her beloved dachshund, Fritzie. "I'm so excited that we found that lovely little suit for you, honey. You'll see, New York is much more formal than we are out here in California. You'll have to dress up more often. Gloves, hat, the whole shebang," Rosie bubbled.

Priscilla was amazed; she had never seen her mother like this. She was almost . . . normal. She was drinking much less, and had daily voice lessons. She was really taking this New York thing seriously. Priscilla couldn't help but get caught up in the excitement. She couldn't wait to show Daddy her new outfits. He always knew just how to assemble things. He may have moved from costume designer to film director, but he still had a costumer's eye and could show her how to look her best.

"I still can't believe that Edith Head stood you up for that appointment," hissed the young man carrying the packages. "That's no way to treat a star of your magnitude."

"Relax honey," cooed Rosie. "You're too upset. I can't expect Edith to drop everything for me. She's being paid to do costumes for that new film. How was Edith to know that Marilyn would gain fifteen pounds and she'd have to have her entire wardrobe altered? These things happen."

"Well it's not like Edith was going to sit behind the sewing machine herself." he fumed. "That big dyke could have delegated the work to an assistant."

"That's not how it's done. Marilyn's a big star now. Edith has to see to these things herself. I've had my day. Besides, you're angry enough for all of us."

"Rosie, your day's not over yet," he hissed. "I just can't believe how calm you're being about this."

"Well, it wouldn't do any good for me to pitch a fit," she responded. "And besides, this gives Priscilla and me a chance to spend some time with her father, doesn't it honey?"

Priscilla brightened up. "Right, Mommy. I can't begin to tell you what a nice surprise this will be."

Rosie smiled. You two take those packages upstairs; I'll go out to your father's studio and get him. She headed through the sliding doors in the den to the pool house, which had been converted to a studio for Eddie when they bought the property. Rosie glanced over at the truck from the pool maintenance company and saw that it was parked a bit too close to the rose bushes. She'd have to remember to ask the housekeeper to speak to the pool boy.

The door to Eddie's studio was ajar and as Rosie pushed the door open, she saw Eddie, stark naked, bent over the rattan sofa. The pool boy was behind him, his pants around his ankles. He was sodomizing Eddie with great energy. Eddie had his eyes closed and was moaning in pleasure. It took Rosie a second to register exactly what was going on, then she quietly stepped back, shut the door and returned to the main house.

She saw her housekeeper as she entered, "Phyllis, be a darling and go find the pool man and have him move his truck. He's crushing the roses." After Phyllis left, Rosie picked up the phone and called her lawyer. "Phil, this is Rosie, I want you to start divorce proceedings immediately. Just use irreconcilable differences. Eddie won't fight it. I want to make a clean start in New York, so rush this along." She then turned and headed upstairs where Priscilla was waiting.

1961

CHAPTER 13

New York City, Times Square

B ack stage at *the Ed Sullivan Show*, things were tense. Andy Williams, who was supposed to preview Henry Mancini's new song, had laryngitis. The show's director was frantically scrambling for a replacement. On top of this insanity, he still hadn't decided what to do with another of the show's guests, chess champ Bobby Fischer. He couldn't very well sit and play chess on national television and during rehearsal his explanation of the game had been a real yawner. Angelina Ferrara was supposed to do a bit with her father but was busy throwing a temper tantrum.

"Why do I have to do this?" Angelina whined in her father's dressing room. The only reason she had wanted to come on the trip was that her parents had promised her that she could see Priscilla in her mother's new Broadway show. Priscilla and Angelina had spoken long distance at least once a week since Priscilla's mother may have dragged her away to New York, but distance had made the girls even better friends.

"Angelina, cara mia," soothed her father. "Please. I don't usually ask you to do this. It's a special favor. This is a family show; they want to show my family."

"Let Mother go on with you like she used to," snapped Angelina petulantly. "She's used to performing. I don't want anything to do with that puppet. I'm almost 18 years old. Don't you think I'm a little old to play with a puppet?"

"Ingrid, do something," pleaded her father. It broke Angelina's heart to see him so pathetic. Since his show was canceled, he hadn't been the same. He used to protect her from everyone, but now he was so desperate for work and exposure that he'd begged her to perform with him.

"Angelina," Ingrid said firmly. "You knew that this was part of the plan when we came out here. You're just a little frightened, that's all. Don't worry; people won't really be watching you. They always stare at the puppet. They won't even notice you, but you need to be there."

Angelina fumed at this last comment. They wouldn't even notice her! Her mother was right; she had agreed to do this. "Just this once and then never again," she said.

Both of her parents breathed a sigh of relief. "Angelina, honey, we appreciate it. Your father and I are going to talk to the director. We'll be right back." They shut the door to the dressing room and began talking quietly as they walked away.

Angelina walked over to her father's make-up table and opened the carrying case that held the infamous Wilbur Wormly. She took it out and went over to the small sofa in the corner. She held Wilbur up and began cursing at him. "Damn you! I wish Daddy paid half as much attention to me as he does to you."

She sat down and put the puppet between her legs to steady it and began twisting its wooden neck back and forth. She knew that the puppet felt nothing, but it gave her gratification none the less. As she started wringing its neck, the puppet slipped and she clenched her legs together tighter to hold on to it. The puppet now pressed tight against her upper thigh. She felt a tingling that she had not experienced before. The sensation increased as she moved the puppet between her legs and higher. A shiver ran through her as she brought the wooden form up higher between her legs, rubbing it against her panties. A sheen of perspiration developed on her forehead and she pushed the puppet's tail end harder against herself. Her fingers pulled her panties aside and she rubbed Wilbur against herself harder and harder, the painted enamel coating becoming slick with her lubrication. The tingling grew more and more insistent. She lay back on the sofa and pulled her panties around her knees. She leaned back and took Wilbur's tapered tail end and inserted it in her vagina. Soon she had the tail end of the puppet deep inside of her, thrusting up to meet it and panting like a collie.

Angelina had read her share of forbidden novels, but she never imagined that the pleasure could be so divine. The puppet's smile seemed to be an obscene leer, so she turned it to face away from her. The twisting of the object between her moist vaginal lips sent her over the edge of her first orgasm. She writhed back and forth, her thighs clutching the doll tightly. It was like nothing she had ever experienced.

She was in such a state of pure lust that she didn't hear the door open as her mother and father returned from their meeting with the show's director. They both stood at the entrance to the dressing room staring at their daughter in disbelief. Angelo's gasp brought Angelina back to earth with a shock.

There was no use denying what had happened. Angelina was chaste, but not so innocent that she hadn't known what she had done. Her mother shut the door and guided her father to a chair at his make up table as he wept silently.

CHAPTER 14

Beverly Hills

Justin Mason sat on the bleachers with the rest of the fathers cheering on his son. No one was more delighted than he was when Jonny had asked to join the junior high school baseball team. Even Jonny seemed surprised by the fact that he had a natural affinity for the sport. It was his one chance to shine.

In every other aspect of his life Jenny was the outstanding one. She was a better student, a fine singer, and a gifted speaker, heading up the school's debate team. Jonny made only slightly better than average grades and preferred to take part in more of the school's behind the scenes activities. Jenny starred in the school play; Jonny built the sets and filled in on crowd scenes. Jenny was class president and on the honor roll. Jonny was in the chess team and head of the Audio-Visual Club. He didn't seem to mind; in fact he idolized his twin sister. To Jenny's credit, she always made certain that Jonny was included in her social activities. His gentle good looks and kindness ensured that he always had a girlfriend, usually the same girl for a year or so. Jenny had a different boyfriend every semester, usually three or four boyfriends at a time.

Justin and Ani sat on the benches along with the other parents cheering on their son as he struck out yet another player from the opposing team. Jenny cavorted on the bench with the other cheerleaders, waiting for the break between innings to do a new routine. Every once in a while she glanced over her shoulder to see if her parents were watching. Ani always was. She didn't understand baseball, but she understood Jonny. He talked to her all the time. He had accepted her as a part of his life. Not his mother, but someone who loved him and cared about him. Not Jenny. Jenny was polite towards Ani, but remained aloof. Ani felt as if she would never break through the wall Jenny had erected.

"She gives me the creeps," Jenny whispered to the girl next to her on the bench. "She's always staring at me."

"That's what mothers do," responded the girl as she watched the game. "My mother stares at me all the time."

"She's not my mother!" Jenny hissed, a little louder than she intended to.

"It doesn't matter," said her friend. "They all stare at us. I think they forgot what it's like to be young."

"She's only ten years older than I am," said Jenny.

"Really? Wow, she's the same age as my sister."

Jenny stood up, "I'll be right back, I have to go to the bathroom."

"Don't be too long we have . . . ow. That was my foot you stepped on," shrieked the girl.

"Sorry," said Jenny. She turned around, smiled and headed off under the grandstand where Ani couldn't see her. She lit a cigarette, inhaled deeply and leaned against a support beam. Within a few seconds she was joined by one of her numerous boy friends, Terry Cozanicki. Terry was as big and dumb as they come, but he was handsome and he had something else that Jenny appreciated; a very active libido.

"Hey, Jenny," he called. "Aren't you worried that the coach will miss you?"

Jenny smiled at him "There's only one out and even my brother's not foolproof. There's at least 15 minutes before the inning's over. I think that's enough time, don't you?"

"I guess so," he said unzipping his fly. "If you want to, I'm not going to argue." He hauled out ten inches of flesh, already firming up in his hands. Jenny wrapped her lips around his cock, taking extra pleasure in the fact that her father and Ani were sitting not more than ten feet above her oblivious to the action taking place below.

CHAPTER 15

New York City, Greenwich Village

Sonny Lewis almost fell off his kitchen chair when Frankie delivered the good news. "They want me to fill in for Andy Williams? And I get to preview a Henry Mancini song?"

"Yeah, pretty good, huh," responded Frankie. "So, do you want to do it?"

"What kind of question is that? Of course I do. The question is, can I learn it in time?" he worried aloud.

"You're a musical genius, or haven't you been reading the press releases we've sent out about you?" Frankie laughed. "Henry Mancini himself will coach you this afternoon and they're going to have it set up like a rehearsal session, sheet music in front of you, the whole bit. You'll be fine, let's get over to the studio now. You've only got three hours until show time."

At that moment, Lavinia came into the kitchen. "There's something wrong with Francie, she's got a really high fever. I can't get her to stop crying. I think that we should take her to the hospital."

Frankie and Sonny just stared at each other. Frankie took charge, "Sonny, you grab a cab to the studio. Lavinia, go get Francie ready, I'll get the car and take you to the hospital." And, as if they had dealt with crises like this every day, they all proceeded to do what needed to be done in a calm, almost numb, fashion. Lavinia scooped up the six-year-old as if she were a doll, grabbed her purse and coat and headed toward the door.

She passed Sonny on the way to the door; he gave her a quick hug and told her everything would be all right. "Let Rochelle know what's happening," she called as she headed to the curb where Frankie already had the car running.

Sonny nodded automatically. It wasn't until that moment that he realized that he didn't know where Rochelle and Richie were.

CHAPTER 16

New York City, Midtown

Rochelle wrapped herself in her arms as she spoke to the kindly woman in the overstuffed chair; "It's so hard to keep up the charade. I feel as if one day something's going to happen and everyone will find out what a liar I've been."

"Do you want everyone to find out?" her therapist asked, as she idly twirled a lock of hair between her long, elegant, fingers.

"God, no," Rochelle spat out in an almost reflex reaction. "I hope that never happens. It would be disastrous."

"Why?"

"Why?!?!?! Well for one thing, both Frankie's and Sonny's careers would be ruined. But, it's not only their careers; it's what would happen to our families. Everyone, well almost everyone, holds us up like some paragon of racial integrity. So many people look up to us, what would happen?"

"Why don't you tell me? What is the worst thing you could imagine?"

"We'd never be able to face our families," Rochelle mused as she unconsciously glanced toward the door to the waiting room.

"Don't worry, Richie can't hear you," she reassured Rochelle. "The door is soundproof and my receptionist is keeping him busy."

"I want Richie to grow up without that kind of pressure. It's not fair, but that's the way it is."

"I see," the woman mused. "So you think it's the best thing you can do for your son?"

"Well, isn't it?" Rochelle queried. "What do you think? Am I being fair?"

"What I think about this doesn't matter. What's important is how you feel about this, isn't it?"

"But that's the problem," sighed Rochelle. "I don't know how I feel about this. That's why I'm coming here. I can't talk about this with Frankie. Usually, I can talk about anything with Lavinia, but I don't think she'd understand, either. I feel so all alone."

"Have you thought about talking to Richie's father?"

"No, that's not an option," Rochelle responded quickly. "I can't put this decision on him. It's up to me to learn how to deal with this on my own. I can't even tell Frankie until I know what I want to do. Or if I want to do anything at all."

CHAPTER 17

Ingrid calmed her husband while Angelina arranged her clothes and sat up. After a few seconds she realized that she was still holding the Wilbur doll on her lap. She quickly set it aside and sat with her hands folded, not certain what to do or say. She needn't have worried; her mother was going to handle the situation, as usual.

"Well," Ingrid sighed. "I don't think I need to tell you that your father and I are shocked. I don't want to discuss what just happened. As far as I'm concerned, this matter will never be brought up again. When we return home after this trip, you will pack your bags. I was going to wait until you graduated to send you to Europe, but I think right now would be better."

"But Mother," sputtered Angelina, not certain what to say. She looked at her father for help, but he just lowered his head and sobbed.

"This is not a punishment. I want you to be very clear on that," continued Ingrid. "You will attend a convent school for your last year of high school, and then you'll stay at the convent while you go to college. We're sending you to Paris as soon as I can make the arrangements. There is a lovely school there that your Godmother Claudette knows of which teaches not only scholastics, but also deportment, something sorely lacking in American girls, something I obviously have not been able to instill in my daughter. There will be no more discussion. This subject is closed."

"Yes, Mother," sighed Angelina. "Will I still get to visit Priscilla before we head back home?"

"You may attend the show tonight with us and may visit for a few minutes back stage afterwards to give her the box of chocolates we brought for her, but otherwise, no," said Ingrid with finality.

Angelina knew better than to debate the point. "Poppa," she pleaded. "I just want to say I'm sorry." She rose to give her father a hug.

Ingrid took her standing up as a cue for them to leave and guided Angelina to the door. "Let's go back to the hotel to change clothes and give your father a chance to get ready for the show." Angelo didn't turn away from the wall.

After they left, he sat and stared at the closed door for a few minutes. He then crossed the room, picked up Wilbur from the sofa and returned to his dressing table. He reached for some tissues from the pop up dispenser and began wiping the puppet clean as his tears fell upon the polished wood.

CHAPTER 18

Beverly Hills

Jonny Mason struck out the last man at bat with ease. In a matter of moments his fellow teammates had swept him up on their shoulders and were carrying him around the bases. Jonny looked up at his Dad and Ani in the stands. His father was on his feet giving him a thumbs-up sign and wearing a grin that any moviegoer could recognize. Ani held on to her husband's arm for support as she stood in the stands and threw a kiss at her stepson. Jonny waved back with joy. It was the first time in many years that he felt as if all was right with his world. He turned toward the bench along the first base line and saw his sister Jenny coming around the corner and leading a cheer. She was so happy that she didn't realize that her lipstick was all smeared. She still looks beautiful; thought Jonny as the guys lowered him to the ground.

Jenny rushed over to her brother, "A no-hitter, huh, big guy! Who'd have thought that my little brother was such a jock? We all thought you were going to be the next Allen Ginsburg, and here you're turning out to be the next Mickey Mantle."

"Maybe I can be both," smiled Jonny as he responded to his sister. "Get me out of here, will you, I can't stand all this noise."

"Hey, girls," Jenny shouted, "Let's give the guys a big cheer; let them know how much we enjoyed the game." As she led the girls to the side of the diamond, the team members followed. The merest suggestion from Jenny was followed like a command; she was a natural born leader. As the girls started their cheer, Jonny went over to his parents and smiled sheepishly.

"Good game today, son," said Justin offering his son his hand and pumping it vigorously. "I don't mind telling you I like what I see out there. Didn't I always tell you sports were fun? A lot more fun than locking yourself in your room and writing poetry all day."

Jonny's smile faltered, just a second or two, but enough for Ani to catch it. "Now, Justin," she chided good naturedly, "There's enough room in Jonny's life for both. I think it's wonderful, not many young men can do either as well as he does. You should be very proud of him."

Justin turned to his wife; "You've actually read his poetry? I didn't know he shared it with anyone."

Jonny looked at his stepmother horror stricken. She wasn't supposed to have told anyone that he had shown her his poems.

"Just one," she covered. "He asked me about a word once. But if the others are as good as the one I saw, he's great."

Jonny smiled again as he saw how well Ani covered for him, as she had done in the past. Justin stared at his son incredulously as Ani winked at him.

CHAPTER 19

New York City

Frankie pulled up to the emergency room door and opened the car door for Lavinia. "I'll park the car and be right back," he said. "Why don't you take Francie inside?"

The nurse at the emergency room desk, who had her face in some paperwork, took one quick look up at Lavinia and said, "Please take a seat. I'll be with you in a minute."

"But my daughter is very sick," pleaded Lavinia. "Her fever is nearly 105°. Can I see a doctor right away?"

"I said I'd be right with you, please sit down." the woman snarled. She might as well have said nigger, for it was quite clear that's what she was thinking. Lavinia looked around. There were no other doctors or nurses visible. She dejectedly turned to take a seat when Frankie entered.

"What's wrong?" he asked.

Lavinia looked at him. "The nurse said to wait," she sniffled.

Frankie turned red. "Nurse," he barked "This woman's child is very sick. She needs to see a doctor now."

The large woman sat more erect in her chair. "And I told her to have a seat. I will be with her in a minute. There are other people ahead of her." Just then Francie started to shiver uncontrollably.

Frankie took one look at Francie, and grabbed Lavinia by the arm and led her through the doors to the right of the nurse's desk. "Is there a doctor available?" he bellowed as he entered the treatment room. "We have a child having a seizure here."

Within seconds medical staff surrounded Lavinia. Francie was swept from her arms to an examining table and covered with ice packs. The sudden shock made her cry, but far from upsetting Lavinia, seeing her daughter cry was somehow reassuring. At least Francie was reacting and wasn't the listless child she held only a few minutes ago. The seizure subsided as quickly as it started.

A doctor brought Lavinia and Frankie to the side of the room while the staff worked on Francie. After some preliminary questions he informed them that Francie probably had some form of meningitis. "You got her to us in the nick of time," he said.

"Is she going to be all right?" asked Frankie.

"Probably," assured the doctor. "Meningitis can be fatal if left untreated, but it responds well to antibiotics. Since you said that she wasn't sick for very long, I think the prognosis is excellent. But, we'll know more after a few tests."

Lavinia breathed a sigh of relief and collapsed against Frankie. The doctor gave them a strange look, and then added, "Why don't you stay with your daughter, while your husband goes out to the desk to fill out the paperwork?"

"My husband?!?!?" answered a confused Lavinia. "Oh no, doctor, he's not my husband."

"I'll go call Sonny," offered Frankie, taking note of the blush crossing the man's cheeks.

"I'm so sorry," sputtered the doctor. "It's just that I assumed, I mean the child . . . and he seemed to be . . ."

Lavinia smiled and nodded, "That's perfectly all right. He's a very good friend and my daughter's godfather. Please don't think about it again. When can I take my daughter home?"

The doctor straightened up and regained his professional demeanor. "I'm certain that she's going to be fine, but I'd like to keep her overnight for observation, to be certain. The nurse will get you registered and assigned to a room." He turned to leave as Frankie entered the room.

"I've let Sonny know that everything's all right. I told him to stay at rehearsal and that I'd take care of everything here, I hope you don't mind," Frankie explained as he crossed to the bed and unconsciously stroked Francie's cheek.

Lavinia started to giggle uncontrollably. Frankie stared at her, unaware of what to do. "He thought that you were my husband. You should have seen the look on his face . . . it was priceless." She walked over next to Frankie and smoothed her daughter's hair as she continued. "Thank you, I don't know what I would have done without you. The way you handled that nurse and took charge of things."

Frankie put his hands on her shoulders, looked her straight in the eye, pulled her towards him, and kissed her deeply. "Lavinia, I probably acted rashly. But I didn't know what else to do. I couldn't let them mistreat the love of my life and put my daughter's life in jeopardy. But I shouldn't have been so careless. Obviously that doctor picked up on it. Maybe I'd better call Sonny back and have him come over here to allay suspicion."

"Not right now," sighed Lavinia as she melted in his arms. "Let's make certain that Francie is all right."

CHAPTER 20

42nd Street, a few days later

The stage manager was at his wits' end. This was supposed to be just another pick-up rehearsal. He had a page of notes from the director about corrections and performance tips he wanted instituted. Most of the notes were about Rosie's performance. He already knew from experience that he couldn't sit down with the star and give her the notes, she'd sit and nod her head and continue doing things exactly as she had done them before. He was going to have to run through the whole damn show and give useless notes to everybody else, then pretend as if the notes he was giving to Rosie were to help someone else's performance. If Rosie thought that she was helping someone else, she would cooperate.

Bless her heart; Rosie Campbell didn't have a mean bone in her body. After appearing in all those back stage musicals for MGM, she had really come to believe that on stage everybody was working towards the best show possible. That was the only thing that made this production bearable. So, he'd ask Rosie to work on remembering the business for this scene so that her leading man would have time for his costume change. Then she'd be able to keep focused and remember what she was supposed to do. Otherwise, if she forgot something, she'd jump ahead to the next part of the script that she remembered.

Nobody could ever get complacent in this show. Working with Rosie was a challenge; they all had to be on their toes because you never knew what would happen next. One night Rosie sang the lyrics to her first act finale song to the tune of song at the end of her first scene. That was quite a sight! The actors froze for just a second until Priscilla led them into the chorus' dance.

He had to admit that Priscilla had earned her place in the show. When they first arrived, everyone thought that the 17-year-old girl was just there because she was Rosie's daughter, but she soon won over everyone in the cast. First, she had refused her own dressing room, choosing instead to share the communal dressing room with the other chorus members. Then she worked harder than anyone else, learning all of her dances easily, and all the while tutoring her mother in the lead role. By the time the show opened, the cast had all adopted her. She even got to wear the coveted gypsy robe on stage opening night.

The tradition of the gypsy robe was fairly new, but had already been adopted by the cast of every Broadway production. According to the legend, a wardrobe mistress had made a robe for herself using costume scraps from every show she had worked on. A year or two ago, she died on opening night of what was supposed to be her last show before she retired. As a tribute, one of the cast wore her robe during the vocal warm-ups on stage just before the curtain rose. The show, which everyone predicted would flop, was a smash hit.

Show biz folks are a superstitious lot. Ever since that night the wardrobe mistress for every musical that opened on Broadway added a scrap of fabric from one of their show's costumes to that very same robe. The cast member chosen by their peers paraded the stage just before opening night's curtain, while the entire cast reached out and touched the garment. Wearing the gypsy coat was a true honor and usually went to the cast member with the greatest list of credits, or one who had recently overcome an obstacle. Priscilla was floored when the cast unanimously chose her.

After years as a pampered Hollywood princess, Priscilla found her place in the chorus and loved it. She didn't yearn for the spotlight like the others; she had already lived her life in the glare of publicity. For once, she was just one of the gang and she blossomed in the freedom. Priscilla also loved New York, as much to her surprise as to anyone else. In New York she made the transition from child to adult overnight. Soon, everyone stopped thinking of her as a teenager, and treated her as a peer. She was just another dancer, someone who would go out with them after the show to unwind.

Priscilla loved the fact that there were no publicity agents guiding her every move. Even when she was with her mother and Rosie's ever-present dog, Fritzie, shopping at Bloomingdale's, or walking down Park Avenue, they weren't gawked at. Sometimes there were awkward moments when someone on the street would stare. But then they'd shake their heads as if to say, "No, that couldn't be Rosie Campbell. She wouldn't be walking down the street like that." Priscilla loved it, Rosie, on the other hand, did not.

Between divorcing Eddie and leaving Hollywood, Rosie had made massive changes in her life, changes that she knew were necessary, but difficult none the less. It wasn't that Rosie even knew exactly what was wrong, it was just that she wasn't used to having to do things for herself. She had never had to go to the grocery store or pick up her own dry cleaning before. Overwhelmed, she avoided having to cook and clean by dining out and lived in a mess until her cleaning lady came by. She hadn't realized how much she relied on the boys in her entourage until they weren't there anymore.

True, she did have a few of "her boys" left, the queers who doted on her. They didn't hang around as much anymore, though. Without money to throw around, Rosie couldn't take care of them. They had to find jobs. Oh, a few still called on her every evening, but they worked during the day now and along with these paid gigs came lives of their own.

The boys would accompany her to dinner, if Priscilla wasn't available, and more and more often, Priscilla wasn't. Rosie felt abandoned, even though she knew she shouldn't, and she started drinking again. She'd have one or two drinks after the show, then some wine with dinner. After running around the clubs with the boys, she'd be dropped off to her empty apartment. Always an insomniac, Rosie would pop a couple of sleeping pills and then wander around the apartment for an hour or so until she dozed off, usually in a living room chair with her beloved Fritzie in her lap.

When she woke up, it was invariably time to go to the theater. She'd pop a couple of her "perky pills" and get to her dressing room an hour before the show, and have a drink or two while she put on her make-up. She never drank during a show and prided herself on that fact. Today, however, she did pop a couple extra pills. She wasn't used to performing during the day, and this rehearsal was not part of her routine.

Priscilla knocked on her mother's dressing room door. "Hey, Mommy," she chirped cheerfully. "All ready for a pick-up?"

"Darling, you know I don't drink while working," Rosie scowled.

"Not a pick-me-up," Priscilla laughed. "A pick-up rehearsal. How about grabbing some lunch between the rehearsals for act one and act two? My treat!"

Rosie looked at her daughter with newfound respect, "You know, Darling, you amaze me," she said as she stroked her daughter's cheek. "I can't believe my little girl's all grown up and buying her Old Lady lunch."

Priscilla smiled, "You're not old, but you do need something to eat. You're as thin as a rail!"

Rosie laughed "Yeah, ain't it a kick, after all those years of the studio guys telling me I was too fat, I can't keep the weight on. Let's get down there so we can get out of here now so we can have a nice leisurely meal."

Priscilla took her mother's hand and they headed downstairs to the stage where the rest of the cast was waiting. "Mommy, let's make it just the two of us, None of the boys okay?"

CHAPTER 21

Priscilla helped her mother crawl out of the cab as it pulled in front of the stage door. Rosie was a little unsteady. Priscilla wondered if her mother was tired or if it was the martinis she at lunch. They still had about three minutes to spare until the pick-up rehearsal for act two started. Priscilla knew from experience that her mother would snap to attention as soon as she walked onto the stage. But, the question remained, how cognizant would she be?

Rosie had given some of her best performances when she was a little high. But, that was always in front of an audience, not to an empty theater. Rosie seemed to draw some inexplicable strength from her fans. Priscilla took her mother's coat and purse from her, handed her over to the stage manager and ran over to join the rest of the chorus members for their second act opening number.

There was no turning back now. The director was sitting out front and had given word that the second act was to be handled as a full performance, sans costumes, and they weren't supposed to stop the action unless the theater caught fire. This was an unusual method for a pick-up rehearsal, but Priscilla had figured out the true reason; it was to help her mother get down the routine. Years of movie work had conditioned Rosie to a different pace than what was needed for a live stage show. Rosie couldn't seem to comprehend that there were no second takes. Every night she would stop in mid-song, or mid-speech and start over, throwing the rest of the cast into a panic.

The chorus was just about finished with the big opening number. Priscilla was in place alongside the others on the grand staircase and turned, expecting to see her mother appear at the top for her entrance. They had worked up this routine to accommodate the thunderous applause and cheers following Rosie's first appearance in the second act. This time though, when the chorus gestured to the top of the stairs, Rosie didn't appear. Priscilla held her breath, and, after an eternity that lasted three seconds, Rosie appeared and delivered her line, "Don't worry kids, I'm right here!" Rosie then belted out the lyrics to the song, not holding back one bit. Her eyes sparkled, that famous smile frozen in place, and working it as only she could. Priscilla finally exhaled in time to begin the stairway tap routine. Rosie took one stair at a time, turning to the chorus members as she descended the curving staircase. Only Priscilla noticed the slightest waiver in her step, and gave her an upstage wink of encouragement. Rosie reached the bottom of the staircase and finished the song with her usual bravura. Two chorus boys swept her up and carried her up the stairs where she turned to deliver the repeated chorus, added to appease her devoted fans.

She might have been caught up in the success of the moment, or maybe she hadn't quite regained her balance after the boys spun her around. Whatever the reason, Rosie decided to take a step forward instead of staying in place for the final note of the song. As she put her foot forward, she stepped in front of one of the chorus girls feet. The girl compensated too quickly and tumbled head over heels down the stairs. A couple of the chorus members were knocked down, but most caught sight of the girl in time to step aside. Priscilla couldn't help but think that the scene was like something out of an *I Love Lucy* episode. It would have been funny, except the girl had made such an awful thud when she landed. Despite directions to the contrary, the cast stopped the show. Miraculously, the dancer appeared to be suffering only a broken ankle and wounded pride.

Rosie was beside herself, even as cast members assured her that it could have happened to anybody. And, in fact, it could have, but Priscilla knew better. It was the vodka martinis Rosie had for lunch that caused the misstep. Rehearsal was called and Priscilla accompanied her mother back to her dressing room.

Rosie asked her assistant to go order a dozen roses to be sent to the young girl's hospital room. "Better make that two dozen," she amended. "After all, she is my understudy." After the young man left, Rosie turned to her daughter, "I feel just awful, and everything was going so well up until that point. What horrible luck."

"Luck?!?!?!" Priscilla seethed. "Luck had nothing to do with it. You were drunk. That's why you tripped her. If you hadn't had so much to drink at lunch, this wouldn't have happened."

"Now Darling," soothed Rosie. "Don't be mad. I just had a couple of drinks. I certainly wasn't drunk. You heard the kids, it could have happened to anyone."

"What are they supposed to say to you?" Priscilla snapped back. "You're a drunk and you know it. Sometimes, Mommy, you make me sick. I'm tired of this. I'm tired of taking care of you when you get like this. I want you to promise to stop. Right now!"

"All right Darling, please don't be mad," cried Rosie, her make-up running down her cheeks. "I promise."

Priscilla wasn't placated. "Mommy, I've heard that before. I want you to promise to get help. Will you go see a doctor?"

"Tomorrow, for sure," she noticed Priscilla's wary look. "You can even make the appointment. I'd go right now, but I need to rest before tonight's show."

Priscilla kissed her mother. "I'm going to make some calls right now. Daddy said he knew of someone who could help."

"You talked to your father about this?"

"Of course," Priscilla said. "He still loves you, you know."

"I know," sighed Rosie. "And I love him too. But, I'm not what he wants. Maybe I should get some help. Why don't you see if he can come East?"

Priscilla brightened up. Her parent's divorce wasn't acrimonious, but her mother had been hurt. Her asking for Eddie was a sign that Rosie wanted to start their relationship again, but this time fully aware of their differences. "I'll go call right now. Why don't you take a little nap?"

"Good idea, dear. Give me a kiss and then turn off the lights on your way out." After Priscilla left, Rosie went over to her dressing table and opened a side drawer. She took out a pill bottle and emptied three sleeping pills into her hand. She swallowed them dry and stretched out on the chaise. For a good half-hour, she lay in the dark, fretting over the day's events. Then, she got up and took another four pills out of the bottle and swallowed them as well. In a few minutes she felt her eyes getting heavy and, eventually, she fell asleep.

CHAPTER 22

Priscilla returned to the theater at 5:30 p.m. after visiting her injured cast-mate in the hospital. Everything was in an uproar; the stage manager was pacing and screaming orders to the costume mistress, choreographer, music director, and publicist for the show. She stood in the shadows and watched with awe as another chorus gypsy sidled up beside her.

"You poor kid," the chorus girl murmured.

"What's going on?" asked Priscilla.

"They're trying to figure out what to do about tonight's show, of course," she said, looking at Priscilla as if she just arrived from the moon. "Oh my God! You don't know what happened!"

"I just got back from visiting Ann Marie in the hospital. What happened?" Priscilla responded, panic starting to set in. "Is something wrong with my mother?"

"Maybe you'd better talk with Pete," she hesitated. "He's in charge, I shouldn't have said anything. I thought you knew."

"Tell me," Priscilla pleaded, although in her panic, it came out more like a threat. "Is my mother all right?"

"They say she's going to be fine," the nervous girl said taking her by the arm and leading her backstage. "She took too many sleeping pills. They pumped her stomach and they say she needs a few days rest. She's in her dressing room now."

Priscilla ran up the stairs to her mother's dressing room two at a time, and burst through the door as Rosie's dresser was handing the star a cup of tea. She pushed the cup away.

"Now Rosie, the doctor said you needed lots of fluids," the young man cajoled. "I put lots of honey in it to help soothe your throat. Drink!"

Rosie took the cup, but had to hold it with two hands to keep it steady. Priscilla appeared at her mother's side and held the cup for her. "Mommy, are you all right?"

"I'll be fine, darling," she croaked out. "I took a couple of pills to help me sleep and then took a couple more later. They piled up on me. Thank goodness Danny here found me. I feel so foolish. Darling you're dripping. Danny, please get Priscilla a towel."

"Don't worry Mommy, everything's going to be all right," Priscilla said as she put the cup aside.

"But, it's not," wept her mother. "I won't be able to perform tonight, and I can't sing for a week or two. The tube from the stomach pump scraped my vocal cords."

Priscilla pulled back in shock. "Your voice! It will be all right, though, won't it?" She knew that singing meant everything to her mother.

"Eventually, Darling," said Rosie, mustering all her strength to reassure her daughter. "I'm worried that they might have to close the show. Pete's trying to contact the producers now."

There was a knock on the door, and Pete, the stage manager walked in. "How ya' feeling Rosie?" he asked with false humor.

"Like three day old shit," Rosie smiled at him. "I'm really sorry, Pete. What do the producers say?"

"They want to close down," he answered. "Without an understudy, they have no choice. The insurance will cover it, but they'd rather keep going, we've had good box office."

Rosie tried to sit up quickly and she did so, if a little unsteadily. "Would they keep going if we had someone to fill in for a week?"

"Yeah," he answered. "But we don't with Ann Marie out of the picture. Even if we could get someone in, it would take nearly a week to prep them."

"Not Priscilla," Rosie offered. "She knows every one of my songs and all my dialogue. She rehearsed with me, and you know she knows the dances. All she needs is a little practice with the blocking."

"It could work," mused Pete.

"Wait a minute!" protested Priscilla. "First of all, I don't know it that well. Secondly, my mother's fans come to see her, not some chorus kid."

"Not just a chorus kid," answered Rosie. "A chorus kid who's my daughter. Come on, Honey, otherwise we'll have to close the show."

Priscilla looked at Pete who nodded in agreement. "I've gotta check with the guys upstairs, but I'm sure they'll go for it."

"All right," she agreed. "Maybe I'm nuts, but I'll try." Pete led her off to go over all the details. "Have you got any chocolate on you, Pete?" she asked.

As soon as they left, Rosie picked up the phone and dialed her ex-husband. Priscilla would need both of them behind her to pull this off.

1963

CHAPTER 23

New York City, Midtown

Rochelle and Lavinia seldom visited the studio until the day of the show's taping, and they never brought the children, but both kids loved Chubby Checker. They were among the millions who had fallen in love with Checkers' hit song, *The Twist*, and Frankie thought it would be cute to have the kids dance on the show. Rochelle wasn't too keen on the idea. She didn't want to parade the kids in front of the public. There were too many bigots around who might get some ideas in their heads. Lavinia agreed, but they both saw the good that could be accomplished by showing a seven-year-old and an eight-year-old of different races enjoying themselves together. They finally agreed when Sonny suggested that the children of other staff of the show join Francie and Richie.

The Sonny Lewis Show had become one of the season's biggest hits when it debuted, and now, in its third year, they could afford to be a little more daring. But, they still were only going to show the children dancing the Twist. Frankie figured that this was one way they could avoid any kind of conflict with interracial dancing. Who could protest a group of little kids dancing together? And, since the staff of the show was like a family, it was a perfect excuse to get together for a party, not that they needed an excuse.

Frankie and Sonny had assembled a crew like no other in the business. They not only worked together; they all truly enjoyed each other's company. A weekend never passed when they didn't all gather at someone's house for a picnic, a kid's birthday party, or a grown-ups' night out. Sonny swore that's why the show was such a success. He felt that the care and devotion everyone felt for the show came across the screen. Every reviewer commented on how much fun everyone seemed to be having. Sonny was such a phenomenon that he made the cover of *TV Preview*, the first Negro entertainer to do so. And, with a few exceptions, there were no protests from subscribers. The times were changing, and as the popular song went, "The answer was blowing in the wind."

Not that Sonny would ever perform that song, or any protest song, on his show. Frankie always pointed out that Sonny's success was a direct result of being non-threatening. It was sometimes frustrating to all of them. The NAACP had approached them to appear in a documentary on race relations and in an advertisement for racial equality, and they had to decline. They had all decided to avoid the issue and simply be an example without saying a word, although it was increasingly more difficult, especially with the children growing up so quickly.

Rochelle, in particular, wanted to "go public" about their relationship, hoping to make things easier for others, to encourage interracial friendships. She felt that they should take a stronger position, but was also realistic enough to know that right now was not the time.

"In a few years," Lavinia always told her. And Rochelle respected Lavinia's opinion more than that of anyone else, so she complied.

CHAPTER 24

London

R osie sat up in bed and called for room service. "Send up a pot of coffee, a glass of tomato juice and some vodka, please." She grabbed her robe from the table by the side of her bed and noticed that the other bed was not only empty, but had not been slept in. She went into sitting room, flipped on the television and lit a cigarette. She was watching the news from the States, so transfixed on Martin Luther King's "I Have a Dream" speech that she didn't hear the door to the suite open.

She jumped across the room when Allen said "Morning, Luv." He stood there holding his jacket over his arm, looking every bit as handsome as he had the day they met at Covent Garden. "Sorry darling, I didn't mean to startle you, but I'm surprised to find you awake so early. How are you feeling today?"

Catching her breath, Rosie settled back onto the sofa. "Much better, dear, and where were you last night?"

"I spent most of the night talking with those four blokes from the band we met. Then I went back their manager's place so I could hear some tapes of their music. Brian, that's their manager, thinks you should add one of their songs to your album."

"What do you think, Allen?" Rosie replied, picking off the remnants off her nail polish.

"It might be a good idea," he responded. "It's not the kind of thing you usually do, but with the right arrangement, it might work. Besides, they're going to be releasing an album in the States just before we return for your concert at Carnegie. It could bring in a younger generation of fans." There was a knock at the door; Allen signed the room service bill after deleting the vodka and sending it back. "Rosie, darling, we agreed, no more drinking and you need something more substantial to eat." He picked up the phone, "Please send two orders of bacon and eggs with rye toast to Miss Campbell's suite, and another pot of coffee." He hung up the phone. "I want you to have plenty of energy for our studio session today."

"Fine," answered Rosie, taking the cup of coffee he had poured for her. "But two pots of coffee?"

"The second one is for me, Rosie." He began to loosen his tie and head toward the bathroom.

"I thought all you Brits drank tea," wisecracked Rosie.

"First of all, how many times do I have to tell you? I'm an Kiwi, not a Brit. Secondly, we do not drink tea after we stay up all night sweet talking a rock band's manager into letting our star record one of his boys' songs," he called from the other room.

"Sweet talked, huh?" snapped Rosie. ""Is that all you did? I noticed your bed wasn't slept in."

"Well, mine may not have been, but his certainly was." He came out of the bath dressed in a white terry cloth robe with his hair wrapped in a towel. "The things I do for you. This was not what I had in mind when I signed on as your musical conductor."

"Is that a complaint?" queried Rosie slyly.

"More like a fringe benefit, darling," he said as he hugged her. "Wait until the world hears that Rosie Campbell is going to cover a tune by the Beatles."

"The Beatles, huh" mused Rosie. "What an ugly name for a group."

CHAPTER 25

Paris

Angelina Ferrara sat in a sidewalk cafe sipping her coffee and reading "The Bell Jar." She happened to look up from her book in time to spy the Mother Superior crossing the street. Luckily, Mother Superior hadn't seen her yet. She'd convinced the nun that she had "female problems," which allowed her to cut class once a week for an alleged doctor's appointment. She spent the day exploring Paris instead. Usually she'd go to see an American film. Today, after seeing her idol, Audrey Hepburn in *Charade*, she decided to do what any 19-year-old might do, take a walk and enjoy the beautiful Paris sunshine.

She leaned her chair back behind a potted plant, hoping to escape Mother Superior's sight. As she scooted backwards, the leg of her chair caught the edge of a brick and she toppled right into the lap of a handsome dark-haired man.

"Well, I knew the women in Paris were beautiful, but I didn't think they fell from the sky, like raindrops," he said in surprise.

Angelina was worried that the noise might attract Mother Superior's notice, so she threw herself into the man's arms and buried her face in his neck. "Please put your arms around me," she whispered.

"My pleasure," replied the stranger as he encircled her in his strong limbs and caressed the back of her head. "But, shouldn't I at least know your name?"

"Gina" Angelina murmured, not knowing why she shortened her name. No one had ever called her that, but it somehow seemed right at the moment. Mother Superior must have surely passed by now, but Angelina couldn't bring herself to release the handsome stranger. Finally after what was most certainly too long an interval, she pulled away. "I'm so terribly sorry, there was someone going by I didn't want to see."

"Oh, the formidable nun?" he asked.

"How did you know?" Angelina asked, pulling away in surprise.

"I have hidden from a few nuns in my lifetime too," he answered, his eyes sparkling. "My name is Jean, Jean Beaubien."

"Ange . . . Gina Ferrara," she responded, staring into his eyes. "Please, let me buy you another cup of espresso, yours has gone cold." Jean accepted the coffee and the two of them spent the next three hours talking. It was as if they had known each other forever.

Jean was a moderately successful photographer, working with some of the smaller design houses, shooting home furnishing layouts and the occasional fashion spread. At one point Gina, as he continued to call her, looked at her watch and realized that it was now the middle of the evening.

"I've got to go back to the convent, they'll kill me for being out so late," Gina offered, rising to leave.

"If you're in trouble all ready, why not make it worthwhile?" asked Jean, caressing her hand. "Come, stay with me tonight."

She didn't think twice before accepting. If you were going to lose your virginity, it might as well be to a Frenchman that you met in a sidewalk cafe.

CHAPTER 26

New York City, 44th Street

Priscilla felt the blood leak into her shoes but she kept on dancing. She was going to get this dance combination right if it was the last thing she did. She took a deep breath and began counting . . . five, six, seven eight and step, two, three, four, five, six, seven, eight and leap, turn, two, three, four, and back, six, seven and kick, bend back, leg out, leg in, arm up, turn, and point.

"Perfect!" Toby called out from the darkened house. "Priscilla, I can't believe that you got that step down so fast. It was absolutely perfect!" The choreographer came down to the edge of the stage. "You'll knock them out with this number. I can hear the applause now. Miss Priscilla . . . , no cut that. You need a trendier first name, Miss Cilla Best please pick up your second Tony Award!"

"No," Priscilla muttered. "Let's do it again. I should have extended my arm more in the middle of the kick. It was too limp."

"Too limp?" exclaimed Toby. "Honey, I wish my last boyfriend was so limp. That arm was perfectly placed. You're being too hard on yourself. Let's go grab some dinner and chill out. You've been rehearsing for nine hours."

"Practice makes perfect," she said, and counted out again. She ran through the same routine from start to finish. As soon as she finished the work lights on the stage went out and she was left in the dark.

"Enough," Toby chided her. "Being 18, doesn't make you indestructible. Let's go to dinner and then I'll take you home to soak in a hot tub." Cilla panted, the sweat dripping from her brow as Toby handed her a towel and put her coat over her shoulders. "Girl, you sweat like a racehorse, but you are one hell of a dancer. By the way, you were right, the extension on your arm was much better the last time."

"I told you I could do better," Cilla smiled.

"Sometimes you don't need to do better," said Toby. "You've got to learn to pace yourself; this wasn't even a full rehearsal. Take it easy, there's still two weeks until opening night."

"I wish I could take it easy, Toby," she whispered. "I'm so tired, but I just hear my mother's voice in the back of my mind going, 'Make Momma proud!'"

"If Rosie got any more puffed up with pride she'd be a balloon at the Macy's Parade," Toby laughed. "You've already proved yourself, honey. Taking over that first show for your mother and then going right into the next one. Cilla, you don't have to worry about living in your mother's shadow any more. You're a star on your own."

"It's not her shadow I'm worried about," she murmured as she settled down in the taxi. "Momma's going to be back in town for the opening. I want to show her that I can headline on my own. Maybe then she'll stop worrying about me so much."

"Ain't that a kick," said Toby. "With you on Broadway, and your mom at Carnegie Hall, it's like Christmas for queens."

They stared at each other a moment both shocked at what Toby just blurted out, and then they both burst out laughing.

CHAPTER 27

New York City, Central Park

Rochelle and Lavinia walked arm in arm as the kids skated ahead of them. Francie was really flying in her new shoe skates while Richie valiantly tried to keep up. The women laughed as Francie skated a circle around Richie, then took his hands and led him along. Suddenly Francie skated up to the women and announced that she needed to pee.

"You mean that you need to use the rest room," Lavinia corrected her.

"Why do they call it that?" asked Francie. "I don't need to go there to rest, I need to go pee!"

Lavinia turned her head in order to keep from laughing, while Rochelle intervened.

"I need to go, too. I'll take you, Francie."

Lavinia, still stifling a laugh, announced that she would take Richie and wait over at the refreshment stand. Richie, hearing this, begged for an ice cream. Rochelle looked at Lavinia and they both smiled.

"I'll get Richie's now," Lavinia offered. "Then Francie can get hers when you get back."

Lavinia headed to the small outdoor cafe, settled Richie in, and returned with a dish of ice cream for him. In the meantime, Richie had enchanted every woman in the cafe. With his curly chestnut hair and light tan eyes he was stunningly good looking. Richie was having a great time out with his "Aunt" Lavinia. As the boy swallowed another spoonful of ice cream, one of the women from the next table smiled at them.

"He is certainly a beautiful little boy," she said while stroking his hair.

"I'm not a little boy," Richie protested "I'm almost seven years old."

The woman continued, unfazed. "It's unusual to see such copper colored hair on a little one. Does he favor his father or mother?"

"Actually he's a little of each," answered Lavinia, smiling up at the woman. "I agree, he is just about the sweetest little boy in the world. You can see why he's won my heart."

"He certainly is," the matron nodded in agreement. "Now, don't feed him too much ice cream or your missus will be upset."

"My missus?" asked Lavinia, a bit confused.

"That's what all the girls called the lady of the family they worked for, in my day," the woman explained. "Do they use another name now?"

"Excuse me," said Lavinia, as she gathered up Richie. "Come on, Richie, we need to be going."

Rochelle and Francie were just coming out of the ladies room as Lavinia approached with Richie in tow. Rochelle at first thought Richie had done something wrong.

"Lavinia, what happened?" she asked. "What did Richie do?"

"Nothing," spat Lavinia. "I'm not mad at him. I just had to get way from those women."

"What women?" Rochelle asked, truly mystified. She had never seen Lavinia so mad.

"Those ladies thought Aunt Lavinia was my babysitter," offered Richie.

"More like his mammy," cursed Lavinia.

Rochelle started to head over to the women to give them a piece of her mind. Lavinia put her hand on Rochelle's arm and stopped her.

"Don't bother," Lavinia said, "They're not worth it." But the truth was that she was afraid. She had never seen her friend so furious, and didn't know what she might do or say.

CHAPTER 28

Paris

"Gina, you are so beautiful. So round and luscious," murmured Jean. He kissed the back of her neck as they snuggled after their lovemaking. "I wish you had told me it was your first time, I would have been more gentle."

Gina leaned against his slim, almost bony, body and caressed his chest, twirling the hair on it in her fingers. "I wouldn't have wanted you to change a thing," she cooed. "Now that I know what all the fuss has been about, I can't imagine a better introduction than what I was given. Are you ready to go again?"

Jean reached over and tousled her hair, "Patience my dear, we have three more hours before dawn and I need a little time to recover. Four times is usually my limit." He rolled over to reach for his cigarettes and pulled the sheet with him, uncovering Gina's naked body. She snatched the sheet back.

"Are you cold?" he asked.

"No, I just don't feel comfortable naked," she answered. "In my family, we never walked around undressed."

"You Americans," he sighed. "Always covering up. Gina, you have a marvelous, rich body. You should revel in it. Let me photograph you in the nude." He reached for his ever-present camera.

"NO!" she yelled as she leapt out of bed and wrapped herself in the sheet. Jean came over and began to kiss her. She tingled in places that she didn't even know she had. He began kissing her throat, then slid down to her breasts and murmured

"Four times may be my limit, but there's no reason why you can't enjoy another time." He then slid his hands under the sheet she held, stooped before her and began licking her inner thigh. With a sigh, she leaned back on the bed, spread her legs and gave in to the passion, once again.

Half an hour later, she was sitting on a stool, nude, except for a strategically placed scarf, and Jean was taking her picture. And she didn't care that she was naked.

CHAPTER 29

New York City, near Times Square, a few days later

Cilla sat in the rear of the cab, "Just sit for a few minutes," she told the cabbie as she rummaged through her purse. "Let the meter run, this may take a while."

"Whatever you say, Lady," the cab drive yawned as he picked up the newspaper sitting on the seat next to him.

Cilla wanted to collect her thoughts, be ready for anything. Ever since she had interceded after Rosie's accidental overdose, things had been a little strained. Her mother just couldn't handle the fact that Cilla had grown up and moved on with her life. Cilla realized soon after that if she stayed and took care of her mother, Rosie wasn't going to get any better. Cilla's therapist helped her see that she had to go out on her own, for her sake, as well as her mother's.

Rosie had wailed and cried, but Cilla stood her ground. First, getting an apartment with a couple of the other girls in the chorus, and then leaving the show soon after her mother's return. When the show closed ten days after Rosie took over the starring role again, Cilla almost relented. Then the offer came for Rosie to star in the national tour of "Who's Afraid of Virginia Woolf?" It was like a godsend for Cilla. Rosie would be touring for six months and that gave Cilla a chance to establish herself in New York.

It wasn't hard to find another job; she'd gotten rave reviews as her mother's replacement. Everybody was shocked though, when Cilla took a supporting role in a small off-Broadway show. She was the featured dancer, but didn't have many lines and only one solo. It was the perfect role for her, and again she garnered rave reviews.

After the national tour, Rosie took her show to London and had been there for a year and a half. The Brits loved her. She hosted retrospectives of her films, attended society parties, and did a few concerts. During that same time Cilla quickly garnered a following among New York's theater community. They especially loved her cabaret act, which she performed at the Bon Soir and a few other clubs frequented by theater folk and queer guys. The queer guys practically swooned over her.

At first, she was certain it was because she was Rosie Campbell's daughter, but when they came back to see her night after night, she knew it was more than just the novelty of her celebrated parentage. Oddly enough, Poppa had convinced her of that. One night he introduced her to his latest "protege", a kid of no more than twenty, after the show. He couldn't stop raving about her performance and he never once mentioned Rosie. It turned out he had grown up in El Salvador and had never seen one of her movies or heard any of her records.

Cilla knew her Poppa was queer for many years. He had to know that she'd figured it out, but they never spoke of it. Some of the dancers in the show made allusions to the fact that he was, but she pretended not to pick up their hints. As far as she was concerned, it wasn't anyone else's business. If Poppa felt it was a private matter, she certainly wasn't going to confirm or deny anything.

Part of the difference between her father and the boys she knew was a generational thing. The guys Cilla's age were a bit more obvious about it. They were quite outrageous, at least in private. Poppa came from a time when it wasn't discussed, even among the gay boys themselves. Part of it was his personality. He was more subdued, not exactly fey, but refined. She knew that everyone thought that she was blind to the obvious because he was her father, and she didn't do anything to contradict them.

She wished Poppa was here; the meeting with Momma was going to be tense. It was the first time that they were coming face-to-face as peers.

Thank God Cilla's show had opened before Rosie got to town. Cilla was thrilled when her show got good reviews, and the critics' mentions of her were even more complimentary. It would have been impossible for Cilla to face her mother if the show had been anything less than a hit.

Cilla was a hell of a dancer, she knew that. And, after years of watching her mother perform, Cilla knew how to sell a song. Singing was another matter. She had a powerful voice, genetics, she figured, but she had a limited range. Just an octave and a half, so Don, the composer, wrote the songs especially for her. The big notes she held in his songs were her strongest.

She was sometimes concerned that she was going too far, that she was too over the top. Ted, the playwright and lyricist, told her to go for it. He was right; she could tell by the way that the queer boys responded. They loved her and the more dramatic she got the more they begged her to continue. Now, she was appearing on Broadway at the same time that her mother was doing her show at Carnegie Hall.

Rosie had a new musical director who put together a concert program for her that the critics loved. She had had to extend the run of her show in London three times. However, while in London, Rosie lived far better then her means, as usual, and needed to raise some money right away. Her music director, who was also her manager, arranged for a month-long run of her one-woman show.

Cilla found a couple of Hershey's Kisses in the bottom of her purse, unwrapped them, popped them in her mouth, and paid the taxi driver. She took a deep breath and headed in to Sardi's to meet her mother for lunch. Rosie was already there, tucked into a booth and holding court. Cilla tiptoed up and peered around the crowd, waving to her mother.

Rosie spied Cilla and shooed away everyone but a tall, slim man with a goatee. He looked like a younger version of her father. Cilla was wary, her mother had had a series of managers and agents with whom she became involved, and they all took advantage of her financially and emotionally.

"Allen, this is my baby, Priscilla. Isn't she beautiful?" Rosie asked lovingly. Priscilla, this is the new man in my life, Allen Warner."

"The new man?!?!?!" Cilla sputtered as she plopped into the booth.

"Oh, no! Not that way," smiled Allen as he extended her hand. "I'm just your mother's music arranger and manager," he smiled.

"And the best friend I've ever had," Rosie exclaimed as she hugged them on each side of her. "He takes care of your Momma almost as good as you did. I don't know what I would do without him."

Allen, to his credit, blushed. "I was always a big fan of your mother. So when I got the opportunity to accompany her I jumped at it. It was so lucky; I was just visiting England . . . ."

"He's from New Zealand," interjected Rosie. "I'd love a martini. Where's that waiter?"

"I already ordered for you, dear," he responded. Noticing Cilla's frown, "The waiter will be back with your iced tea right away. What can I get for you, Cilla?"

"Oh, that's right, everyone calls her Cilla now. It is more grown up," her mother smiled and stroked her hair. "It may take me a while to get used to that." Rosie opened her purse and took out a pill bottle. She saw Cilla eyeing them suspiciously. "Oh, it's all right darling, these aren't sleeping pills or diet pills. It's real medication from my doctor."

"Pills? What's wrong? Are you sick?" she began sputtering.

"No," said Allen as he patted Rosie's hand. "This is just something to calm your mother down. They're called Valium and they're absolutely harmless."

Cilla smiled at Allen. She liked him already. "Good. You know, I am thirsty, I'll have a Tab. I'm just addicted to it."

"The tab???" asked Rosie. "No, no honey, this lunch is on me."

"Tab is a new soda. I love it, and it tastes so great, you'd never know it was a diet drink, Momma."

"You're on a diet?!?!?!" asked Rosie incredulously. "You can eat anything you want and never gain a pound." She turned to Allen, "I adore my daughter, but I hate the fact that she never has to diet."

"We must try it then," said Allen ordering three Tabs from the waiter. "Now Cilla, let's get down to business. How about doing a guest spot in your mother's show on opening night?"

"What?!?!?!" Cilla gasped. "I can't, I'm appearing in a show, too."

"Yes, dear," coaxed her mother. "But, we open next Sunday and your show is dark that night. Please, it would mean so much to me to be able to work with you. Just one duet?"

Cilla composed herself. She needn't have worried about her mother accepting her career. Rosie wanted her help. Cilla knew that having her there to count on would make Momma more self-assured.

"Okay," she answered. "But not just a duet, I want a solo, too. That way I can give my show a plug"

Allen laughed out loud. "Rosie, she certainly is your daughter!"

CHAPTER 30

Beverly Hills, a few weeks later

Justin Mason led his wife Ani down the aisle of the high school auditorium, looking for their seats. There were as many stars in the audience this morning as there were at the Academy Awards. Ed Begley's son was a student here, as was John Carradine's. He waved to them and a couple of other folks in the business before settling in to the seats that their neighbors had saved for them. Justin was bursting with pride; today they were going to present awards to the outstanding students in the school. Jenny had been chosen sophomore homecoming queen and Jonny, Jon he corrected himself, was being presented with a trophy for making the All-State baseball team for the upcoming season, the only underclassman in the state to do so.

"Justin," his wife whispered, "If your grin gets any bigger, I'm going to have to move over a seat to make room." She nudged him playfully in the side.

He couldn't help it; things were going so well. Finally. Jenny had made her peace with Ani, and Jon was beginning to come out of his shell. He was still much shier than his twin sister was, but he was more comfortable in small groups and among the family. The recent changes in the family dynamics meant more to Justin than all the awards he had won for his last film. It was worth taking the morning off from the set to show his support for the kids.

As the house lights dimmed, Ani stole a quick peek at her program. Before the presentation of the awards, there was going to be a skit of some kind. To her surprise, she noted that Jon was listed as one of the participants, which she found odd. Jon usually didn't like to perform. If he could have played baseball without fans watching him, he would have been much happier.

The skit began, a corny take-off on Alfred Hitchcock's new film, *The Birds*. As the skit progressed it was clear that it was an excuse for the students to poke good-natured fun at their favorite teachers. Midway through the skit, Jenny entered and was attacked by some "birds". Ani smiled, thinking that she should have realized that the listing in the program was a mistake. Jenny was the type to ham it up on stage, not Jon.

As the skit neared its ending, one of the "birds" landed on Jenny's head and flew away with her hair. It was then that Ani, and Justin, realized that it was, in fact, Jon disguised as Jenny. The audience roared with laughter. Most everyone knew that

Jon and Jenny used to do that as children all the time. Ani looked over at Justin; his wide grin had been replaced by a scowl.

"What's wrong?" Ani whispered.

"I thought that those kids were over that nonsense," Justin huffed.

"They are, Honey, that's what makes it so funny," she soothed. "I'm surprised that he could fool even us."

Jenny came out in a baseball uniform; her hair tucked up under her cap, and started swatting the birds. The audience roared even louder. As the skit ended and Jenny began to deliver her welcoming speech, the principal came onto the stage and stopped her.

"I'm sorry to interrupt," he choked out and began sobbing. After a few tense seconds when the parents and students in the audience began looking at each other, confused, he continued. "I'm sorry to say . . . we have to stop . . . it's just horrible, horrible." A few people tittered; thinking it was part of the show. "Please, no," he pleaded. "President Kennedy has just been shot."

The collective gasp by the audience seemed to suck every ounce of oxygen from the hall. People began muttering and whispering. Many of the women were sobbing; people began to get up from their seats. A sense of panic began to build.

"Everybody, please stay calm," Jenny commanded, and they did. People returned to their seats as she continued speaking, "Dr. Zimmerman," she said, speaking to the principal, "What do we know about this?"

The principal came to the microphone and related what he had heard on the radio moments earlier and then said, "I'm afraid that we need to cancel the ceremony. School is being dismissed immediately. Parents, please meet your children in front of the building. That's all I know for now."

With that, Jenny and Jon ran down the stairs from the stage and hugged their parents. Justin Mason wept openly as they walked to the car. They rode home in silence; Jenny and Jon still in their costumes. They entered the house as zombies, Justin and Ani settling in the den before the television, Jenny and Jon going upstairs to remove their costumes.

Jon shut the door to his room, leaned back against it and wept. As he went into his bathroom to remove his make-up and wash his face, he caught sight of his reflection in the full-length mirror on the door and was startled to see how feminine he looked. In spite of his sorrow, he felt his penis becoming firmer. He had often masturbated while wearing a pair of women's panties that he had stolen from Sears. Afterwards, he always felt so ashamed that he promised himself he would never do it again. He had already broken that promise so many times, and now, fully dressed like this, the urge was uncontrollable.

He put the wig back on and began rubbing his crotch, enjoying the sensation of the silken panties sliding back and forth. He took off the cheerleading sweater and looked at the bra filled with socks. They almost looked like real breasts. He lifted the skirt and started stroking his penis, excited by the incongruity of the feminine attire and his bright red, throbbing cock. He began fondling and stroking his moist warm shaft. It didn't take long for his breathing to become labored as he stared at himself in the mirror while he shot his wad.

Guilt soon took the place of the animal passion he had just felt. He sobbed as he cleaned up after himself. He was soon slumped on the floor and began weeping, ashamed that he couldn't control himself even as he mourned the death of President Kennedy.

CHAPTER 31

New York City, a few days later

Pacing in her dressing room at Carnegie Hall, Rosie was beside herself. She was devastated and considered canceling her show. She'd loved President Kennedy, had, in fact, campaigned for him. He had been so sweet to her the few times they met. Whenever she performed at a fundraiser for him, he always requested *Will I Ever See You Again?*, a snappy number, and her first hit song. Like the rest of the country, she was in mourning. It had only been a few days since the president had been assassinated. She wasn't certain if people would even show up for the concert, which was supposed to start in four hours. She had to make a decision soon.

Allen burst into the room. "Rosie, it's incredible."

"What's going on?" she asked. Allen was usually so composed, she couldn't even begin to guess what got him so excited.

"You've got to see it," he said as he led her down the hall to a window. "Look!"

Rosie looked out and saw a line of people that stretched around the corner and out of sight. "What's going on?" she asked.

"Those are people waiting in line for the doors to open," screamed Allen. "Some of them don't even have tickets, they're hoping that there may be some available at the last minute."

Rosie started laughing uncontrollably. "And to think that I was worried that people wouldn't show up! Well, I guess we won't have to cancel tonight's show, but maybe we should anyway, out of respect."

"Don't be silly. People need to have something to take their minds off of their grief," said Allen. "I respected Mr. Kennedy a great deal, even though he wasn't my president. That doesn't mean that we have to put our entire lives on hold, though."

"I suppose that you're right Allen," sighed Rosie. "I'd better call Cilla and let her know what's happening."

"There's no need, Luv," he smiled. "She's in her dressing room right now. We shared a taxi coming here."

"But our hotel isn't anywhere near her apartment," responded a confused Rosie. "Wait a minute! Is that why you didn't come home last night? Did you two spend the night together?" Allen nodded in assent. Rosie frowned, "Allen, Darling, I love you dearly, but I'm not going to have Cilla go through what I went through with her father. Don't lead her on. Unless . . . Oh my god! Is Cilla the right girl?"

"Right girl?" asked a puzzled Allen.

"Yes. You know, they say you guys are the way you are because you haven't met the right girl. Is Cilla your 'right girl'?" Rosie asked expectantly. "Oh, that would be too wonderful. I think of you as a son already. This would be . . ."

"Hold on baby," laughed Allen. "Rosie, I am what I am. Have you thought that maybe you're the way you are because you haven't met the right girl?

"Oh no, darling, Tallulah tried it years ago on me and it didn't take." Rosie laughed. "I found the thought of sex with a woman revolting."

"That makes two of us," said Allen.

"Then what happened?" asked Rosie.

"Cilla is much wiser than you think. We're just going to be very good friends, explained Allen. "She had me figured out from the get-go. We're just pals. Last night we went club hopping and then I crashed at her place. No funny business. Now get your famous fanny on stage. Cilla's probably waiting for us now."

"Isn't it early for vocal warm-ups?" asked Rosie.

"No, that's not it. I have an idea," he said. "I know that you want to do something special in honor of the president tonight, so I've worked up a special arrangement of *Will I Ever See You Again?* for you and Cilla to do as a duet."

"Allen, I'm not certain that changing something this late in the game is a good idea." pleaded Rosie. "I'm nervous enough already."

"Don't worry," he said calmly. "Cilla and I worked on it last night; she'll lead you through it. I knew it would be hard for you to perform that number, knowing how special it was for the president. But, it's your signature song, so we can't leave it out. All you'll have to do is introduce the song, I changed the tempo, made it a ballad. Cilla will start it off as you usually do, then slow it down, and then you'll join her for the finale. You'll be fine. Don't worry. Now let's go work on it."

At the show that night, Rosie introduced the song, choking back tears. When Cilla started, the audience applauded as they always did when they recognized the tune, but with the tempo slowed, the song took on an entirely new meaning. The audience gave them a standing ovation at the end of the song, tears streaming down their faces.

The next day the New York Times called it ". . . a balm for the wounds of a nation." Rosie and Cilla recorded the song and it became the number one hit of the year, ". . . I still remember your face, though you are in another place, my love for you grows stronger, and I can't take it much longer. Is this really the end? Will I ever see you again? Will I ever hold you again, my friend?'"

1966

CHAPTER 32

New York City, midtown

It was the last show of the season, and, as had become a tradition on *The Sonny Lewis Show*, it was a family production. It had been ever since they had had the staff's kids on with Chubby Checker years ago. The public seemed to love the idea of seeing the children grow up and learning about the folks behind the scenes. Sonny and Frankie were especially happy because, in a *Life Magazine* profile of Martin Luther King, Jr. and his wife Coretta Scott King, the couple had said that seeing Negro and white children together on the show gave them hope for the future. Sonny and Frankie used that quote whenever a sponsor seemed hesitant.

This year was going to be extra special because their own kids were going to be performing a duet. Richie had proved to be a musical prodigy. By the age of four, he could plunk out tunes on the piano, playing them by ear after one listening. Now that he was ten, he could read sheet music and play difficult concertos as well as pop tunes. He loved anything having to do with music.

Francie had been a little more reticent to display her talent. A shy girl, Francie usually kept to herself. One day though, Frankie had walked in on her playing alone in the living room and stood behind her for a few minutes as she softly sang to herself. He tiptoed out of the room and fetched Sonny. The two men stood behind Francie and listened to her sing for a few minutes. As Sonny then softly began to sing along, Francie matched him note for note. He slowly raised his volume and Francie joined him, rocking back and forth with her eyes closed. All of a sudden, Francie started singing harmonies and counter-melodies, shifting the tempo and ended up wailing. She sold the song as professionally as Sonny ever did. When the song was over, she opened her eyes and began playing with her dollhouse again.

The two men stood and stared at each other, their chins practically resting on the floor. "Francie, Honey," stammered Sonny. "How come you never told us that you could sing so good?"

"Nobody ever asked," she responded very matter of factly.

"Will you sing with me again?" he asked.

"Okay, but only if Uncle Frankie sings too," she said without looking up.

"Oh Francie, Honey, you don't want to hear Uncle Frankie sing," he sputtered. I'm a terrible singer."

"Oh, I know you are," she smiled up at him. "But I like to hear you sing anyway."

"I don't know any songs," he protested.

"You know *Three Blind Mice*," she shot back.

"She's got you there," laughed Sonny.

"All right," Frankie gave in. "Three blind mice, three blind mice . . ."

Francie joined in, skatting around the melody in a way that would have made Ella Fitzgerald jealous. Ever since that day, Francie had become a singing fool.

You couldn't stop the child, to the delight of both families. About a year ago, she and Richie began learning songs together, and the two performed together as if they were one.

Oddly enough, as they progressed, Richie became a little more reticent and Francie took the lead. Lavinia and Sonny were always encouraging Francie to pull back a little and let Richie shine. One day as the kids were performing for their parents, the Lewises were about to caution Francie again when Richie turned to them and said, "Uncle Sonny, Aunt Lavinia, don't worry about it. I like it like this, I can play the piano more and it's funner this way."

The shocked adults sat back and let the kids have their way. Before long they had a rhythm going, and, indeed, it did seem to work for them. From then on, the kids took lessons together, as well as individually.

Now, all four proud parents stood in the wings as Richie and Francie performed their first number on live television. They were all amazed at how mature the kids looked.

"They look like teenagers," whispered Lavinia.

"I can't believe how fast they're growing up," agreed Frankie.

The kids were about half way through their rendition of the Mamas and the Papas' new hit, *California Dreamin'*. The audience was mesmerized, as were their parents. Richie and Francie had performed well enough at home, but really got into it in front of an audience. They weren't fazed by the fact that they were performing in front of people, or that millions more were watching on television. In fact, it seemed to increase their pleasure.

A production assistant snuck up behind them and whispered, "The switchboard's going crazy. Everybody loves the kids. We'll have them do an encore, even if it puts us into overtime."

Rochelle and Lavinia stared at each other. "I think we've created a monster," they both whispered in unison, smiling ear to ear.

After the studio audience quieted down a bit, the kids repeated the last 16 bars. When they took their bows, they impulsively kissed and hugged each other.

That's when things began to unravel. Again, the switchboard lit up, but this time the callers didn't have compliments. They were outraged to have an interracial couple kissing on television. Never mind that Francie was only eleven and Richie was just ten. Never mind that the viewers had watched these kids grow up together over the years. Something about that kiss triggered some deep-seated fears across America, and it wasn't only from white viewers, either. Many Negro callers were offended, or more likely, threatened, by the act.

Perhaps it was a reaction to the racial unrest in the country at the time, but that simple, impulsive act, by two children, who thought of themselves as sister and brother, created a maelstrom of controversy. Their motives were innocent and related to their elation, but that didn't matter. The incident became the center of a national debate that raged for weeks. The Lewises and the Kayes refused to apologize or make excuses for the action. National leaders made speeches, both pro and con, about the incident. Surprisingly, many supporters of the civil rights struggle seemed to be upset as well, even though many of them had been promoting understanding between the races.

Sonny and Frankie decided that their only comment was going to be "No comment," but that approach seemed doomed to failure. A few very liberal folks, both White and Negro, spoke up in their defense, but it was too little, too late. Later that summer, race riots began to break out. Although there was more to those riots than two little kids kissing, you wouldn't have known it from the news surrounding the events. It wasn't long before the network called in Sonny and Frankie to discuss the situation. By the end of the summer, it was announced that *The Sonny Lewis Show* wouldn't be returning for the fall season. A spokesman for the network said it was temporary, that they expected the show to return at a later date, but everyone knew otherwise.

CHAPTER 33

LAX

Justin and Jon stood at the end of the corridor and waved to Jenny and Ani as they boarded the jet bound for New York City. After the plane took off, they headed over to the international terminal to catch their own flight. Jon seemed even quieter than usual.

"What's the matter, Jon?" asked Justin.

"Nothing," the young man responded, not looking up.

"I think that you're going to love Japan," Justin said in an attempt to cheer the boy. "Just think of the adventure! When you go back to college in the fall, you're going to be the envy of everyone."

"I suppose so," ventured Jon.

"Don't worry about not knowing the language," Justin continued. "The studio has hired Japanese students to help out on the set, and as my assistant, you have your own personal translator."

"Dad, I'm sure it's going to be great and I'm looking forward to it, but, well, there's something I wanted to talk to you about. It's kind of weird . . ." Jon trailed off.

"Boy, Ani is certainly tuned in to you kids," Justin said in shock.

"What?!?!?!"

"She told me that this would be something to be concerned about," Justin explained to his astounded son. "At first I poo-poohed the idea, but maybe there's something to it. I know what's bothering you, son."

"You do?" asked Jon with a mixture of surprise and embarrassment. "How did Ani find out? I'm so ashamed. I don't want to feel like this, Dad," he whispered, "but I can't seem to help myself."

"I don't think it's anything to be that concerned about," Justin said with a wry smile. "Ani says that you're bound to have some separation anxiety. It's the first time in your life that you and Jenny have been apart for more than a few days."

A few hours later

Jenny and Ani fastened their seat belts as their jet landed in New York City. After the limo driver met them and they claimed their luggage, they headed towards Manhattan.

Jenny stared out the window as the car sped down the highway. "You know, Ani, I haven't been to New York since I was a little kid. The last time I was here, my Mom's aunt and uncle met us at the train station. I don't think they had jets then."

Ani smiled at her stepdaughter, "I'm sure they did, but it was probably easier to travel with kids on the train. Planes weren't as luxurious as they are now. I'm sorry your mother's aunt and uncle retired to Florida. I'd feel a little better about leaving you all alone in New York for school if I knew that there was someone nearby."

Jenny gave her one of those "Oh, please" looks that only a 19-year-old girl can give. "Ani, it's my second year in college, I'm not some inexperienced child. Just because I've transferred from UCLA to Columbia, it's not like I'll be living in some ghetto! I'll be in a dorm instead of an apartment, just like we agreed. Don't go getting all misty-eyed and over-protective on me."

"I promised that I wouldn't, didn't I?" she said, stroking Jenny's arm. "I sometimes forget how strong you are. I'd be scared to death to move half way across the country at your age. Shoot! I'd be a little scared to do it even now."

"You're not afraid of anything." Jenny shot back.

"I'm terrified of flying," confessed Ani. "I'm also not too fond of snakes."

"Why didn't you say you were afraid of flying? I could have come here on my own." Jenny asked with surprise.

"I knew that I'd feel better if I made certain you were all settled in," Ani answered.

"You mean that my father would feel better."

"Well, maybe both of us," smiled Ani, grateful when Jenny smiled at her and hugged her arm.

"Ani," Jenny bubbled, "I'm so excited I could pee."

"Please wait 'til we get to the dorm," laughed her stepmother. "This limo is pretty fancy, but I don't think it has a potty."

"A potty!?!?!" laughed Jenny. "Ani, really . . ."

"Sorry," Ani added. "Maybe it's just my way of denying the fact that you're all grown up and don't need me anymore."

"Wait a minute, I didn't say anything about not needing you," protested Jenny. "I still get to come home for visits to taste your muffins, don't I?"

"Yes, and I'll even ship them to you, if you want. I'm already sending some to Jon. Won't you be lonely without him?" Ani asked, hoping to open the door to an area she was worried about.

"Of course I'll miss him, but this is the first time in my life where I get to be me, not half of a set. Oooh, look, there's the dorm."

Ani smiled, she knew that Jenny would be the stronger half of the two, as she climbed the stairs she hoped that Jon was faring as well with Justin; communication between those two wasn't always easy.

Jenny plopped her suitcase on her bed and surveyed her dorm room. "It's kind of small, isn't it?"

"I guess it is, compared to what you're used to," replied Ani. "Remember though, most people haven't grown up with your advantages."

"I know that, Ani. I was just a little surprised." Jenny said, feeling a little chastised.

"Sweetie, you need to be careful about what you say," explained Ani. "A lot of people will be resentful of the fact that you grew up with a famous father. They'll judge you faster than they would other people, and they're more likely to take things the wrong way. This is really your first time interacting with people who didn't grow up the way you did."

"My life wasn't that easy," she said defensively.

"You know that, and I know that, but these people don't. They're going to expect you to act like some rich spoiled brat because your father is a movie star," Ani explained. "I know, because when I first came to work at your house, I thought that."

"You did?" gasped Jenny. "But you were always so nice to us . . . and Momma. I would have never guessed."

"Well, it didn't take me long to see how terrific you and Jonny were," Ani explained to her stepdaughter. "I fell in love with you guys in about two minutes. I just want other people to be able to learn how nice you are, so watch what you say, and how you say it. Even the most innocent comment can be taken the wrong way."

"Okay," Jenny answered, piling her suitcases in the closet. "I'll unpack later. Let's go explore the city. I'm starving and I want to get one of those hot dogs I see everyone eating in the movies about New York."

"Why don't I ask someone in registration where we should go?" offered Ani.

"Where's you sense of adventure?" giggled Jenny as she headed for the door. "Let's walk and see where we end up. That's why I decided to come to New York for school. If I wanted to play it safe, I would have gone to one of the Seven Sisters."

Ani picked up her purse and followed Jenny. She wondered why she was ever worried; she should have known that Jenny would be able to fit in anywhere.

Tokyo, a few days later

Jon smiled at the beautiful Japanese woman who was assigned to him as his interpreter. He didn't know what to say, so she took the lead, "My name is Keiko, Mr. Mason. I am happy to meet you."

Jon turned around looking for his father. "Mr. Mason? Oh, you mean me," laughed Jon. "Please, call me Jon. It's nice to meet you, too."

"I thought that today I would show you around Tokyo and then we could discuss what you would like to see in further detail. If that is satisfactory with you, Mr. Mason," she bowed slightly.

"That sounds fine, Keiko. But, please, call me Jon; I am not old enough to be Mr. Mason. Mr. Mason is my father," he bowed slightly as well.

"Oh, no. That would be a sign of disrespect, Mr. Mason. I couldn't call you by your first name," Keiko bowed a bit lower.

"Well," said Jon slyly, "Wouldn't it also be disrespectful to call me by a name I didn't want to be called?" He bowed even lower than he had the last time.

Keiko looked confused. "Yes, I suppose it would." She brightened slightly, "May I call you Mason-san? Adding san to the end of a name is a sign of respect." She bowed again, lower.

Jon bowed even lower and replied, "Yes, that would be fine. I want you to be very honest with me about matters of etiquette. I did some reading about Japanese customs and I know that etiquette is very important. Don't feel that you will embarrass me," he bowed again.

"Mason-san, bowing is not a contest," she smiled.

"What?" he asked.

"Bowing is a sign of respect. The person with a higher position of authority does not bow as low as someone of a lesser station. To do so would be very rude," she smiled up at him, clearly happy to be able to be forthright. "I am working for you, so I shall bow lower."

"But, that doesn't seem right," protested Jon.

"By whose standards?" quipped Keiko. "You are in Japan now."

"You're right. Thank you, Keiko. What do you have planned for today?"

Keiko smiled, "I know you love baseball, so I thought you might like to see a Japanese baseball game."

"That sounds terrific," said Jon. "Let's shake a leg."

"You got it Mason-san," joked Keiko. Noticing Jon's surprised look, she explained. "I may be a Japanese girl working in a traditional role, but I went to Stanford."

Jon smiled and realized that he was going to like spending time with Keiko this summer.

Jon loved exploring Tokyo with Keiko. They had developed quite a rapport in the past few weeks. They conversed in both English and Japanese. To his surprise, he found that he had an ear for the language, and even Keiko was amazed at how well he was doing. Last night she suggested that perhaps he didn't really need her services anymore. He assured her that, even if he spoke the language well, he still needed her guidance in cultural matters.

Jon had fallen in love with Japanese culture. He had never felt so at home back in the United States. He loved wearing kimonos and hapi coats. The soft fabrics and the drape of the garments allowed him to keep his bad habits in check. He felt as if he was gaining a strength of character that he'd been lacking. Jon was truly happy for the first time in a long time.

Today was going to be even better. As a way to get a little publicity for the movie his dad was working on, the studio had arranged for Jon to play a demonstration game with one of Japan's baseball teams. Jon's first instinct was to refuse to participate, but Keiko had urged him to take part. She knew that he loved baseball and that he would enjoy himself. She reminded him that he would be just one member of the team and wouldn't be in the spotlight alone. That made him feel better. Keiko always knew the right thing to say. When he shared his poetry with her, she made thoughtful and incredibly insightful comments.

So, here he was, sitting on the bench waiting to enter the field. He realized as soon as he got in the locker room that he wasn't going to be only a member of the team. He was a good foot taller than anyone else in the clubhouse. The guys all seemed a bit taken aback by him, but, when he introduced himself in Japanese and exhibited the correct behavior; they seemed to understand that, although he looked like a big, clumsy American, he had the heart of a son of the Empire.

An hour later, the game was underway, and Jon was playing exceptionally well. It was one of those games where everything seemed to be orchestrated. He made two or three double plays, got a few good hits and seemed to be popular with the fans, although it was a little hard to tell. The behavior of a crowd at a Japanese game was decidedly different from what Jon was used to. The spectators were very reserved, with the exception of two Japanese businessmen who were sitting near the dugout. Throughout the game, they talked excitedly. They were louder and more animated than Japanese usually were in public, and they drew stares from the other spectators. They were a too far away and speaking a little too fast for Jon to keep up.

After the game, Jon was taking pictures with his teammates and thanking them for sharing the game with him. Keiko came down on the field with the two businessmen. She was glowing behind a smile as sweet and mysterious as Mona Lisa's.

"Mason-san," she started. "It is my honor to present Mr. Maruyama and Mr. Matsumoto," she said as she bowed.

The two men reached forward to shake hands. Jon, a little startled by the Western gesture, put out his hand; they pumped it vigorously, thanking him for the pleasure of watching such a gifted sportsman play.

Jon demurred that he really wasn't that good, but thanked them all the same. The fact that he responded in Japanese surprised them and, for some reason, caused them to give each other a knowing glance. They then asked him a question in Japanese. Jon was glad that Keiko was there, because he thought he didn't understand the men. He turned to Keiko, and before he could speak, she told him the answer to his unasked question.

"Yes, Mason-san, you did hear that correctly," she smiled. "These two honorable gentlemen offered to make you the starting pitcher on the baseball team that they own. They want you to play professional baseball here in Tokyo!"

CHAPTER 34

Paris

Gina adjusted her sunglasses as the cab sped along the Champs d'Elysse; Ingrid was looking at her appointment book. "Angelina, Darling, after this morning's photo shoot I was wondering if we could have lunch with Claudette. She asked me last night and I told her I'd check with you."

"Mother, feel free to make your plans, you don't have to check with me. I love having you here visiting me, but I'm certain it must be boring for you to sit around during these photo shoots." Gina offered, squeezing her mother's hand slightly.

Her mother had been a bit at loose ends since her father had died last year. After running his life for so long, she felt a terrible emptiness, Gina knew. But, at 22 she didn't want her mother to start running her life. They'd finally reached a point where they were beginning to rebuild their relationship, so Gina was a bit cautious in her reply. "Besides, you know I don't eat lunch."

"Claudette would love to see you. She says that she runs in to you from time to time at parties, and you chat for a while, but that's it," Ingrid offered. "She jokes that when you first started modeling, you were always referred to in the society photos as 'Claudette Colbert's goddaughter, Gina Ferrara' and that now it's 'Gina Ferrara's godmother, Claudette' and they don't even mention her last name. Not that she minds."

Gina slid the sunglasses down the bridge of her nose and looked at her mother.

"Well, maybe a little," Ingrid laughed.

Gina smiled at her mother. "All right, we'll go, but tell her not to prepare any lunch for me. Just some coffee and toast."

Ingrid looked at her daughter with concern, "Darling, I know that you have to watch your weight, I used to be 15 pounds lighter when I modeled. But, you really are getting too thin. Have you seen a doctor? Nothing's wrong, is it?"

"No mother," Gina sighed. "It's just this new look. Since Twiggy came on the scene, the fashion editors all want that stick look. Unfortunately, with Daddy's Italian peasant stock in me . . ." She spied her mother's disapproving look. "Don't get all upset, I love my heritage, but let's face it, Daddy's people weren't exactly going to be blown away by a strong wind. Every pound I gain shows up on my face." She then added, "Don't worry, this trend will pass and when it does, the first thing I'm going to do is order a plate full of eclairs."

"All right, Sweetie," Ingrid said, stroking her daughter's arm through her bulky sweater. "I feel guilty for all those years I made you take all those exercise and sports classes. Maybe that wasn't the right thing to do."

"Just the opposite, Mother," Gina reassured her. "What you taught me was incredible self-discipline. I don't think I would have lasted a month as a model without that. I've seen so many girls come and go. They're used up and tossed aside if they can't handle it. I've lasted as long as I have exactly because of what you taught me. Oh, here we are! Driver pull over at Chanel."

They entered the salon and went upstairs where a crew of fashion coordinators and make-up artists were waiting. Ingrid found a quiet corner and took out her knitting as Gina went into the make-up room. A few minutes later, Ingrid saw Jean Beaubien approaching. He was clutching some proof sheets and scowling. They nodded at each other stiffly before he pushed open the door to the make-up area and entered.

Within a few minutes the entire make-up staff came out and quickly disappeared. Jean's temper was infamous and it wasn't uncommon for him to explode during a shoot. Those that weren't the direct recipients of his rage always scattered, lest they be added to the target list. Since Gina hadn't come out of the room, Ingrid assumed that it was she who was the focus of Jean's anger.

Within months of meeting Jean, Gina was appearing on the cover of Europe's top fashion magazines. At first Ingrid and Angelo were angry; they didn't like the idea of Gina dropping out of school. Gradually though, they warmed to the idea, and were genuinely happy for Gina. She finally seemed to have found something that she liked to do. There was no denying Gina was beautiful; the mixture of classic Roman beauty and the height from the Scandinavian side of the family seemed a perfect combination. In less than a year she was the world's top model.

When Ingrid and Angelo had flown to Europe for Gina's first fashion show at Balenciagga, Ingrid thought that it would remind her of her days as a model, but Gina was in a league far beyond anything Ingrid had experienced. It was a social whirl, but Gina seemed to be happy, so they were happy. Seeing Gina established seemed to bring some measure of peace to Angelo.

Ingrid never liked Jean, though. She didn't trust him. What kind of man seduces a teenaged girl, encourages her to drop out of school, and has her move in with him? It wasn't long before she and Angelo began to suspect that Jean was using Gina to further his career. Unfortunately, they couldn't convince Gina of that.

Ingrid would never say it, but she was certain that Angelo's heart attack was brought on by his worries about Gina and "that man". Jean's screaming interrupted Ingrid's reverie. It was so loud that she could hear it through the closed door of the make-up room.

"You cow," she heard Jean say. "All of these photos are useless. The clothes look horrible because you look horrible. I told you that if you didn't lose weight, I wouldn't photograph you any more. I take pictures of fashion models, not livestock."

Ingrid was about to get up and put a stop to his tirade, when the door suddenly flew open. Jean stormed out of the make-up room and continued out of the salon. Ingrid ran in to comfort Gina. She was huddled on the floor crying, her make-up a mess. She was clad only in a bra and panties and Ingrid gasped in horror. Her daughter wasn't just thin, she was emaciated. Her elbows were wider than her upper arm, Ingrid could only think of the pictures she had seen of starving children in Africa.

"Oh, Mother," Gina cried as she tried to stand. She was so weak that she couldn't even pull herself to a standing position; she got half way up and started to collapse. Ingrid caught her daughter and draped a robe over her shoulders.

"What has that man done to you?" she asked, her voice catching in her throat. "Gina, what's wrong with you. Are you sick?" Ingrid thought that her daughter must have cancer, she looked like a skeleton.

"No mother, I'm just too fat," Gina said in disgust.

"Too fat?!?!?!" Ingrid said incredulously. She spun her daughter around to face the mirror and removed the robe she had thrown over Gina's shoulders. "Gina, look at yourself. You weighed more than this when you were twelve."

Gina kept her head down. "I can't," she cried. "I can't stand to look at myself."

Ingrid put her hand under Gina's chin and forcibly raised her head. "Gina, you are not fat. You are nothing but skin and bones. This cannot be healthy."

Gina looked in the mirror and nodded. For once, Ingrid was grateful that she had been such a stern parent. In the past she had had some doubts, thinking that if she'd been a little less regimented, Gina wouldn't have rebelled so much. Now, however, there was no doubt in her mind. In her weakened state Gina had fallen right back into obedience. Ingrid sensed that Gina's life might just depend on her following Ingrid's directions exactly. It was obvious that Gina was in no condition to make any decisions on her own.

Ingrid took Gina back to her apartment and kept a bedside vigil. She prepared broth for Gina, for that's all she would eat. Each day she added a little cream to the broth, the next week some vegetables. All along she insisted that Gina take vitamins. She accompanied Gina to the bathroom and sat with her, for once she had caught Gina forcing herself to vomit up what little food she ate.

Ingrid fielded all her phone calls. She had her lawyers try to arrange to have all of Gina's contracts canceled. When the agencies wouldn't relent, Ingrid sold off her stock portfolio and bought out the contracts. Thank God she had invested Angelo's income wisely and had enough money to do so.

In the past month, Gina had gained four pounds, and Ingrid felt it was at last safe to bring her home. She sold Gina's apartment in Paris and severed all of her daughter's French contracts. Then she called Claudette and asked for her help in arranging medical transportation to the States, and a nurse to accompany them. Claudette knew of a doctor in Switzerland who would prescribe a course of treatment and she was flying him to Paris that night.

The next day, Ingrid was introduced to Dr. Harry Shadrow. As Claudette sat with Gina, Ingrid sat at the kitchen table with Dr. Shadrow. "What?" she pleaded "What would cause someone to do something like that to themselves?"

Dr. Shadrow explained to Ingrid that Gina was suffering from a rare psychological problem, one in which she viewed herself as too fat, no matter how thin she was. He prescribed extensive counseling sessions with a psychiatrist and recommended a doctor in California who had agreed to take on Gina, although he almost never accepted new patients. Ingrid reached over and clasped the doctor's hand and tried to thank him, but all she could do was sob.

The next day, Gina, Ingrid and the nurse boarded a plane for the United States. Ingrid thanked the nurse for her help. "God has already taken my Angelo," she muttered. "If he wants Gina, he'll have to fight me first."

The nurse didn't think that even God would stand a chance against Ingrid.

CHAPTER 35

Hollywood

The tall blond man looked Cilla squarely in the eye and cursed, "You are absolutely depraved! Do you know that? I don't know what I ever saw in you. Get out! Get out before I throw you out, you wrench!"

Cilla had stood her ground when he began speaking to her. She matched his steely glare, right up until the last word out of his mouth. "So, that's what you think of me?" she said. "The truth finally comes out. Well, you're nothing more than a, than a . . . power drill." She collapsed against his chest in a fit of laughter. He held on to her as the two of them teetered precariously on the curb.

"Cut!" yelled the director. "Reset the lights and get make-up in here," he said as he saw Cilla's mascara running down her face. "Take 10. We'll try that again." He walked over to the two giggling actors. "That was pretty good Cilla. I actually thought that you were going to be able to get through that scene."

"I'm sorry Joel," Cilla said as she stood still so the make up girl could fix her face. "I didn't know if you wanted me to keep going after Derek's flub, and I started to, but then I just lost it. Sorry."

"No, it was my mistake. I don't know what's gotten in to me," said the matinee idol. "I guess that I'm just a little tired today," he said looking off toward the edge of the set.

"That's okay," offered the director. "We've been making terrific progress up until now. We're actually a day ahead of schedule. Tell you what, let's nail this scene, and then take off early for the day. Derek, get ready for your entrance. We'll start shooting in a minute." As soon as the actor was out of earshot, the director leaned in toward Cilla and whispered, "You're doing great, Cilla. Try to pull him through this scene. I'm beat."

"Not a problem," Cilla reassured him. "Unless he calls me a wrench again." The scene went off the second time without a hitch, or a wrench. Cilla was in her trailer when the door opened and Allen popped his head in.

"I hear that you're getting off early today," he said chipperly. "How about if we go out for dinner tonight? I don't have a rehearsal tomorrow"

"I'm beat, let's stay in," she replied, putting a chocolate in her mouth. "I think we've had enough pictures of the happy newlyweds in the fan magazines. The people at immigration can't expect us to go out every night."

"I think we've got them convinced that it's not just a marriage of convenience so I could stay in the States." he laughed. "If they only knew!"

"Listen, Allen, Honey, you've got to do me a favor," she cooed.

"Anything, Luv," Allen said, folding his lanky body into an overstuffed chair. "I owe you my career, my life, my citizenship. Whatever you desire is yours."

"It's really not that big a deal," she said trying to look serious. "Just get my co-star to bed at a decent hour, so that he can remember his lines the next day. I don't want your active libido interfering with my chance to win an Oscar," She batted her eyes in an exaggerated way and they both melted in laughter.

1969

CHAPTER 36

Tokyo

Jon stood tall, closed his eyes for a second, wound up and threw a slider. The batter swung, but just couldn't connect with the ball. The umpire signaled the third out of the inning, and the end of another winning game. Jon bowed toward the ump, then turned and bowed to the fans in the stadium. They went wild. He took off his cap and waved it toward the crowd as he headed for the dugout.

He stopped to sign some baseballs, mitts, programs, whatever his admirers thrust in front of him. He joked with them in Japanese, and in English for those who preferred to speak to him in his native tongue. Oddly enough, he was more comfortable speaking Japanese now. After three years in Tokyo, he felt that this was his home.

In the locker room he congratulated his teammates, changed into street clothes, and headed to the players' parking lot. Keiko was waiting in their red convertible. He kissed her as he got in the car and they sped off for home where there would be just enough time for a shower and a few minutes of meditation before meeting Keiko's parents for dinner. It was their second wedding anniversary, and his in-laws were honoring them with a small party at their favorite restaurant. It would be just them, Keiko's elderly aunt, and a few close friends. He felt very lucky to have such a loving family and such a wonderful, understanding wife, he thought, as he gazed at Keiko.

The past three years had been the happiest of his life. When his father's movie finished filming, Jon decided that he wanted to stay in Japan. His father had little reason to protest, as Jon had a good offer to play professional baseball, already made some wonderful friends, and, of course, had Keiko. His only regret was that his father and Ani were halfway around the world. Jenny was even farther away than that.

Who'd have ever thought Jenny would end up a Political Science major at Columbia? But, then again, he would never have guessed that his life would take the path it had. Here he was living in Tokyo, with a wonderful wife and a job he loved, a job that left him plenty of free time to study and write poetry. He was proud of the fact that his sensei, his master teacher, had admired his first attempts at writing poetry in Japanese.

Jon pulled the sports car into the parking garage for their building. As they rode the elevator up to their penthouse apartment, Keiko smiled at her husband.

"You seem awfully pensive tonight, Jon," she said softly.

"I was just counting my blessings," he responded, as he reached over and took her hand. "I was thinking how lucky I am to have you."

"Funny, I was thinking the same thing." she smiled. "We made such good time driving home from the stadium that we'll have time to relax before we go to meet everyone for dinner."

He unlocked the door to their apartment, and held the door open for her. "I can think of one way I'd like to relax. Just let me take a shower first."

"I was hoping you'd say that," she smiled. "You go hop in the shower and I'll open a bottle of champagne. We can have our own private anniversary celebration before we leave for the restaurant."

Jon came into the bedroom, wrapped in his favorite midnight blue kimono. Keiko was sitting on the futon in her bright pink kimono. Her face glowed in the light of the candles she had lit. The champagne was chilling in a silver bucket on the nightstand. In front of Keiko there was a large white box with a red bow on top.

"What's this?" asked Jon, with a smile.

"Oh, just a little something to show how much I love you," she said reaching for the sash of his robe. The sash fell open and Keiko leaned forward and began to fondle Jon's already thickening cock.

"Mmmmm," moaned Jon. "Don't you want to see your present?" he asked.

"Later," said Keiko as she swept his gift aside and pulled him on top of her. He reached between her legs and was surprised at how moist she was already. "We don't have much time and it would be rude to keep everyone waiting," she gasped as she wrapped her legs around him and forced him inside of her.

Their coupling was passionate, athletic, and brief. Afterwards they lay back and snuggled together, sipping champagne.

"Open your present," Keiko offered, pushing the box close to him with her foot.

"No, you open yours first," he insisted as he pulled an envelope out from under the futon.

"Very sneaky," she said eyeing him and stroking his smooth chest. "Jon, you didn't!" she exclaimed as she looked at the contents of the envelope. There were five airline tickets enclosed. "You promised that we'd go to the States soon, but I didn't think this soon," she squealed. "Why five tickets, though?"

"I want our families to get to know each other, more than just meeting at the wedding," he said.

"That's only four," Keiko said. "Why the extra ticket?"

"We both know that your Aunt Nobuko is dying to go to Disneyland!" he laughed

Keiko kissed her husband excitedly. "They're going to be so happy. Can I tell them tonight?"

"Of course," he smiled, loving the fact that she was so happy. "We'd better start getting dressed soon."

"You haven't opened your present yet," she pouted in fun. "It's not a trip, but it is something I know you want."

"I wonder what that could be?" he said as he untied the ribbon. Jon opened the box, pulled back the tissue paper and almost cried. Keiko had gotten him the most beautiful present.

"Go ahead, try it on. I want to see you in it," she urged him.

"Keiko, it's just so beautiful. How did you know?" he asked.

"I saw you looking at it in the catalog, and I knew you'd look great in it."

Jon held up the garment before him. It was a beautiful black satin corset, with silk garters. A pair of black hose and stiletto heels were still in the box.

"Put it on, put it on," Keiko cried. "I'll help you," she said as she fiddled with the hooks in the back. "See, it even has an attached, padded bra."

Jon looked at himself in the bedroom mirror, "It's beautiful," he stammered.

"So are you," Keiko concurred, as she lay back on the bed. "I think we have a little time before we have to go."

Jon smiled as he reached for his wife. He really was the luckiest man on earth.

CHAPTER 37

New York City, Upper West Side

After school let out, Francie hopped onto the low stone fence in front of the building and waited to be picked up. Her mother and Rochelle were taking Richie for an audition at the music academy, so Uncle Frankie was going to pick her up. Her friend LaWanda, the prettiest Negro girl at the school, kept her company. LaWanda was so beautiful that even the white boys said she was pretty. Francie was surprised when LaWanda said that she wanted them to be best friends. She always thought that LaWanda was stuck up, but she found out later that she was just really shy. They shared all the secrets that 14-year-old girls shared.

"Did you see how Miss Johnson gave Tisha whatfor this afternoon?" asked LaWanda.

"What for?" Francie said. Sometimes LaWanda used terms Francie didn't understand.

"She yelled at her," LaWanda sighed. "Sometimes girl, I think that you ain't Negro at all."

"Just because I don't know some of the stuff you say doesn't make me any less Negro," Francie defended. "We just don't talk like that in my house."

"I know. You talk so white that, at first, I thought that you might be a mulatto." explained LaWanda. "My mother says you look like one. I heard her say, 'That's girl's high yellow."

"What's a high yellow?" Francie had never heard those words.

"A high yellow is someone who is only part black, but mostly white," LaWanda explained patiently. "A Negro who is so light they could pass for white. Someone like you."

"What a terrible thing to say," Francie started crying. "My mother and father are both Negro and you know it!"

LaWanda suddenly remembered that her mother told her not to repeat what she had just said to anyone. "Oh, don't get all worked up," she said quickly. "I didn't mean anything by it."

"Maybe you're a high yellow too," said Francie, hurt by the knowledge that her best friend talked about her behind her back. "You're not much darker than I am. That's why the boys all love you. Even the white boys want to kiss you."

"Take that back," said LaWanda, pinching Francie's arm.

Francie gave LaWanda a playful shove and chanted, "The boys want to kiss LaWanda 'cuz she's high yellow and she wiggles like Jello."

The two girls began taunting each other good-naturedly. Francie started to get off the fence when she saw Uncle Frankie's car approaching. She turned as she hopped off, planning to tease LaWanda once last time. LaWanda gave her a playful shove. Francie lost her balance and fell backwards onto the sidewalk; she hit the ground hard. The last thing she remembered was her Uncle Frankie yelling, "Hey stop that!"

Frankie carried Francie into the emergency room. A nurse approached and when Frankie explained what had happened, a doctor rushed Francie into an examination room.

The nurse took Frankie over to a cubicle. "I just have to get some information while the doctor examines your little girl. How old is your daughter?"

"She's not my daughter," answered Frankie numbly. "She's my god daughter."

"I'm sorry," said the nurse. "It's just that she looks so much like you that I assumed . . . ." her voice trailed off. "Can you reach one of her parents? We'll need their consent if we have to perform any procedures."

"I work with her father. I'll call him, and her mother." Frankie muttered. "Is she going to be okay?"

"You can never tell with head injuries," explained the nurse. "But, I wouldn't be too worried. Kids have hard heads. My boys are always knocking theirs into something. Here, use this phone, just dial the operator and have her connect you."

Within minutes Frankie had reached Lavinia at home. She, Rochelle and Richie were on their way over. He caught Sonny at the studio, just as he was getting ready to head into the recording booth. He was also on his way over to the hospital.

Hours later, the doctor came out to find the two families sitting quietly in the waiting room. He spoke to them gravely, "I'm afraid that I don't have much to report that is positive. The blow to her head must have been pretty severe. There's a lot of internal bleeding. We've put in a shunt to drain off some of the fluid, so that pressure doesn't build up and cause brain damage."

"My baby," sobbed Lavinia. "Is she in a lot of pain?"

"No," said the doctor. "She's unconscious, most likely comatose. At this point, it's really a matter of wait and see. I'll let you know as soon as we know something. She needs to rest now; you can visit her in about an hour. I would suggest that her parents go down to the labs and have some blood drawn. I don't foresee her needing much blood, but she's AB negative, which is pretty rare. It's always a good idea to know who's the best match in case we do need blood."

Lavinia sobbed into Rochelle's shoulder. Sonny stood in shock with his arm around Richie. Frankie sobbed, "If only I was a few minutes earlier, I could have prevented all this," he said, turning to Lavinia. "I'm so sorry."

"How could you know? Accidents like this happen," soothed Lavinia. "We'd better go down to the lab and have blood samples taken now. By the time that's done, we should be able to go in and visit Francie."

"Let's go," said Frankie, as he took Lavinia's arm. "This isn't going to be easy." The two of them walked down the hall.

Richie watched them for a second then turned to his mother. "Mom, why is Daddy going down to the lab with Aunt Lavinia? Shouldn't Uncle Sonny be going?"

Rochelle sat down and pulled Richie to her side, "This isn't exactly the way we'd hope this would come out. We were going to wait until you were older, but I guess that there's no getting away from it now. You see Richie, your Daddy isn't your real father."

Richie's jaw dropped open. "What?!?!?! Well, if he's not really my father then who is?" the boy asked.

Rochelle stared at Richie, unable to speak.

"I am," said Sonny as he put his arm around the boy's waist and pulled him close. "Your father, uh, Frankie, is Francie's real father."

"Wow that makes her my sister," said Richie.

Sonny took Richie's hand. "Not really. You see, I'm your real father. We were going to tell you this in a few years, when we thought that you both were old enough to understand."

The boy just stared, first at Sonny, then at his mother.

"This doesn't mean that any of us love you any less," she explained.

"But, how, why?" Richie stammered. "Does Francie know?"

"No, we were going to tell both of you at the same time," explained Rochelle.

Sonny took Richie's hand, "I've always loved your mother, and Frankie has always loved Lavinia. People who aren't the same color if they get married, well it can be hard on them and their kids. So I married your Aunt Lavinia and your mother married your father, . . . uhm, Frankie."

"Honey," she soothed. "We don't expect you to understand this right now. When we get home with Francie and everyone, we'll sit down and explain the whole thing. But, for right now, you can't tell anyone. Promise?"

Richie nodded in assent, too stunned to speak.

CHAPTER 38

Beverly Hills

G ina walked down the stairs of her parents' house thinking about how many times she had done this as a child, as an angry teenager, and now, as a grown woman. Her mother beamed at her from the bottom of the staircase.

"What is it mother?" she said lightheartedly.

"It's just so good to see you looking so well," smiled Ingrid. "I keep thanking God for hearing my prayers when you were sick. Every time I see you, I thank Him again," she started crying.

"Mother, if you're going to cry every time you see me, it's going to get very difficult for me to stay here." Gina cautioned her mother. "That's all behind us now. Don't dwell on it."

Gina supposed she couldn't get too cross with her mother. She owed the woman her life, literally. Whether with God's help or not, Ingrid had devoted the last three years to nursing Gina back to health, both physically and emotionally. Gina looked back on the situation now and couldn't believe what she had let happen to her. It started so slowly, at first, changing her hairstyle to please Jean, trying a new color lipstick because he said it photographed better. Dr. Shadrow had helped her see that who she was didn't depend on how she looked. Oddly enough, she felt better now than she had in years, and she was ten pounds heavier than when she first met Jean. Screw him! She had more energy now, at 25, than she had had at 18.

Looking back she found it hard to believe that she was the same person who lived in Paris. She hadn't realized how totally Jean had begun to dominate her life until her mother saved her from him. What she thought of as Jean's all encompassing passion was really Jean cutting her off from everything in the world except him, she now realized. And, while it would be easy for Gina to blame everything on Jean, she knew that she had to accept some of the responsibility.

A few months ago, Gina wanted to go back to school and finish college. Her mother was a little hesitant, but Dr. Shadrow had reassured Ingrid that it was a good sign, and, finally, she relented. Gina signed up for only a few courses, in easy subjects, art appreciation, composition and photography. The first two classes she liked well enough, but it was photography that really sparked her interest, ironically. Her professor said she had a real feel for the camera and she readily gave her encouragement. This coming semester, Gina was taking two photography courses concurrently, and working in the professor's lab two afternoons a week. She felt more exhilarated than she had in years.

Gina smiled at her mother. "How about if we do a little shopping and then stop for lunch?" she offered.

"I don't need anything," Ingrid said brightly. "How about if I make us lunch here?"

"Who said shopping was about getting something you need, Mother? Let's just go out. It's such a beautiful day." She saw the slightest hint of a frown cross her mother's face. "We don't have to spend a lot. We don't even have to buy a thing."

"It just that . . . ." Ingrid trailed off.

"I know," sighed Gina. "Mother, it's true that we don't have as much money as we used to, but we've cut back on expenses, too. No more servants or nurses, just the gardener and a cleaning lady. The money from my trust fund and the residuals I get from my commercials allow us to get by. So, please, permit me the pleasure of my mother's company for lunch at some inexpensive cafe." Gina laughed as she took her mother by the arm and led her out the door.

CHAPTER 39

Los Angeles

"Cilla, honey, enjoy your last night of anonymity," Allen saluted his wife. "After your movie opens tomorrow, you're going to belong to the public."

"I thought that this thing would never open," laughed Cilla. "Can you imagine the studio keeping this in the can for three years?"

"You've got it, but now we can enjoy the moment," wheezed her co-star Derek, as he took a hit off the joint and passed it to the nameless redhead sitting next to him in the back of the limo. "Here . . . darling, what did you say your name was?"

"Denise," she cooed. "Denise Gold. I just want to say Mr . . ."

"Derek, Darling, just Derek," he corrected her. ""You're my date for the evening, and dates call people by their first names."

"Yes, Mr . . . Derek." she stuttered. "I'm just so excited that you wanted to take me out. I didn't even think that you noticed me on the set. My part being so small and everything."

Peter choked on the smoke as he passed the joint to Cilla. "It's not your parts I'm interested in Miss Gold. Besides, haven't you ever heard? There are no small parts, only small actors."

"And actors with small parts," joked Allen.

"My dear, that is so pithy, you are positively elegant." Cilla applauded facetiously, as she passed on the untouched joint and took a bite out of the chocolate bar she had in her purse.

"Yes, you might even say, pith elegant." Allen lisped jokingly.

"I don't get it," said the puzzled starlet.

"And you won't be getting it later," smirked Derek. "Honey, didn't your agent explain it to you?"

"Explain what?" she asked.

"Oh my lord," Derek cried. "We've got a genuine Doris Day ingenue on our hands. I'll kill her agent!"

"Sweetie," Cilla said in a comforting tone. "How can I explain this to you? You're only here tonight as eye candy." Cilla looked into the young woman's blank eyes and explained further, "You're here to make Derek look good, to appear on his arm. In return, you get your picture in the papers and he gets to make all the men drool with envy and all the women swoon. After the premiere, you'll go home and call your mother in Kansas City, or wherever, and that will be that."

"But, I'm from Portland, Oregon. Why would I call Kansas City?" she asked.

"This one's a few sandwiches short of a picnic, isn't she?" sighed Derek. "You don't have to call anywhere, Dear. This date is just for show. After the movie is over, I'll send you home."

"Did I say something wrong?" asked the befuddled beauty. "Don't you like me?"

Allen leaned forward, took a long drag on the joint, and looked the girl straight in the eye. "Nothing is wrong with you, Darling, it's just that Derek's a poofter." Noting her blank look, he continued, "A sissy, a fairy, a fag. He likes boys. Got it?"

You could practically see the light bulb go off in her head. "Oooooh! Okay," she said agreeably. "That's much better. I was worried that I'd have a real battle on my hands when you dropped me off. You have a reputation as a terrible ladies' man, you know."

"And he wants to keep it that way. That's precisely why you're here," Cilla explained. "After tonight, you're going to tell everyone how he wouldn't keep his hands off of you."

"Okey-dokey," she smiled. "Now, can I have hit off that roach?"

They all looked at her and everyone burst out laughing. The window between the driver and the passengers rolled down a notch, and the driver announced that they were just pulling up to the theater. Derek opened the windows, ostensibly to wave to his fans, but, in reality, to give the smoke a chance to clear out before they pulled up in front of Rona Barrett.

As the limo stopped, Derek got out and reached for Miss. Gold's arm. She clung to him like condensation on a glass of beer on a hot day. Allen got out next, just as Rona Barrett was announcing Cilla's entrance.

"And now, here's Derek's co-star, Cilla Best. What many of you folks don't know is that Cilla is the daughter of Rosie Campbell, and a star in her own right, having won a Tony Award for her performance in the Broadway production of this movie. Cilla, how come your mother's not here tonight?"

Cilla smiled brightly and muttered through her teeth, "Nasty bitch." But, she turned to Rona and announced; "Now, Rona, you know that my mother's in London. She did call me, though, to wish me luck. She said if I should run into you to give you something." She leaned over to kiss the tiny woman on the cheek and at the same time, ground a spike heel into her instep. "That's from my mother and me!" She then took Allen's arm and entered the theater.

After the film screening, she and the boys made the round of parties with Miss Gold. When they dropped her off at midnight, Allen said, "Now, let's go have some real fun."

"I know just the place," offered Derek. He tapped on the glass and gave the driver an address in West Hollywood. "This is probably the last time you'll be able to go anywhere without your fans mobbing you," he said. "And I really think you should see this act at least once in your life."

The limo pulled up in front of a run down looking building in a seedy section of town. Cilla looked a little apprehensive getting out of the limo. "Are you certain this is the right address? It looks like an abandoned warehouse."

"Don't worry, Luv," comforted Allen. "It's much nicer inside. They leave the place dumpy on the outside to make it less noticeable." As he was speaking, he knocked on the door. A peephole cover slid open, and then the door opened. The blast of music, lights and smoke erased all thoughts of an empty warehouse.

Cilla and the boys slipped in and were led to a table at the side of a small stage. Cilla did a double take; the performers on the stage looked remarkably like the Andrew Sisters. There was a little buzz of excitement as some of the crowd recognized Derek. Cilla took in the crowd of attractive young men and leaned over to Derek whispering,

"Aren't you worried about being seen in a gay bar?"

"They can't tell anyone they saw me here without admitting that they were here too," smiled Derek. "This place is filled with people in the industry. No one is going to drop the beads on anyone. I can't wait for you to see this act, you're going to plotz."

"Cilla, there's a queen here who does an impersonation of your mother," explained Allen. "I thought that it would be the next best thing to your mother being here," he said kissing her on the cheek.

There was a break between acts, which Allen used to signal the waiter and order a bottle of champagne. The trio settled in with their drinks, waiting for the show to begin. There was an unusually long silence before the emcee of the show entered. She immediately squelched the applause.

"Ladies and Gentlemen," he began ominously. "I have very sad news. We've just been informed that Rosie Campbell was found dead in her London apartment a few hours ago." There was some tittering. "This is no joke, Rosie died of an overdose. They're saying it was accidental." Moans and sobs filled the air. Cilla, Allen, and Derek sat in stunned silence. "As a tribute, Tess Tickle would like to dedicate her next performance to the late, great, Rosie Campbell, a Hollywood legend."

Wisps of stage fog drifted across the footlights, and then the lights came up on an incredible facsimile of Rosie Campbell. The performer stood stock still for almost a full minute, then began singing,

"I still remember your face, though you are in another place, my love for you grows stronger and I can't take it much longer. Is this really the end . . ." Tears streamed down the performer's face as he sang.

Cilla sat and stared, frozen in shock. Her mother was dead. She couldn't believe it.

CHAPTER 40

New York City

It was a hot and sticky night in New York City, unusually hot for the end of June Jenny was eating an ice cream cone as she walked through Sheridan Square. Even though it was late and she knew she should head back up town to her apartment, she couldn't bring herself to leave. This was why she wanted to come to New York City. As late as it was, the streets were still teeming with people. People of every race, religion and possible persuasion. Nothing like white bread Beverly Hills, with its upper class homes filled with middle class lives. Jenny doubted that she'd ever move back to California. After she finished grad school, she was staying in New York

A tall woman bumped into her as she rushed by, knocking the ice cream out of Jenny's hand. "Hey, watch it!" she yelled as the amazon whizzed past. To her astonishment the woman turned around. That's when Jenny realized that it wasn't a woman at all, but a man dressed as a woman.

"Sorry," the drag queen muttered, then a look of shock crossed her face, and she turned quickly to leave.

"Wait a minute! I know you!" Jenny called. She'd recognize his voice anywhere. She tried to imagine the person before her without all the make-up and the wig. "Aren't you in my statistics class?"

"Busted," she said. "Hi, Jenny. Yeah, it's Dominic Donzetti."

"What's the deal?" a stunned Jenny asked. Dominic was hardly what you'd call a good-looking man, but he was a stunning, if not pretty, woman.

"I'm gay," he confessed. "Please don't tell anyone. I could get thrown out of school."

"Hey, it's nobody's business but yours," she reassured him. "Besides, someone I care a great deal about likes to dress up in women's clothes."

"I knew you were good people," he said. "Thanks."

The two of them walked together for a few blocks talking. Dominic explained that his girl name was Anita Mann. Unlike Jenny, Dominic/Anita didn't come from a well to do or wealthy family. He worked as a drag performer to make enough money to pay for school.

"I figured I like to get dressed up anyway, so I might as well make some money at it. My folks found out, though and threw me out of the house. So, now, it's

112

even harder," he said, but didn't mention that he sometimes hustled to make ends meet.

"You're kidding," Jenny said, not so much in disbelief as shock. She couldn't imagine a parent turning a back on their child. She knew that her Dad and Ani wouldn't ever do such a thing, but then again, maybe she was näive. Jon had told her about his transvestite activities, but made her promise not to tell anyone else. After he confided in her, she did a lot of research on the subject, so she knew more than most people would guess. "So, you only dress up to perform, you don't get turned on by it?"

"Well, I sometimes get excited, because I kind of make a pretty girl, not to be immodest, or anything," said Dominic blushing. "I guess the excitement is more in thinking about how guys look at me when I'm in drag. I get treated much better as Anita than I do as Dominic."

"So, you don't feel like a woman trapped in a man's body?" Jenny asked.

"More like a man trapped in women's undergarments!" joked Dominic. "Oh well, there is no beauty without pain."

The two turned a corner and saw a crowd of people gathered around outside a bar.

"What's going on up there?" asked Jenny.

Dominic saw the cop cars and paddy wagons and spun Jenny around. "Let's go the other way. That's The Stonewall, a sleazy bar where a lot of drag queens hang out. It's probably being raided."

Jenny asked, "Why?"

"Why what?" asked Dominic.

"Why are they raiding the bar?" she asked. "They've got to have a reason to arrest people."

"They can pick any number of reasons. For example, it's against the law to serve drinks to homosexuals. It's also against the law to wear clothing of the opposite gender," he explained.

"That's ridiculous, I wear boys' jeans and shirts all the time," she answered

"The rules are different with drag queens and dykes, it seems. No surprise. The cops bend the laws to fit what they want," said Dominic. "They don't really need a reason, and most of us are too afraid of being found out to put up a fight. Come on, let's go," he urged.

"Let's go see what's going on," said Jenny. She took his hand and led him down the street. "We'll stand on the other side of the street. I won't let anything happen to you."

As they arrived on the corner, about five or six police cars pulled up. The cops emerged from the vehicles and began to harass the crowd. One of the cops reached his arm back and punched one of the drag queens in the nose. As the blood gushed, the crowd became angrier. A very masculine woman started yelling at the cops. Someone picked up a garbage can and threw it at the cop who had punched the drag queen. It hit him square in the back and he stumbled forward.

The crowd began to revolt. In a matter of minutes the bystanders had turned on the police, throwing whatever was handy; soda bottles, stones, coins, even a fence post. The cops had nowhere to go but into the bar. Even when they were inside, the crowd didn't let up, pelting the storefront and the windows with pebbles and rocks. A few even threw bricks. Soon the crowd was chanting "No more!" and "Dirty Pigs". Jenny started chanting, and before she knew it, she was throwing things, too.

The reporters and photographers showed up slightly before the additional police squads. Eventually, Jenny was rounded up, along with Dominic, and others. They were taken to the police station where they were booked. Somehow Dominic and Jenny got separated. While she was being booked, she asked about Dominic, but the cops at the station wouldn't tell her anything. They treated her like scum. She didn't like to use the fact that her father was famous, but she had promised Dominic she would look out for him, and she couldn't do that if she was in jail herself.

"My name is Jenny Mason," she announced to the startled desk sergeant. "My father is Justin Mason, the actor. I want to call his attorney." As soon as the police verified her identity, she was released and pushed out a side door of the precinct house onto the sidewalk. She was about to head to the front of the station to bail out Dominic when a reporter stopped her.

"Are you Jenny Mason?" he asked. When she confirmed that she was, he asked for a statement. As she had seen her father do a hundred times, she stood on the sidewalk and gave him a brief interview. She was in the middle of explaining how unfair she thought the whole situation was when a commotion caused them to turn around. Dominic had tried to escape the building by jumping out a side window. He ended up impaling himself on the wrought iron fence surrounding the building. Jenny stood in stunned silence for no more than a few seconds before she began screaming for help.

Jenny rode in the ambulance with him to the hospital, removing his make-up and wig. At the emergency room, she was forced to sit in the lobby and wait. A few minutes later, the doctor came out and told her Dominic was dead. She asked for his clothes and the doctor handed them to her in a brown paper bag.

"I noticed that you'd removed his make-up, I figured that you didn't want his parents to see him that way," he said. "I'm sorry."

Jenny walked down the streets of Manhattan as the first flickers of sunlight began. As she passed a newsstand, the headline of a newspaper caught her eye, "Queers Battle Police" the headline read. Underneath the headline there was a picture of Jenny with a rock in her hand. She read the caption, "Movie star's daughter joins the fray, as queers fight the police. Jennifer Mason, the daughter of film actor and director, Justin Mason, was among the hundreds of people arrested late last night in Greenwich Village."

CHAPTER 41

New York City, Greenwich Village

Richie sat eating his cereal as his mother and father—real father, Sonny—went about their morning routine. Since Francie's accident a few weeks ago, the entire family sat down and had a long talk. The grown ups explained everything about why they did what they did. Richie didn't really understand the whole thing, but it didn't make that big a difference to him. He always knew that Uncle Sonny had loved him like a son, and now he knew why. So, now he had two dads and two moms. No big whoop.

Francie was a little more freaked out. Hey, if you got conked on the head and woke up two days later to find out that your dad wasn't really your dad, you might be freaked out, too.

"Richie, don't dawdle," Sonny urged. "You start your lessons with your new piano teacher today, and you don't want him to think that you're always going to be late."

"Okay, Uncle Sonny. I'm almost finished. Can I put on the radio until we leave?" He was supposed to still call his real dad Uncle Sonny, at least for a while. "I want to hear that new Monkees' song again."

"You know, Richie," his Mom said as she packed his music into his book bag, "I think you write songs even better than that stuff." She smoothed his coppery wavy hair. "It's almost time for a haircut."

"Mom, I want to grow my hair long, like the Beatles and the Monkees," he said. Richie turned the radio dial trying to find music, but all that was on was news. He decided to leave it on one station and wait for the news to end. He finished the last of his cereal and began drinking his juice. He listened intently to the newscaster. Just then Uncle Sonny and Dad entered the room.

"Ready to go see your new music teacher," Frankie asked. "This guy's supposed to be the best, and he teaches music composition at Julliard."

"Sure," Richie said as he gathered up his stuff. "There's something I don't understand."

"What is it, Honey?" asked his mother.

"I just heard the guy on the news say that a bunch of gay people were rioting last night. I just wondered why."

"Well, Honey," Rochelle began slowly, trying to pick just the right words. "A lot of people don't think some people shouldn't love other people."

"Oh, like our family!" Richie said.

"No, not at all," said Sonny. "This is very different."

"But, it sounds like what you said a lot of people think about you and Mom," protested Richie. "And you said, that just because some people think that it's wrong, doesn't mean that it is.

"Now, Sonny," Rochelle tried to intercede.

"Now, nothing," said Sonny grabbing his hat. "We're late enough as it is. No more talking." He then hustled Richie to the car.

*   *   *

Richie picked up his sheet music and looked through it while they sat in the waiting room of the rehearsal studio. He pretended to be looking at it and studying it intently. He found that if he looked busy, the grown-ups thought he was deaf or something and talked right in front of him, thinking he wasn't paying attention.

"Are you certain about this guy, Frankie?" Sonny asked. "He's only 22. That's just a little older than Richie."

"Eight years older. Listen Sonny," Frankie reassured. "He's supposed to be a genius. You've heard him play and listened to what he's written. Richie is so far beyond what either of us can teach him. He needs someone like this Chris Carlson guy."

"There's no denying his talent. He's good," Sonny mused. "That doesn't mean he's a good teacher."

"Henry Mancini swears by him," offered Frankie. "He's also worked as a substitute conductor for the Met, so I'm certain he can handle Richie."

Just then the door into the rehearsal room opened and a tall, surprisingly muscular young man stepped forward. He was clad in tight hip-hugger pants and a flowered shirt. A headband barely contained his long, blond, wavy, hair. When he smiled, he showed a row of perfectly formed white teeth. He introduced himself to Sonny and Frankie, then sat down in the chair next to Richie and started talking with him.

After a few minutes, he rose and said to Richie, "Why don't we head into the rehearsal room so that we can get started? I'm anxious to hear what you can do." He turned to Frankie and Sonny. "We'll be busy for about 2 hours, why don't you come back then?" He didn't even wait for an answer as he led Richie into the adjoining room.

The time flew by. Suddenly Richie realized that he and Chris, that's what he said to call him, had been talking about music for almost an hour. Chris was the first person who ever treated Richie like a grown-up. He was great.

"Let me watch you play," suggested Chris as he stood to the side of the piano.

"What should I play?" Richie asked.

"Anything you want," Chris offered. "Nothing fancy. Play your favorite song."

Richie played a Bob Dylan song while Chris watched. Richie wasn't nervous, but he did feel like there was an electric charge going through him. He wanted Chris to like him, to be impressed.

"That was really cool, man," Chris offered. "Now, I want you to play that again, and some time during the piece, I'm going to say 'freeze'. When I say that I want you to stop and don't move. Leave your fingers positioned exactly as they were when you were playing. Okay, start."

Richie played, paying extra attention to what he was doing. He couldn't figure out what Chris was looking for. Suddenly he heard "freeze" and he did. Chris was behind him; he leaned over Richie and put his hands on top of Richie's.

"Here, Richie," Chris said indicating Richie's right hand. "Do you see how this hand is arched? If you flatten that arch, you'll increase your stride and your hands won't get so tired. You have large hands for a boy your age, but if you do it this way, you'll be able to add half an octave to your stretch. See?"

Richie tilted his head a little in order to look at Chris when spoke to him. As he turned, he could see into Chris' open shirt and admired the beautiful muscles of his chest. He was so close; he could hear the young man's heartbeat. Chris' hair brushed across the back of Richie's neck as he leaned forward to position his hands. Richie felt a shiver come up from his toes, almost like an electric shock.

Chris stepped back, unaware of the effect he stimulated in Richie. "Go ahead try playing that again, with the change I told you about." He looked down at Richie's hands. "Hey, relax! Your hands are shaking. Loosen them up a little; don't be nervous, you're terrific. I'm just here to help you do the best you can do." He leaned back against the side of the piano and Richie began to play. "Yeah, that's it. You're doing great, Richie, really great."

At that moment Richie came to the conclusion that his father was wrong. He hadn't been able to name his feelings before. He knew that he liked boys in a way he shouldn't, but he didn't think that he was gay. Now he knew not only that he was gay, but that his Dad wouldn't understand. He knew that this was something you didn't tell people about. At least not when you're only 14 years old.

1972

CHAPTER 42

Tokyo

Jon fastened the latch on the carry-on and placed it next to the door. With the Olympics in town, it would be a madhouse at the airport. He and Keiko were heading there in less than half an hour and he didn't want to take a chance with lost luggage. That's why he had sent everything else ahead and kept just the essentials in one bag. All the stuff that they would need for the plane ride back to the States was in his hands: their passports, yen and dollars, a change of clothes for him, Keiko and Yoshi; books and toys for Yoshi, a book and a pillow for Keiko, and his ever-present journal. Jon had picked up with his poetry again when Yoshi was born almost two years ago. He was as surprised as anyone was when his first book of poems, "Prayers for Yoshi" became a best seller.

In Japan, it was not deemed odd that one of the country's most popular baseball players would write poetry. The people of Japan were more surprised, he imagined, by the fact that a 25-year-old American could write poetry in Japanese. He first thought that it was the novelty of that fact which made the book so popular, but after all the recognition his work had received, he had to face the fact that the people of his adopted homeland really liked his poetry. Even some of the more important literary journals praised the book beyond what could be brushed aside as courtesy.

He couldn't believe that he was heading back home after all these years, but the chance to play for the Dodgers was a dream come true. He was a little old to be starting in the majors, but even if he got to play for a year or two, it would be worth it. Playing for the Tokyo team was great, but these were the Dodgers! He was also grateful for the offer, because he could be close to his Dad. The last few years had been rough on the old guy, his health was failing, and it was getting harder for Ani to care for him by herself. With Jenny due to finish grad school by the end of the year, they'd soon all be living in the same city again.

Keiko waddled into the living room carrying the baby and rested against the window ledge. Jon took Yoshi from her arms. At a little over two years old, he was already a big boy and a bit too much for Keiko to be carrying, especially in her last trimester. Jon knew it was a cliché that pregnant women glowed, but Keiko didn't just glow, she radiated. He knew Yoshi had been conceived the night of their anniversary party three years ago. They hadn't been trying for a baby, but they weren't taking any precautions, either. With this new child, it had been different. Keiko had had a difficult pregnancy and the doctor had advised them to wait a few years. So they had been taking precautions. Keiko couldn't take the pill, so she used a diaphragm.

However, one night, they were so excited; they rushed and must not have inserted the device correctly. The doctors seemed to think everything would be all right if Keiko took it easy. They even said that it was all right to fly, as long as she could elevate her feet. Luckily, the Dodgers were flying them to Los Angeles First Class.

The buzzer on the intercom went off, Keiko started to rise, but Jon motioned for her to relax. "It's probably just the cab driver here to take us to the airport," he said. "Let me load the bags and then I'll come help you downstairs." She started to protest, then thought better of it and relaxed. "Hello," Jon said into the intercom. "Western Union with a telegram," came the reply.

Jon buzzed the Western Union guy into the building, "We're on the 22nd floor," he said. He turned to Keiko. "Do you have any idea what this is about?"

"No," said Keiko. "Maybe it's a farewell message from my family. The phone was disconnected yesterday, so they couldn't call us."

"But, they're meeting us at the airport to say good-bye," he responded. "That can't be it. Oh God, I hope my father is all right!" There was a knock at the door and Jon opened, bowed to the Western Union deliveryman and took the telegram, his hands shaking. He opened it, and read silently.

"Out loud," said Keiko. "I'm not a telepath."

"Dear Mr. Mason," he read. "We are pleased to inform you that your recent book of poetry, *Prayers for Yoshi*' has won the Faulkner Prize. Please contact our office immediately to confirm your acceptance of the prize." He stared at Keiko, before slumping onto the window ledge next to her in shock.

CHAPTER 43

New York City

Francie waited outside of school for the car to pick her up. The 17-year-old had begun to blossom during her first year of high school, and by her sophomore year she went from being a gangly teenager into a lovely young woman. She held her books in front of her, trying to hide her breasts. She didn't like the stares from the men as she stood on the corner waiting for her father's driver to pick her up.

Francie took a slip of paper out of her jacket and read the information carefully, then slipped the paper back into her pocket. At last she saw the car rounding the corner and stepped forward to the curb to get in. She opened the back door quickly and practically collapsed onto the seat.

"Good afternoon, Miss," said the driver. "I'm sorry to be a few minutes late, there was a traffic jam on Fifth Avenue."

"S'okay" she muttered and kept her head down. She was glad that Dad-Frankie stopped sending a limo to pick her up. The kids gawked at her enough; she didn't need them to think she was a rich snob. She wanted to be like all the other girls in school and walk home, but her parents (all four of them!) were in solid agreement that it wasn't safe for her to walk, or take the subway, from 53rd street all the way downtown to their house in the Village. She had begged and pleaded, but they wouldn't budge. Since she was a year younger than most of her classmates, they acted like she was a baby. They were so over-protective. Maybe if she had a friend from school that lived nearby, they would relent. The trouble with that plan, thought Francie, is that I don't have any friends at school. They're all a bunch of rich white girls and they're all stuck up.

They didn't treat her different because she was black, thought Francie, although they'd all faint dead away if they knew she was half "white". They treated her differently because she was younger than they were. Sometimes she wished her parents didn't let the school make her skip a grade. True, the work the older kids did was more interesting, but it wasn't any harder for her than the stuff kids her own age did. The school actually wanted her to skip two grades, but Lavinia and Frankie wouldn't have it.

She wished she had a real friend. Richie was great, but he was more like a brother than a friend. She wanted a girl her own age to talk to, like she had before LaWanda moved away. She reached into her coat pocket and pulled out the piece of paper again. She looked at the article about the choir. Maybe there'd be some kids like her there. She knew she should talk to her parents first. The article said that the choir met in a church pretty far uptown. Francie was sure her family wouldn't want her to go there alone, but, if she went and then got in the choir, how could they say no?

She looked up at the driver, "Is it okay for me to use this?" she asked, indicating the phone in the back of the car.

"Hey, your father pays for the use of the whole car," he said. "If he don't mind, I don't mind."

She dialed the house. There was no answer, but she pretended there was. "Hi Mom, I just remembered, today's my choir practice," she said to the phone, still ringing at the other end of the line. "Is it all right if I have the driver take me to practice and pick me up? Thanks." She pulled herself up to the edge of the car seat and leaned over to talk to the driver. "My Mom asked if you could take me to choir practice instead of bringing me home," she lied. "I'll only be there an hour or so and then you can pick me up. All right?"

"Where's the practice?" he asked.

Francie looked at the article in her hand. "Oh, it's not too far, 175 East 159th Street," she said casually, although she had no idea where that was never having been past 63rd Street in her life.

"Are you sure about that address?" the driver asked quizzically. "That's clear uptown, all the way in Harlem."

"Yes, I know," Francie feigned disinterest. "Is that a problem? If it is I can call my father and arrange for someone else to take me."

"No, no problem," said the driver. He never understood rich people anyway, especially rich black people. He swung the car around the corner and headed uptown. He traveled the rest of the way in silence and tried to figure out how to arrange his other customers so he could get back to Harlem in time to pick up this girl. "Miss Francie," he said. "You know, it might take me a bit longer than an hour to go get my other customers and get back to you in time. Do you want me to get another driver to pick you up?"

Now Francie was worried. If another driver picked her up and dropped her off, her parents might find out. "No, that's okay. I can wait for you."

"I'm not sure about that," he said. "It looks like the address is for that big church ahead. Is that it?"

"Yeah," said Francie. "You can let me out at the corner. I want to walk the rest of the way."

"I don't think that's a good idea," he warned. "This isn't the best neighborhood you know."

He was stopped at the light and Francie just opened the door. "I'll be fine," she said and hopped out.

She was shutting the door when he called after her. "You wait inside that church for me. Don't wait out front. I'll come in and get you."

"Okay," she said as she dashed away.

Francie walked in to the massive church and stood in awe. Her parents weren't really churchgoers, so Francie didn't have much to compare the place to. She thought it was the most beautiful room she'd ever seen. The Church of Everlasting Glory was impressive, it may have seen better days, but the sheer size of the place was still breathtaking. Suddenly she heard a booming voice.

"Hello?"

Francie jumped about 15 feet in the air. She was so entranced that the voice startled her. She turned her head from side to side, not certain where to look.

"Up here, Honey." As she looked up, the light from the stained glass window shone on her face. "No, Child, turn around." Francie turned and saw an enormous black woman standing in the balcony. "Honey, I'm sorry I scared you. What do you want?" The woman asked moving her hand from side to side.

It was then that Francie saw that the woman was polishing the balcony rail. It was a cleaning lady! Francie felt foolish about showing the cleaning lady how frightened she was, and wanted to run out of the church, but, for some reason, all she did was stammer, "I want to sing."

"Don't we all," said the woman as she set down her cloth. "You wait right there. I'll be down in a minute." She lifted her massive body and lumbered up the steps of the balcony toward the door at the back.

Francie sat in a pew and waited for the woman to come to her. She was more than a little nervous.

"Slide over, Child," the woman said as she plopped herself next to Francie. "My name is Prudence, but everybody calls me Miss Peaches. What's your name?"

"I'm Francie, ma'am," she replied and then thought better of giving her real name. "Francie Kaye," she said using Frankie's last name as if she had her whole life. "I want to join your choir. I read about it in the newspaper."

"A thing as young as you reading the paper?" said an obviously impressed Miss Peaches. "Most children don't like to read at all, much less the paper. How old are you Francie?"

"I'm a senior in high school," Francie said with a smile, deciding to let the pleasant woman think she was a bit older than she actually was. She reached in her purse and handed Miss Peaches her hankie. "You look tired. Is this not a good time?" Francie's mother had always emphasized good manners and Francie knew she shouldn't say to the woman, "Boy, do you sweat a lot," but that's what she was thinking.

"Why, thank you," said a surprised Miss Peaches. "I don't know any families named Kaye. Your parents aren't members of our church, are they?"

"No," replied Francie. "They don't go to church much. But, I really want to sing in the choir. Can I still do that, even if my parents don't come to church?"

"Of course you can, Sweetie," said Miss Peaches. "Do you know any hymns?"

"Not really," admitted Francie. "I mostly sing stuff I hear on the radio."

"Sing something for me, something you really love," the woman encouraged. "Go on up there by the pulpit and sing."

Francie walked up and tried to think what she should sing. She had just seen "Grease" with her family, but didn't think any of those songs would be appropriate. Suddenly, the perfect song popped into her mind. She turned to face Miss Peaches, lifted her head and sang, "The first time ever I saw his face, I felt his love shine down on me . . . ." At the last second, she had altered the lyrics of the song slightly. As much as she loved that song, it had never seemed so personal or to have meant so much. When she was done, she looked at Miss Peaches. She knew she had sung well. She just wondered if she had chosen the right song.

Miss Peaches walked up to her and regarded her with a sense of wonder and awe. "Child, you sing as if the sweet Lord Jesus were standing right next to you. I have never heard a voice as pure as yours in my life. Of course you can sing in our choir. We practice every Wednesday night."

Francie smiled as Miss Peaches hugged her close to her massive bosom. Now, all she had to do was tell her family. "Thank you Miss Peaches," she said excitedly. "I'll be here." She looked at her watch.

"You waiting for somebody?" Miss Peaches asked.

"My Dad's driver . . ." she corrected herself. "My Dad's driving here in a minute. He said to wait inside the church. Is that all right?"

"It sure is, Sweetie," Miss Peaches patted the pew with her hand. "Why don't you sit right here, I got to go finish my chores."

"Are you the cleaning lady?" asked Francie.

Miss Peaches looked at her for a long second and Francie worried that she said the wrong thing. Then the large woman burst out laughing. "Honey, I am the preacher, the book keeper, the handyman and the cleaning lady! It's pretty much a one-woman show."

"Not any more," said Francie. "Now you've got a helper." She picked up a rag and began polishing the pew.

CHAPTER 44

Los Angeles

Gina parked her car on Santa Monica Boulevard, locked it and tossed the keys in her purse. She wasn't used to being in this part of town, but the directions she had were pretty clear. Gina looked forward to seeing Penny. Penny was once Gina's college instructor, and had been the first to spot Gina's talent as a photographer. She'd urged Gina to pursue studies in that area. Over the course of the past couple of years, she and Penny had developed something of a professional friendship. Now Gina often took some of Professor Nichols' students as her interns.

Gina started working as a free-lance photojournalist as a lark, something to keep her busy while she decided what she wanted to pursue as a career. It wasn't until she had gone back to Paris to see some of her past haunts and, truthfully, to confront some of her demons, that she began to feel as if this was the thing she wanted to do for the rest of her life. She sold some of her photos of everyday Parisian street scenes to a number of travel guides. Those led to a show in a small gallery in Venice Beach and, finally, the assignment from *National Geographic* that made her professional reputation, a study of the life of the sisters in the convent her mother had sent her to a lifetime ago. Gina wasn't too certain about tonight's events. Penny had asked her to take some shots of a meeting of authors at a feminist bookstore.

Gina didn't think of herself as a feminist, in fact, she and Penny had spirited debates about that very issue from time to time. Penny insisted that any woman making her way in the world had to be a feminist. Gina couldn't help but picture a frizzy haired Earth Mother with dirty fingernails whenever she thought of a "feminist". Gina agreed with equal pay for equal work, and she felt that a woman could do just about any job a man could do, but she wasn't a feminist. She liked girly things too much. She couldn't bear to think of living without bubble baths, nice clothes, hundreds of pairs of shoes, and manicured nails. Maybe it was a holdover from her days as a model, or her mother's upbringing, but Gina liked to look good, and to her that meant well groomed.

She entered the small bookstore and took note of the lighting. The store was bright, thank goodness, perhaps a bit harshly lit, but adding a filter to the lens would remedy that situation. As she began to assemble her camera, she spied Penny and gave her a quick wave. Penny came over with a couple of women. Most of them were pretty fierce looking, but one, with frosted hair and over-sized, tinted, glasses seemed friendlier than the rest.

Gina was introduced to each of them as Penny explained that they were a group of feminist writers who were going to read some of their work tonight and discuss some upcoming plans. Gina was about to ask them if they wanted to freshen up before she began shooting, then thought better of the idea. These women didn't care how they looked, except for the one with the streaked hair, who didn't seem to be around at the moment.

The owner of the bookstore, Stacy Crane, was a short woman who looked even shorter because she was wearing a man's sport coat that was two sizes too big for her. Gina decided to take headshots primarily, which would emphasize her large, expressive eyes and clear complexion. Most people who claimed not to care about how they looked were amazingly vain when it came to seeing themselves in a photograph. Gina's success came, in part, from her ability to automatically discover and emphasize her subjects' assets. Most of the time, this meant getting her subjects to relax and be themselves. This, however, was not one of those times. Her aim was to help these women get their message across, and that meant showcasing their earnestness and compassion.

The woman with the streaked hair was the easiest to capture. Although she was extremely photogenic, she also came across as intelligent and sincere. Gina sighed, without meaning to, and a few women turned her way. One leaned back and muttered under her breath, "I know what you mean, she's beautiful. But I hear that she's totally straight."

Gina hadn't been thinking in that direction at all, so the whispered comment took her aback. She focused her attention on the matter at hand and continued shooting the event. Afterwards, as she was packing up, the woman with the streaked hair came over.

"Thanks for doing this. We're really trying to get the word out."

Gina was a little confused, "I'm sorry, I was so focused on taking the photos that I didn't really hear a word that was said, uhm . . ." Gina stammered, embarrassed that she couldn't remember the woman's name.

"Oh, that's all right. I get a bit absorbed in what I'm working on, too," she responded. "I'm Gloria, and the reason we're here tonight is to try and drum up support for a new feminist magazine we're starting. I've seen your work and you're good. Would you like to work with us as a staff photographer?"

"Well, I'm not sure," stammered Gina. "I'm flattered, but I'm just starting out and I don't want to limit myself to just one outlet."

"You wouldn't have to. Believe me, with what we can afford to pay, we're not expecting exclusivity," she laughed, handing Gina a card. "Call me when you make a decision."

Gina looked at the card in her hand, "Gloria Steinem, Editor, *Ms. Magazine*".

CHAPTER 45

20,000 feet above Kansas, a few weeks later

Cilla and Allen had been out partying all night. It had been a hell of a week. First Cilla's latest movie, a dark, cynical look at Paris in the 1920s, had its premiere. The critics loved it, saying that it ". . . redefined the American musical." The studio was already pushing Cilla for an Oscar nomination, which was why they were in New York in the first place. Cilla had done the morning news shows, then a round of interviews in the afternoon. They even had cocktails with Cubby Broccoli. He was trying to convince Cilla to sing the theme song to the next James Bond film.

She had barely had time for a short nap when it was time to head over for the opening of their friend Ben's new show, "Pippin." Then they headed over to Andy Warhol's Factory where the quirky artist insisted on taking pictures of Cilla all night using a new camera that developed the pictures right in front of your eyes. They'd had entirely too much to drink, not to mention the drugs he put in his body about as often as Cilla ate chocolate.

Then they had to get up at the crack of dawn to catch this red-eye flight to Hollywood where Cilla was in negotiations with Warner Brothers about a new movie. She also was set to meet with her publicist, do the Tonight Show, make an appearance at a charity benefit, and lay down a few tracks for her new album. Allen was exhausted just trying to keep up with Cilla. It was no wonder she had crashed the moment they got on the plane. She was sitting next to him; her mouth wide open and snoring like a buzzsaw.

"Excuse me?" a timid voice in the aisle began. "I was wondering if Miss Best could sign an autograph. I'm a big fan."

Allen turned his head, slid his sunglasses down the bridge of his nose, and took a look at the speaker. It was a young man. He couldn't have been more than 19. Tall and handsome with wavy hair that shown like copper, and the most beautiful eyes he'd ever seen. Allen pulled himself up to a full seated position, gently pushed on the bottom of Cilla's jaw to close her mouth and spoke to the boy.

"Sweetie, Cilla's resting right now. She's had a very tough weekend," Allen explained. "Why don't you leave your autograph book and I'll have her sign it when she wakes up.

"You're her husband, aren't you?" the boy asked, his voice cracking. "Didn't you write the song, *There's A Lady* on Cilla's "Bittersweet" album?"

"Yeah, I did," said a surprised Allen. "Not many folks read the credits. I'm impressed."

"Oh, I read every word of the liner notes," said the kid proudly. "I'm a songwriter too. I'm going to a music composition workshop in L.A.," he said, trying to sound sophisticated. "My family, er, I'm from New York."

"Do you write lyrics or melody?" asked Allen, impressed by the kid's knowledge and amused by his attempts to sound worldly.

"Both, actually, just like you," he said. "I read an article about you in *After Dark*, but it never said which comes first for you, music or lyrics."

"Well, it depends," said Allen. "Sometimes it's one way, sometimes it's the other. But it's usually the melody. And you?"

"The same," said the kid. He took a deep breath and continued, "I like After Dark, it has such interesting articles, and the photographs aren't so bad either. You should pose for some."

"What?" said a shocked Allen as he sat up quickly.

"Oh, nothing." stammered the kid. "I meant because you're so talented. Well I'd better go." He started to rise, and Allen could see the kid's erection through his tight pants. It reached halfway down his thigh.

Allen hadn't been cruised in a long time. He looked the kid in the eye and asked, "How old are you?"

"Uhm, 19," he answered.

Allen watched the kid quiver, then he smiled. "Take it easy, we're alone up here in First Class, no one heard you. Tell you what, I'm going to go to the bathroom, if you're interested, I think it's time for you to join the mile high club. I'll be in there," he said as he gestured to the first class rest room door.

The kid set his book on the empty seat, looked about the cabin, opened the door to the rest room, and darted inside.

Cilla opened one eye, saw that he was gone, and reached for his book. She opened it, looked at his name inscribed inside, and wrote, "Thanks for being such a big fan, Richie. I hope your career goes miles high!" She signed her name and drew a picture of an airplane next to it. Then she sat up and signaled for the stewardess. "Do you have any chocolate?"

CHAPTER 46

Somewhere over California, a month later

Cilla left the spa in Northern California two days early. Allen had booked her into the place as a part of her recovery from exhaustion. She was certain that the papers would chalk it up to drug abuse or drinking. Let them think what they liked; they all assumed that she was a chip off the old block. Ironically, Cilla never drank anything more potent than a glass of champagne. As for drugs, she wouldn't even take an aspirin. She'd seen what the combination of drugs and alcohol could do to someone first hand. The strongest combination she ever opted for was a bottle of Yoo Hoo soda and a bag of M&Ms.

As she sat in the Cessna on the ride from San Francisco she worked out in her mind what she wanted to say to Allen. She loved him and knew he loved her, but they were both party animals and she now saw that they weren't good for each other. She wanted a real marriage and knew that Allen wanted to have the freedom to be a tramp. They'd been married long enough, so a divorce wouldn't threaten his citizenship. She wanted to part friends and have each of them go on with their lives. Cilla was so caught up in her own thoughts; she nearly jumped through the roof of the small plane when the man across the aisle tapped her on the arm. "What?!?!?!"

"Sorry to startle you," said the attractive gray-haired man. "But, we're about to land, so you'd better put on your seat belt. You just seemed to be thinking so intensely that I thought that you hadn't heard the pilot's announcement," he explained.

"I hadn't," she said. "Thanks. I'm Cilla, Cilla Best."

"I know," he said. "Our parents were in a picture together years ago. I'm Tim, Tim Caine, Jr." and he extended his hand.

"Imagine that," said Cilla. "What brings you to L.A.?"

"I was up in San Francisco securing funding for my new movie. I'm a producer, and I'm working on a new documentary."

"Really, that sounds so interesting," said Cilla flirtatiously.

"It's about the great leading ladies of the early years of the movies," he explained. "Hepburn, Davis, Garbo, Shearer, I'm including them all. And of course, your mother," he hastened to add.

"I'd love to see a rough cut, when you're ready," Cilla said, with genuine interest. She loved old movies and, even though she spent her youth in Hollywood, she was as big a fan as any farm kid.

CHAPTER 47

New York City, 1 month later

Richie stood in the dressing room buttoning his shirt; he looked down at his hands. They looked as if they belonged to some strange man. He'd had that feeling a lot lately. His folks said that it was because he had entered puberty and his body was growing so fast. They weren't kidding. In the last year he'd grown six inches and was now six feet tall. When he stood next to Frankie, he towered over him. People were starting to make jokes about how Frankie, at five foot six, had a 16-year-old son who was so tall. If people would open their eyes, they'd see that Richie took after his real father. Sonny was six three and had broad shoulders, just like Richie.

Richie thought back to his plane ride to the music conference last month. When he talked his parents into letting him fly alone, he argued that someone from the workshop would meet his plane. They reluctantly agreed. But never in his wildest dreams did he expect to have the experience he did. He couldn't believe he had been so bold. He'd acted like a man, not a kid. He certainly looked like a man. He'd started growing pubic hair a few years ago and now he had a massive bush. But, the thing that so amazed him was his cock. Richie had seen enough guys his age naked, like when he changed at the swimming pool, to know that his dick was bigger than that of most guys his age. But, until Allen Warner had made such a big deal about it on the airplane, he hadn't realized just how much bigger. At first he thought that Allen was just trying to make him less nervous for his first time, but, after a while, he realized that Allen hadn't even figured out that it was his first time with another guy. He just kept sucking on his dick and saying how big it was.

He often woke up in the middle of the night with a hard-on. Last night it was so stiff that it felt like it was going to burst. He didn't know what made him do it, but he went over to his book bag and took out his ruler. He laid his dick along the top of the ruler, hoping to measure it, but his cock was longer than the measuring stick. He stood looking at it in the mirror on the back of his bedroom door; it was about as big around as a closet pole. Then he took a hanger from the closet and put it on his dick. He found that he could make it bounce up and down by clenching his butt cheeks together. For some reason this fascinated him. He ended up taking four shirts out of the closet and hung them on his dick, it was still so hard, it barely drooped. He then added two pairs of pants. Although it was difficult, he could still make his dick jostle.

He'd hung his clothes back up and then began fondling himself. He knew that he wouldn't be able to go back to sleep unless he jerked off. He settled back on the bed and turned on his reading lamp; he had it all down to a routine. He'd fished out his copy of *After Dark* from the pile of magazines and books next to his bed. *After Dark* was supposed to be a magazine about the performing arts, but for some reason, it always seemed to feature the photos of half dressed dancers and actors. An issue from two months ago had an article on a dancer that he found particularly handsome. He had a strong jaw line and a great body, not scrawny like his. The photographer, Rick Dean, always lighted his subjects so that they looked like they were sculpted from butter. He was Richie's favorite photographer and the subject in the issue he held in his hand was his favorite. The tattered, sticky, pages were a testament to that. Richie began stroking himself, using some Vaseline he kept hidden in the back of his night table drawer. He loved how it made his hand slip up and down on his cock so smoothly.

Before long, he knew that he was getting really close, that's when he grabbed an old sock and shoved his cock into it. He held the sock tightly around his throbbing penis and stroked it, all the while looking at the picture in the magazine. He imagined that the dancer was the one touching his dick. The guy had such great lips; Richie wondered what it would be like to kiss him. He wondered if Patrick—that was the dancer's name—would suck him. He then flashed on an image of the guy with his lips around his cock, sucking him just like Allen Warner had. Richie shot wads of cum into the sock. It was the most intense feeling he'd ever had. He almost fainted from the pleasure. He quickly put the sock in the bottom of the hamper, pulled on his pajamas, crawled into bed and went to sleep.

That was last night, and he'd already jerked off twice today. Lately all he could think about was sex. His reverie was interrupted by a knock on the door, announcing that it was time to go on stage. Richie walked out and looked into the darkness of Carnegie Hall. He may have been only one out of a dozen kids performing tonight, but for him it was as exciting as a solo performance would be. His entire family was out there; Mom, Dad, Frankie and Lavinia. Even Francie, who had been so out of it lately, had been excited for him. He sat at the grand piano and waited for the butterflies in his stomach to settle.

Sonny and Rochelle stole looks at each other and smiled. Everybody was so proud of him. Richie had blossomed into quite the handsome young man. His talent seemed to give him a sense of self-assurance that, when combined with his newly developed body, made him seem much older than he was. Richie began playing, softly at first, and then building as the other instruments joined him. The head of the workshop he took in California said that his ear for composition was uncanny. Since he had returned, both Sonny and Rochelle had noticed that he seemed much more self-assured. They had made the right decision letting him go to California on his own, they agreed.

Chris Carlson stood backstage and watched his students with pride. They were an exceptional group of kids, ranging in age from 12 to 18. Richie was the most talented, and had been studying with him the longest. He was also, by far, the one Chris felt closest to: he felt a real connection with the kid. It wouldn't be long before Richie would outgrow him, musically speaking. He had already outgrown him physically. Richie was about two inches taller than Chris.

The group finished and Chris applauded from back stage. Richie stole a glance into the wings and Chris gave him a thumbs up sign.

The Kayes and Lewises were the first on their feet cheering. They were so excited that, at first, they didn't notice that Sonny sat down quickly. Rochelle turned to see what was going on and realized that Sonny didn't just sit down, he had collapsed.

"Frankie!" screamed Rochelle over the applause. "There's something wrong with Sonny. Help!"

Frankie pushed his way over to Sonny and tried to rouse him. "Oh, my God! I think he's having a heart attack. Somebody call an ambulance." Lavinia was already half way up the aisle.

"You couldn't have done anything," the doctor reassured the family. "He had a massive coronary, and if it's any consolation, I don't think he suffered much."

Rochelle and Lavinia held each other, sobbing. Frankie had his arms around Francie. The doctor left them just as Chris walked in with Richie.

"Is everything all right?" Richie asked, even though, in his heart, he knew it wasn't.

"Your father died," Frankie said softly. "I'm sorry."

Chris stood off to the side, not certain of his place. When he overheard Frankie, he was really confused. Frankie was Richie's father. Maybe Frankie didn't know what he was saying. But then, Richie started crying and Chris knew he had, in fact, heard right. It suddenly made sense. That's why Richie had such a dark complexion while Frankie and Rochelle were so light.

Richie turned to Chris and buried his face in Chris' arm. "It can't be true. It can't be true," he kept muttering over and over. Chris just patted his back and held him.

Then Frankie turned to Chris. "I think the kids should go home," Frankie told him. "Will you take them for us?"

"Of course," Chris replied. Frankie gave him money for a cab and the keys to the apartment and they left.

CHAPTER 48

Greenwich Village, an hour later.

C hris sat in the living room and looked at the two sides of the apartment. So many things seemed to fall into place. He had known this family for years, and he'd thought that their family dynamics seemed odd, but he had put those feelings down to his unfamiliarity with interracial friendships. While he didn't consider himself a bigot, he hadn't known many black people growing up. Now that he knew the truth, so many things "clicked". He always thought that Sonny took a special interest in Richie because he was also a musician. That may have been part of it, but mostly it was because he was the kid's father.

Chris felt a closeness with Richie's family, and empathized with them. If must have been difficult for them, to keep a secret like that all these years. As he sat and thought about the situation, he assumed that Francie was probably Frankie's kid. Wow, what a mind blower. He glanced toward the stairs that led to the second floor of the Kaye's apartment. Poor Richie, what a burden to carry. But, no wonder he and Francie were so close. At least they had each other to confide in.

He assumed that was why Richie sometimes acted so strange around him. There were times when he felt that the kid really trusted him, but then, Richie would suddenly step back and become a bit distant. He'd probably wanted to tell Chris, but felt he couldn't confide in him, afraid that he might be rejected. If only Richie knew that it didn't matter to him, that he thought of Richie like a kid brother.

He and Richie and Francie had been sitting in the living room for about half an hour just staring at their shoes. "Anybody want something to eat?" Chris asked, just to break the tension. "I'm not much of a cook, but I'm certain that I could make you guys a sandwich or something." They both just shook their heads. "You haven't eaten since this afternoon," he offered.

"I'm really not hungry," sighed Francie. "If you don't mind, I think I'll go to my room." As she stood, the phone rang and she jumped to answer it. After listening for a few minutes, she handed the receiver to Chris. He spoke with Frankie for a few minutes, and then Rochelle asked to talk to Richie. While Richie was on the phone, Chris told Francie that the adults would be home in about two hours.

"I'm going to lie down for a while," she said. He gave her a hug, which she held for a few minutes.

"Are you going to be okay?" he asked. She nodded and went upstairs. Richie did the same on his side of the house after hanging up the phone. Poor kids, thought Chris, recalling the events.

The kids had been upstairs for about 20 minutes when Richie's voice interrupted Chris' reverie, "Chris?"

"Yeah, Buddy," Chris responded.

Richie came down the stairs wearing a sweater and jeans, having changed out of his suit. He plopped down on the couch next to Chris. Chris put his arm across Richie's shoulder and gave him a sideways hug, just like his father used to give to him. It was comforting without being too intimate. He was certain Richie needed some comfort now, but he didn't want to upset him any further.

"It's been a rough day, huh?" Chris asked. "I know it doesn't seem important now, but you played really well tonight. I bet Sonny was really proud."

"So you figured it out, huh?" Richie said and looked up at Chris with tears brimming in his eyes. He was trying so hard to be a grown man, but Chris knew that, right now, he felt like a little boy.

"Yeah, I did. I think," Chris answered. "So Sonny is, was, your dad and Rochelle's your mother?" he asked rhetorically. Richie nodded. "Does that mean Lavinia and Frankie are Francie's parents?"

"Yeah," said Richie. "Sorry I couldn't tell you. It was kind of a secret. I really wanted to, though."

"That's okay," Chris reassured him. "I guess your families were worried about how folks would react. I just want to let you know it doesn't matter to me. I've always thought that you all were great."

"Thanks," said Richie, and he leaned his face against Chris's chest.

There didn't seem to be much more to say, so Chris just held Richie and rubbed his back. This seemed to soothe the boy; he put his arms around Chris' waist and snuggled close.

"You poor kid," Chris murmured. He just sat there holding the boy for a while. Richie may have been taller than Chris, but right now he was just a frightened kid.

"I love you Chris," Richie said, so softly that Chris wasn't quite certain he heard right.

"Thanks," said Chris. Richie changed position and turned his head up to Chris. Chris looked down at Richie and felt a wave of compassion for the kid.

"You've been so great to me," said Richie. "I really appreciate you staying with me now."

Chris was a little surprised when Richie reached up and kissed him. Chris gave the boy a peck back on the cheek. Richie turned his head and kissed Chris full on the lips. Chris froze for a moment, then pushed Richie away for a second. Then, afraid the kid would think he was upset, he hugged him again. "Richie," he stammered, "I think I know what you want. But, no. I can't"

"I'm sorry!" Richie started to sit up and pull away. "That was stupid. Please don't hate me. It's just that I was so upset and I thought . . ."

Chris pulled him close again. "No Richie," he explained. "I don't hate you. It's okay to feel that way about someone. It's just that it wouldn't be right for me to, well, you're a student of mine, and you're too young for me. I love you, too, but not in that way."

Richie sat up and looked Chris in the eye, "I wasn't saying that you were, you know, gay, or anything," he said quickly, afraid he had made a major mistake. "I just meant . . ."

"Richie, it's okay," Chris said, smiling at the boy wryly. "I am gay. And if you were older, and if you weren't my student, and if your parents hadn't entrusted you to me, well maybe. But, that's a lot of ifs. It wouldn't be right; it's very easy to mix up different kinds of love, especially when you're upset. It can be confusing."

"You're gay?" Richie said. "I never knew. How come you never said anything?"

"Well, first of all," Chris said quietly, "It didn't have anything to do with our relationship, or so I thought. I think of you first as a student and then as a friend. Secondly, if people knew, then they might not want me to teach their kids."

"That kind of makes sense," Richie admitted. "I just wish I knew sooner. It would have been easier."

Chris looked at Richie, "Have you had a crush on me? Duh! That's why you've been so distant."

"I didn't think I could let you know," Richie said, almost crying. "I can't let anyone know."

"Yes, you can," offered Chris. "Probably not for a while. But, I bet that when you're older and you tell your Mom, she's going to be okay about this. She's a pretty cool lady, so is the rest of your family."

"So, you think I should wait?" Richie asked.

"At least a few years," Chris suggested. "I think your Mom's gonna have her hands full for a while."

"Yeah," Richie sighed, and snuggled close to Chris, who held him like a brother.

1976

CHAPTER 49

New York, Harlem

Francie was leading the choir through rehearsal, while Miss Peaches went to take a phone call. Francie hoped that the call wouldn't take too long; she wanted to have time to practice her solo before she had to leave. She took a peek at her watch, it was almost 4:30, and she'd have to leave by 5:30 if she wanted to make her acting class. That was, if she could find a cab, which weren't exactly plentiful here in Harlem. She supposed that, if push came to shove, she could take the subway, but she really didn't like to, especially after dark. A few years ago she would have argued with her parents that she should take the subway, but now that she was 21, she understood their concern. So many guys thought that a young black woman out at night was there for their amusement.

Her parents had tried to shield her from the truth for years. Francie had decided that she couldn't be shielded forever after her Uncle Sonny died. She told her parents that it was time to give her some freedom. She argued that they tried to protect her from pain by pretending for too long. It was then that she told them about coming to Harlem for choir practice. They had a fit until she pointed out that she had been doing it for months and nothing had happened. Eventually they began to ease up on her.

Bringing them to a performance and having them meet Miss Peaches was the clincher. Nobody could say no to Miss Peaches, and they could see how well she protected Francie. The entire family, her mom and dad (although she had to be careful to call him Uncle Frankie in front of everyone), her Aunt Rochelle, and Richie all came to see her sing her first solo in the choir. At first people stared at her dad, Aunt Rochelle and Richie, no doubt wondering what the white folks were doing at their church. But, once Richie played the piano at church, no one cared, they were just happy to have such a talented kid in the congregation, especially since he was willing to fill in for the choir's accompanist from time to time. The choir held the high note at the end of the hymn and Francie was about to tell them to take a break until Miss Peaches returned, when the church leader came rushing in to the chapel.

"Sweet Jesus," cried Miss Peaches as she waved one hand over her head. "Sweet Jesus, thank you for your blessings!" The choir was instantly transfixed, awaiting Miss Peaches' news. "That phone call was from Washington D.C.," she explained. "There's going to be a big celebration at the Statue of Liberty for the bicentennial, and we've been invited to sing!"

Francie jumped up and down excitedly amidst calls of "Blessed be!" and "Thank you, Lord!" from members of the choir. "What songs are we going to do?" she asked Miss Peaches. This seemed to stun the choir and they all waited for Miss Peaches' answer.

"Well, we're going to do two numbers. The president himself asked if we would perform *The Battle Hymn of the Republic*," she said excitedly. "The other number is our choice."

"Did you actually talk to the president?" asked Francie.

"No, just the man in charge of the show," explained Miss Peaches. "But, he said that the president had read about us in the paper and saw us when we were on *the Today Show* at Christmas, and he asked him to find out if we could perform at the celebration. Of course I said yes. We're going to have to put in some extra rehearsal time. The Fourth of July is only six months away."

Francie looked at her watch. This was worth being a few minutes late for acting class.

CHAPTER 50

Malibu

Jon sat at his typewriter staring at the page. After three books of poetry, he was experiencing his first case of writer's block. The past few years had been such a whirlwind that he just kept writing all the time. When his first book won the Faulkner Prize, he was offered a contract for an English translation. It made *the New York Times'* best seller list, and Jon and the family were featured in an article in a new magazine, *People*. That was almost two years ago, and since then he had written two more books of poetry. Both had been big hits in Japan and moderate hits in the U.S. He'd come to realize that the fans in the U.S. were fickle.

He loved Japan and would have preferred to live there, but his father's illness had forced them to stay in the States. Keiko was in love with America and they lived here permanently, although they did go back to Japan often. Jon bought a home outside of Tokyo for Keiko's parents and aunt, and they stayed there whenever they returned. He still thought of Japan as home, but the weather here in Malibu was wonderful. He could see why Keiko, city-born and bred, adored it. He walked to the window of his top floor studio and looked out at the beach in front of the house. Keiko and the kids were playing at the edge of the water. Yoshi, now almost five, was like a dolphin, jumping through the waves. Nobuko, his darling daughter, was a little more cautious, playing tag with the water rolling up on the shore.

His second book was about his experiences as a Westerner in Japan. The third was more painful, divided into two parts. The first was a series of poems about his relationship with his father. The second dealt with his mother's suicide. The last book had been his biggest seller, mostly, he guessed, because the public loved taking a peek into the life of a celebrity.

At first Jenny was offended that he opened their family's wounds to public scrutiny, but eventually she relented, saying that it had helped her come to terms with some issues. He certainly hadn't intended it, but the discussions it generated about their family helped the public understand Jen, as she now called herself, a little better. She'd always been a fighter for the underdog and took on a lot of unpopular causes. Along the way she'd earned the nickname Bleeding Heart Jen. The book had made the public a little more sympathetic towards her, though Jon doubted she cared about that one bit. Jen did what she did because she believed in it, damn the consequences.

A perfect example was when she started dating Bruce Goodman. The former hippie and student activist was running for Congress. Jon and his father had been convinced that Bruce was only using Jen for publicity. After he was elected to Congress, with the clearest majority of any candidate in the history of New York, Jon and his Dad thought he'd drop Jen. Ani had more faith in him, and she was proved right. Jon and his dad were never happier to admit they were wrong. The couple married in 1970 and Bruce adored Jen, now more than ever.

Jon turned away from the window and sat at his desk again, nursing his cup of tea. This time he wanted to write a book of prose, just to prove to himself that he could. He'd already written a few short stories and non-fiction pieces about baseball, both about his own career and about the game in general. Now he wanted to try a longer form work. He toyed with the idea of a novel, but he didn't know where to start. He'd even thought of a non-fiction piece about his father, a tribute and biography, but it was too soon after his death. His father had died only six months ago and the pain was still too fresh.

He decided to meditate, a technique that he had developed in Japan. It often helped to clear his thoughts and might allow him to come to a decision. He lit a few candles and stretched out on the tatami mat that lined the floor of the studio. He focused on the crash of the surf outside and let go.

Keiko played with the children on the beach. They were building a sandcastle when Jon approached. He settled down next to Nobuko and watched as she used her plastic shovel to dig in the sand. He reached out and stroked her thick reddish-brown hair. Keiko knew her husband well enough to sense that he had something he wanted to talk about. She also knew him well enough to wait and let him work things out in his mind before speaking.

She was constantly amazed at how Japanese he was in his ways. He thought like a Japanese man, but he had the gentleness and openness of an American. It was the combination of the two that had attracted her to him in the first place. Too many Japanese men put business first and family second; Jon always put his family first. She knew that he would prefer to live in Japan, but she wanted the children to grow up in the States, where she felt they would have more opportunities, especially for Nobuko. Women's roles were still more restricted in Japan. Keiko was lucky in that she was able to experience more personal freedom, thanks to her American-raised husband.

She was also happy that they had enough money to travel back and forth between Japan and America and spend time with both her and Jon's families. The children adored their Gramani, as they called Ani, but were too young to understand about Justin's death. Keiko missed Justin terribly; they had grown very fond of one another. She was glad that her own father was healthy. At least the children would grow up knowing one grandfather.

It was getting late in the day and the children were due for their nap. She called Yoshi in from the water, picked up the kids' toys and started to lead them into the house. Jon took Nobuko and carried her. Keiko took Yoshi's hand and brushed the excess sand from his bottom. She helped him rinse off in the outdoor shower as Jon undressed Nobuko in preparation for the same. They worked as a well-oiled machine, each taking part in the care of the children. That was what Keiko most loved about her husband. Unlike many men, he did not view his softer side as a weakness. They put the children down for a nap and settled in on the rattan love seat on the deck with their tea.

"Keiko," Jon began, "I have an idea for my new book."

Keiko looked at Jon, waiting for him to tell her at his own pace; she snuggled closer to him.

"But, I want your permission," he said.

"Jon you don't need my permission," she smiled. "You write about what you need to write about. I trust you.

"This is different," he began. "I want to write about us. To tell our story."

"How much of our story?" Keiko asked, a slight frown crossing her face.

"Everything," he almost whispered. "I want to talk about why I like to dress up. What it feels like. How you have dealt with it. What it means to me."

"That could be dangerous," she warned. "It could be the last book you write. Are you ready for that?"

"Yes," he said with conviction. "We have enough money to last us the rest of our lives. I really want to do this, but if it will embarrass you, I won't."

"Nothing you do has ever embarrassed me," she said lovingly. "If you have really thought this through and it's what you want to do, then do it. I just ask one favor."

"Anything you want," he smiled.

"I want you to tell your family," she insisted. "Tell Ani and Jen first."

"You're right, I should tell them first," Jon replied. "Telling your family will be the hard part."

"Not so hard," Keiko said. "They adore you. But, I think that I should tell them, and we should do it in person. We'll have to go to Japan before the book is published."

"I want to go before I even start," Jon said. ""I want their permission too. I don't want to dishonor them."

"You still think like a Japanese, Mason-San," she smiled.

He took her in his arms and kissed her deeply. She took his hand and began to lead him inside. They were nearly to the bedroom door when the phone rang. Keiko headed toward the phone.

"Let it ring," Jon said softly. "That's why we got an answering machine."

"But, what if it's important?" Keiko asked.

"That's the joy of those things, we can call whoever it is back," Jon explained. "Come on."

They were halfway to the bedroom, when they heard the voice of Jon's agent on the answering machine. "Hey, Jon, it's Howard. I just wanted to let you know that the President Ford wants to name you the Poet Laureate. I told him it probably wouldn't be a problem. Call me back."

CHAPTER 51

New York, LaGuardia Airport

Gina waited at the International Terminal for Franco DiPaolo. The legendary Italian director was arriving on the first Concorde flight from Europe to film a documentary on the Bicentennial. There had been a lot of debate over whether it was right for an Italian to film a documentary on such an American celebration. Frankly, Gina didn't really care. Get the best man for the job, she thought. Click. Get the best person for the job, she corrected herself.

She hadn't realized how much of our language was sexist until she began working for *Ms*. That's where she first heard of saying "Click" when she encountered something sexist. She'd been doing it so long that she even did it when thinking to herself. Gina hadn't really thought of herself as a feminist, but she had changed her mind. In most of the media, feminists were still portrayed as man-hating hags, and, most likely, lesbians. Gina certainly had every reason to hate men. Both her ex-lover, Jean Beaubien, and her father, Angelo, had treated her as a second class citizen, but, though she counted a number as her friends, she certainly wasn't a lesbian. She didn't think of herself as a hag either, although that had taken years of therapy. Gina was proud to call herself a feminist.

The mainstream press, however, treated Gloria Steinem and Gina as novelties. *Esquire Magazine* had done a feature on the two of them. At first she had been pleased, thinking that if a men's magazine was finally coming around to seeing feminists as "normal," then perhaps the rest of America would not be too far behind. When the issue with their profile came out, she and Gloria were depicted on the cover with the blurb, "Glamorous Feminists: Our Kind of Chicks." She didn't know what irked her more, the fact that they had been duped for the article, or the overly retouched photographs that made them appear as if they should have been on the cover of *Cosmopolitan*.

They even managed to make Gina's book of photographs seem childish. That really hurt because the book had started as a tribute to her mother. In her women's group meetings, she first realized what a strong role model her mother had been. In sharing her story with other women, she began to find others who felt the same way. She'd turned those conversations into the basis for *Mothers' Days*, which combined her photos of mothers and their daughters with Gloria's interviews with the subjects. She knew in her heart that the book was important; it looked at mother-daughter relationships as no one had before. But the Esquire article made it seem simplistic and juvenile. A few years ago, she might have been devastated, but now she was simply annoyed.

The passengers from the plane began to file down the gangway into the terminal. From her spot behind customs, she spotted DiPaolo, or rather, she spotted his wavy, jet black hair. He was short, and it was difficult to see his face as he moved through the crowd.

Gina was excited to be working with Italy's legendary filmmaker. She was not all that excited about the bicentennial. In fact she was tired of all the hoopla. It was so crass and commercial. The anniversary of the country's founding seemed little more than a publicity stunt. It did, however, give her a chance to meet a man she so admired, so she had jumped at it. DiPaolo made it through customs in minutes—the power of celebrity—and walked over to her. He brushed his hand through his wavy hair, straightened his tie and spoke in a low rumble.

"Ms. Ferrara," he said, taking her hand. "I am so sorry to be late. It seems the photographers wanted to take pictures of the plane as it came toward the terminal. What was the use of flying so fast? It took so long to get away from the reporters that it ended up taking the same amount of time to get from Rome to you as if I took my regular flight. Normally I would not keep a woman as beautiful as you waiting."

He's a typical Italian, thought Gina, piling it on like he's making a submarine sandwich. She smiled at him and responded, "I didn't mind waiting. I've been a fan of your work for some time. I'm very excited that you agreed to work with me. We've got a car waiting to take you to the hotel." The next few minutes were filled up with loading his luggage into the trunk and making arrangements for the trip to the city. Eventually the chauffeur shut the door and they had to make small talk again, which Gina dreaded.

"I was very impressed with your book," DiPaolo said, taking off his gloves. "You captured the bond between the women in every photograph you took. It is truly remarkable!"

"Thank you," replied Gina, slightly embarrassed to discover she was blushing.

"The women were all so beautiful," he continued, to Gina's dismay. She'd hope that he'd seen beyond the superficial aspects of her photos. "Not just pretty, though many were," he explained. "But, deeper. With a beauty that came from their souls. That is why I asked to have you work with me on this project. Truly, the reason I accepted this project at all was so that I could meet the artist who created those portraits. Now, I am very happy," he continued, "For now I discover that the woman who created this wonderful art is a work of art herself."

CHAPTER 52

Manhattan

Jen grabbed the bag sitting beside her and hopped out of the cab. While Bruce paid the driver, Jen rummaged through her purse, desperately looking for a stick of gum. They'd been to a luncheon in Chinatown earlier and she could still taste the garlic on her tongue. She figured that it would not do for a congressman's wife to address the American Legion reeking of garlic. This was going to be Bruce's toughest crowd to face since he won the election and she was uncertain how receptive the traditionally conservative group would be to Bruce and his leftist politics. It was times like this that she was grateful for growing up in Hollywood.

It didn't matter if it was a debate, a fundraiser for one of her charity events, or a run for office, she was great at schmoozing folks and getting them on her side. This was where she was the biggest help to Bruce, who came from the tradition of in-your-face radicals. Between them they usually could win anyone over, it was just a matter of . . . she looked up when she heard the shouting. As usual, it was Bruce arguing politics, this time with the cab driver. She sighed and headed over to him.

"Don't you see? It was all a conspiracy by the big oil companies and the government? There wasn't a gas shortage. It was all orchestrated by the Republicans to take the focus off of Watergate!"

"I don't believe you," the cab driver said. His accent pinned him as a recent immigrant, but Jen couldn't pinpoint from where. "The government doesn't do that sort of thing in this country."

"You're a working man, an immigrant, a minority," Bruce shouted. "How can you claim to be a Republican when all they want to do is screw you and then send you back where you came from?"

"Darling," she cooed. This had gone far enough. She had to get Bruce to the luncheon and quick—they were already five minutes late. "I'm certain that this man has enjoyed his debate with you, but I'm afraid we're going to be late if we don't hurry." She took his arm.

"One second, Jen," he said as he turned to the driver.

"Sorry to interrupt, but I really must get him inside," she said to the cab driver. She gave Bruce's arm a yank to let him know she meant business. "Come on, Bruce," she muttered. "If you keep those American Legion members waiting, they're going to hate you before you even open your mouth."

As he followed her up the steps, Bruce stopped for one second and took a look at his wife. He was the luckiest man alive. Not only did Jen share his passion for politics; she had a great rack to boot. The other guys in Congress had what looked like Stepford Wives, all ruffles and conservative clothes, nodding in agreement with their husbands. Then there was Jen, decked out in a short wrap dress. With no bra on under the clingy fabric, she was certain to have the attention of every man in the room. He ran the steps two at a time to catch up with her.

"Aren't you glad I made you start jogging?" she asked. "Otherwise you'd enter the ballroom panting. It wouldn't look good to all of those macho guys." she laughed at the idea.

"The way you look, they'd know exactly why I was panting," he joked. "How about if we cut out of here early? I've got some weed at home."

She stopped so quickly, he almost ran her over. "You have it at home? What if someone came over and found it? Your career would be over."

"Jen, I'm a known radical!" he joked. "Folks would be disappointed to find out I didn't do drugs."

"Suspecting it and having evidence are two different things," she warned. "Now remember, make nice with these boys. You're not going to turn them in to liberals, no matter how hard you try."

"I know," he sighed. "Do you have any idea how much I hate talking to these thick headed goons?"

"Bruce . . ." she began to caution him. "Just remember the key points, which are . . ."

"Worker solidarity, the economy and the need for unions to stay strong," he said with resignation. "It's not that I disagree with those things, it's just that there's so much more that needs . . ."

"Hey, you're preaching to the choir," she interrupted. "Let's just focus on those things, though." She stood with her hand on the door to the banquet room. "Ready?"

He nodded as she smoothed her hair and straightened her back. Then Jen flung the door open and walked in next to him. They stood just inside the doorway for a few seconds, just as she had taught him. The combination of the door flying open and their standing stock still for a moment focused every eye in the room on them. As soon as they had everyone's attention, they began working the room, starting together, so the American Legion members could see she was the dutiful wife, then allowing the group's leaders to separate them, so that they could meet twice as many people.

The men didn't even realize that they were being played like a finely tuned piano. Bruce mingled about the room, talking about the strength of the union and how much union workers added to the economy, knowing that most of the members of the American Legion were working class folks. Jen stood in one area and had a line of people waiting to have their picture taken with her. Before each photo, she took a button with the words, "For a Good Man, It's Goodman" from her bag and pinned it to the guy's lapel. She made certain each man she was photographed with was wearing one. That way when they showed their friends the photo, the slogan would stick in their mind as well. The members of the American Legion might not have started out as fans of Bruce, but they certainly were fans of her father. By the time she was finished with them, they were fans of both Justin Mason and Bruce Goodman.

Pretty soon, it was time to begin the dinner. Jen sat on the other side of the podium from Bruce at the head table. As she chatted with the men sitting on either side of her, she sliced her steak into little pieces, which she proceeded to move about her plate. She didn't eat meat, but it would not do to make that known. It could end up a political liability. She was in the middle of charming the folks seated near her when Bruce caught her eye. He looked a little under the weather. He signaled her and they both excused themselves and met in the hallway.

"Have you got an antacid?" he asked. He looked a little green.

Jen was worried that they might have to go home before he made his speech. "I think so. Are you all right?" she asked as she handed him the tablets.

"Yeah, I just think dinner didn't set too well," he admitted. She was always warning him that he didn't have to eat at every event they went to. "I'll be fine. Let's go back and get this over with."

They were about to go back into the room when a pair of conventioneers came out the same door that they were about to enter. They were holding up a third guy between them. He looked far worse than Bruce did.

"What's the matter guys?" asked Jen. "He can't be sick, my husband hasn't made his speech yet."

"Nah, Ma'am," one responded. "I think he's got the flu or something. We're going to drop him in his room and come right back."

She and Bruce entered the room and returned to their seats. Upon seeing them return, the host for the evening began his introductions. As he did so, a few more of the audience members made their way toward the exits. There were always a few who stepped out to use the bathroom during speeches, so Jen didn't think anything of it. Halfway through Bruce's speech, however, she noticed that more people were leaving. She looked up at Bruce to gauge his reaction; he was sweating profusely and seemed a little disoriented. He was getting to the summation when he collapsed. There were a few gasps in the audience before someone yelled for a doctor.

Jen sat in the ambulance next to her husband holding his hand. She knew the medic really couldn't tell her anything that he hadn't already. Bruce had a high fever, was a little dehydrated, and had a bit of fluid in his lungs. The medic thought that it was probably pneumonia, but the doctor at the hospital would be able to tell her more.

When they got to the hospital, Bruce was whisked in ahead of everyone else. A Congressman got high priority; Jen chuckled to herself, knowing how much Bruce would hate that. After an hour or so, the doctor came out to tell her that he wasn't quite certain what Bruce had, but that they thought it was highly contagious—a dozen other people at the banquet were admitted with the same symptoms. They examined Jen, but she showed no signs of the condition. They were going to keep Bruce in isolation overnight for observation.

Jen wouldn't be allowed in the room, so she went home to pick up a few things for Bruce. While she was at home, she called Bruce's assistant and informed her of what happened. She already knew. It was all over the television. Jen turned on the 11:00 news in the bedroom as she packed a bag of toiletries. Bruce didn't own a pair of pajamas, so she grabbed his old M.I.T. t-shirt and a pair of running shorts. The reporter had just said that nearly two dozen people from the banquet were hospitalized. They still hadn't discovered the cause of the illness. The only thing they could rule out was food poisoning. Jen wasn't worried. Bruce was usually as healthy as an ox. She went downstairs to the front of their town house and hailed a cab.

When she got to the hospital, she saw the nurse who had helped admit Bruce. "Ms. Dixon," she said, reading the nurse's name tag. "Can you tell me what room my husband is in? I brought some things for him."

"I'm sorry Mrs. Goodman, I can't . . . ." she stammered. "Here comes his doctor," she left abruptly.

Jen saw the doctor coming down the hall towards her. She started to walk towards him and then caught the look on his face. She knew before he opened his mouth that he did not have good news.

"Mrs. Goodman," he stammered. "There's no easy way to say this. Your husband is dead."

Jen stared at the doctor as if he was speaking gibberish, then collapsed on the floor.

*   *   *

Ani handed Jen a cup of tea and sat on the chair across from her. It had been a week since Bruce died. Bruce and 14 others, thought Jen. The doctors didn't even know what killed them all. For the time being they were calling it Legionnaire's Disease. The irony of a radical dying from Legionnaire's disease was almost funny, she thought bitterly. She was about to relay this to Ani when the phone rang.

"Mrs. Goodman," the voice said. "Please hold for the president."

"Mrs. Goodman, This is Gerald Ford," the president introduced himself, as if she wouldn't know who he was. "I just wanted to call you personally to offer my sympathies on your husband's passing. Bruce was a real breath of fresh air here in Washington. I'll miss him. If there's anything I can do, please don't hesitate to ask."

"Thank you, Mr. President, I'm fine" Jen stammered. Ani stared at her in shock. Jen just shrugged.

"Mrs. Goodman, I know it is very soon after Bruce's death, but I have a favor to ask you. It is a tradition that when a member of Congress dies in office, his spouse is offered the opportunity to fill his position for the remainder of the term. Bruce still has one year left in his term. Will you fill his seat in the House?"

Jen stared at the phone for a second before replying, "I'd be honored, Mr. President."

"Thank you Congressman Goodman," he replied. "A member of my staff will call you in a few days to make all the arrangements."

After the obligatory good-byes, Jen hung up the phone and stared into space before turning to her stepmother and saying, "Ani, hold on to your chair. Have I got a shock for you."

CHAPTER 53

New York City

"Francie, can I see you for a moment?" Uta Hagen said as she entered the room.

Francie had been talking with two girls in the back of the room before acting class. "Yes, Mrs. Hagen?" she asked. She was a bit nervous; Uta had never singled her out before.

"I'd like to see you in my office for a minute, if you don't mind," the grande dame of acting said as she gestured for Francie to proceed through the door from the rehearsal room into the hall.

Francie turned to her friends. They looked at her as if she had a secret. "I don't know either," she said as she headed toward the hallway. "Mrs. Hagen, can you tell me what this is about?" she asked.

"I have someone I want you to meet," she said mysteriously, then noticed Francie's concerned look. "Don't worry, this is good news. Here we are," she said opening the door to her office. There were three people crowded into the small room. When she and Uta entered, it became positively cramped, "Francie, I've been telling these people how talented you are."

"Mrs. Hagen, you are very kind, but . . . ."

"Nonsense, what is true is true. These people are looking for some actors to be in a television movie and they asked me to suggest some students for them to meet." After introducing Francie to a tall man and a blonde woman, Uta excused herself and went to teach her class. A shorter black man sat in the back of the room. He wasn't introduced.

Francie was very nervous. She hadn't acted in anything except student productions, and truth be told, was about to drop out of class to focus on her singing. "I don't know how much, Mrs. Hagen has told you about me . . . ."

"She speaks highly of you," replied the taller of the two men before Francie could finish. "She says that you haven't had much stage experience, but that you have a natural affinity for the craft."

"Frankly, Honey," croaked out the woman, She was pudgy, with blonde streaks in her hair. Her voice made it clear that she'd spent most of her life smoking. "Your acting ability is secondary. We're looking for someone to play a gospel singer. It's a small role, but Uta says you've got the pipes for it."

Francie smiled. She was much more certain of her singing ability than her acting talent. "I've been told I'm pretty good."

"We saw you on *The Today Show*," said the tall man. "Frankly, this role has been hard to cast, and we're coming to you at the last minute. Alex here," he said gesturing to the gentle looking black man sitting at the rear of the office, "Thinks you'd be perfect for the role. We'll have to do a quick screen test, but I don't think that it will be any problem. If it works out we'd need an answer immediately. As I said, we don't have a lot of time."

"Well," Francie stammered, not sure what to say next.

"Who's your agent?" asked the blonde. "I can hammer out all the details with him."

"The important thing," the tall man continued, not letting her answer the woman, "Is that we need to do the test tomorrow. Give Ms. Mengers your agent's number and she'll set everything up."

"I don't have an agent," offered Francie. "But my Uncle Frankie has one. He used to represent my father, too. I'm certain he can take care of everything. Do you want me to call him?"

"Your Uncle Frankie?" Sue Mengers said. "Who are you?"

"I'm Francie Lewis," she replied. "I thought you knew. My uncle is Frankie Kaye. My dad was Sonny Lewis."

"Holy shit!" said Sue.

The tall man, turned to the shorter man and said, "Alex, no wonder she can sing."

"Even without the pedigree I knew she was going to be perfect. She's exactly what I envisioned Kintana would be," he replied in a soft, refined, voice. "Francie, my name is Alex Haley. I am a great fan of your father's work. When I heard you sing on the television last Christmas, I knew you were perfect for this role. I had to argue with the studio. They only wanted stars for all the roles, but I insisted that I wanted you, I hope it will be worth the wait. We're filming a television movie version of my book, *Roots* and I want you to play Kintana."

Francie was agog. Alex Haley was a legend, and he had searched for her. How could she say no? "Of course, Mr. Haley. I'd be honored."

"Write down your address and phone number, Honey," croaked the blonde. "I'll arrange everything and call to let you know when the limo will pick you up tomorrow."

CHAPTER 54

Coral Gables, Florida

Richie left the rehearsal room weighted down by his backpack, which was filled with sheet music. As he stepped out of the building into the hot Florida sun, he was again grateful for attending the University of Miami. The music school was highly rated and, as a bonus, he got to escape the winters up North. Richie hated cold weather. If he had liked it he might have taken Julliard up on its offer of a full scholarship. Besides, his family could afford to pay for his tuition and room and board, so he was free to attend any school he wanted.

He was also drawn to Miami for a number of other reasons. It was where his mentor, Chris Carlson, had gone to school and it gave him some breathing room from his family. Richie knew he was gay, but he hadn't yet had the courage to tell anyone in his family. He was about to tell Francie one day, but when he mentioned the word gay, a strange look came over her face. Since she joined the church choir, she had gradually become a more devout Christian. At that moment, he'd never felt so alone in his whole life. He was grateful for Chris, who had become Richie's "older brother." They talked about the things that concerned Richie; love, prejudice, and most importantly, sex.

Richie was glad that he and Chris had not become sexually active. Many other guys might have taken advantage of Richie's initial desire, but Chris helped him sort out his feelings. When he did, he realized that his crush was really a need to be accepted. Knowing Chris was there for him made the fact that he still hadn't had a relationship bearable. Almost. Richie had had anonymous sex a couple of times, but he always felt horrible afterwards. He was ready for something more, and had decided six months ago that he was going to wait until he met someone with whom he could have a relationship. Now it was almost Valentine's Day and he was getting tired of waiting. He had masturbated a lot in the past six months to try to keep his libido in check, but the more he held back, the more he thought about sex.

"Hey Richie! You gonna pass right by me and not say hello?" he heard. He turned around and saw Emma Morrison, from his music theories class. She was a nice girl, but she just didn't get the fact that he was not interested in her. She was gorgeous—dark curly hair, alabaster skin and the bluest eyes he had ever seen. He was certain that she was used to men falling at her feet. Richie was tempted to tell her he was gay, just to keep her off of his back.

"Hi Emma," he muttered as he kept moving. If he kept walking and didn't look at her, perhaps she'd take the hint. "I'm kind of preoccupied, thinking about my recital and all."

"Like you need to worry! You're a genius," she cheered. "I was going to ask you if you wanted to join my brother and me. We're going to the Student Union for lunch."

Richie looked up for the first time and his heart almost stopped. Emma's brother was as handsome as she was beautiful. No, he was even better looking. He had light, sandy colored hair, chiseled features and the same incredibly blue eyes as his sister. His body was trim and slightly muscled—Richie guessed that he was a swimmer. Richie could barely think, much less respond to the invitation, so he just mumbled an assent and followed Emma as she led the way. He would follow her anywhere, as long as her brother was there. Richie had never before felt this way when looking at any man; it was lust at first sight.

"My name is Anton," the god offered, extending his hand. "If I waited for my sister to perform the social graces, I'd die of old age."

"That'd take a while," joked Emma. "You're only 23." She continued speaking, but Richie wasn't listening, until he heard her say, "There's a table." She led the way through the crowded room, followed by Anton and, finally, Richie. Anton had a great ass and the movement of his cheeks in his tight pants mesmerized Richie.

After they settled at the table, Emma excused herself to head to the bathroom. Anton turned to Richie, "So, you're a music major? I'd have thought acting."

"Acting?" Richie was shocked, he had been known for his musical ability for so long, that the idea of something else was foreign to him. "God no! If I'm not behind my piano, I'm terrified to be in front of a large group of people."

"It's just that you're so handsome."

"Wow! Thanks. What do you do?" Richie asked, but what he wanted to do was giggle like a little girl and run around the room saying, "He thinks I'm handsome."

"I work for a friend who has his own business," Anton said. "It's kind of boring, but it pays well."

Emma returned to the table carrying a copy of the school paper. "Look at this," she said, thrusting the paper to Anton. "Dade County may pass a gay rights bill. Did you know about that Anton?"

"Emma!" Anton said to his sister, then turned to Richie. "I'm gay. I usually don't make a big deal about it, but my sister has a big mouth. I hope that doesn't make you uncomfortable."

"No," said Richie. It was now or never, he thought. "So am I."

Emma's jaw dropped open a full three inches. "I knew it! Thank God, for a while there I thought that I was losing my touch."

"Not too self-centered, are we?" said her embarrassed brother. "Please let me apologize for her," offered Anton.

"No need," responded Richie, "She's right."

"You know, you two should go out," Emma offered, casually switching to matchmaker. "Anton hasn't dated anyone in months. Anton, ask him out!"

"Emma, you shouldn't put your brother on the spot," Richie chided, hoping all the while Anton would agree. He looked at the man of his wet dreams, "Don't, I mean, you shouldn't . . ." he trailed off.

"That's okay. I was trying to figure out how I could ask you out anyway," he laughed. "You know, you should wear that shade of red more often, it's very flattering."

"What?" asked Richie, looking at his gray sweatshirt and jeans.

"Your face," Anton said. "You blushed so deeply when Emma embarrassed you, and it looked so cute."

It was then that Emma stood up and announced, "I'm giving you guys a chance to talk. I'm leaving." and she got up and rushed off leaving the two men staring at each other before they both burst out laughing.

"Well, that was subtle," Anton joked. "That's my sister, all right. I'm sorry; I can leave if you like."

"No," shouted Richie, a little louder than he meant to. "I'd like to do something . . . I mean see a movie or go grab a bite to eat."

"That sounds good," offered Anton. "How about if you drop off your stuff at home, then we can go someplace for dinner. I've got my car parked in the lot."

"I live in the dorm right over there," Richie said indicating the building across the street from the Student Union's big plate glass window. "I'd like to wash up first; I've been locked in a rehearsal room all morning."

"Sounds good," said Anton. "Do you want me to wait here?"

"No," offered Richie. "My roommate went home for the weekend. You can come to my room." Richie leaned forward and said in a lower voice, "I haven't told anyone else I'm gay, so play it cool, okay?"

"No problem," said Anton, as he rose to leave with Richie.

Richie left Anton in his room and went down the hall to the communal shower. He had butterflies in his stomach and he knew he was grinning from ear to ear. He was lucky that most of the guys were either down at dinner or away for the weekend, because he was sure his face would give him away. He showered quickly, and returned to his room with a towel around his waist. As he reached for the door, he realized that he hadn't thought about this. He'd have to change in front of Anton. He didn't want to appear as if he expected sex right away, but he couldn't very well go into the room and then take his clothes back to the shower room. The thought of sex with Anton made his dick start to firm up. Richie took a few breaths to regain his composure and give his dick a chance to relax. He then opened the door and slipped into his room. Anton was naked on the bed waiting for him. Richie turned off the overhead light, unwrapped the towel and settled next to Anton on the bed. They kissed deeply.

"I've been wanting to do that since the moment I saw you," Anton panted. He reached down to stroke Richie's dick. When his hand found the throbbing penis, a look of shock registered on his face. Then he looked down. "Wow!" he said mesmerized by Richie's huge shaft. "I've seen some big ones in my day, but never like this."

"I hope it's not, well, not . . ." Richie never knew what to say when this happened, and it happened every time a man saw his cock. He was embarrassed, and a little proud, all at once.

"It's fine," said Anton kissing Richie deeply. "It's really just an added bonus. With your baggy jeans, I didn't suspect anything like this."

Richie stroked the side of his face, grateful that he was more than just a huge cock to the man. "Some guys are freaked, and to others it's . . . it's, well more important than who I am."

"Well, you've got to admit, it certainly is formidable," laughed Anton. "I'm certain that I'll be able to cope with it," he whispered as he pulled Richie close.

"Oh," said Richie in surprise when Anton nestled next to him. Anton wasn't as big as Richie, but his was the biggest Richie had ever touched, other than his own.

*   *   *

Miami Beach, a few hours later.

After a great dinner, which Anton put on his expense account, Anton said he had to call his boss and find out if he needed to work the next day. Richie sat with his fingers crossed. His recital wasn't until Wednesday, so he could afford to take a day off to play, and he couldn't think of a better playmate than Anton. He was head over heels in love. When Anton came back from the phone, he announced that he was free all weekend. Seeing Richie's smile, he said, "I hope that means that you feel the same way I do. I'll say it first. I'm crazy about you."

"I like you a lot, too," said Richie. "I've only been with a couple of guys, but I never felt this way about them. I hope it's all right to say that."

"More than all right," Anton said as they walked to his car. "I have a confession. My sister thought that you might be gay and showed me your picture in the school yearbook. I asked her to introduce us. She told me that you were pretty shy, so we took it slow."

"I'm glad you made the first move," murmured Richie. "I would have been too afraid."

Anton reached over from the stick shift and caressed Richie's leg, "Me too," he said, then feeling Richie's cock stir through the fabric, added, "And then there's that added bonus. How about if we go back to my place? Can you spend the night?"

"I'd love to," Richie grinned. Soon Anton pulled into the garage of a luxurious high rise building. Richie was surprised that a guy so young could live in a building so posh. Anton explained that it was one of the benefits of the job; his boss owned the building and even had an apartment in it. He was seldom there because he traveled so much, so Anton fed his cat and collected his mail when he was gone. They made out as they rode up in the elevator. When they got off the elevator, there were only two doors.

"There are only two apartments per floor," explained Anton. "My boss uses that other one as his office, and lets me stay in this one so he has me at his beck and call," he joked.

Richie walked into the apartment ahead of Anton. The room was dark and Richie could see the lights of a few ships out on the ocean beyond the window. Anton flipped a switch which lit a table lamp. The tastefully decorated apartment impressed Richie. Anton flipped another switch and the classic Cilla Best album, "Bittersweet", began playing at a seductive level.

"Let me give you the tour," Anton offered. "This is the living room and terrace," he said indicating the large balcony. "There's the kitchen I never use, and the powder room. And, here's the master bedroom," he said with a flourish, turning on the lights. The room was gorgeous, with a king-sized bed on one side of the room. On the opposite side of the room, mirrors lined the wall. A row of built-in closets lined a third wall, while floor to ceiling windows, shielded by gauzy drapes, led out to a second balcony which also overlooked the ocean. The room was beautifully lit, bright without glare. It looked like a movie set.

Anton noticed the impressed look on Richie's face. "It's not as much of a pleasure pit as you might think. This was my boss's place before he renovated the penthouse apartment, Most of this is his doing, only this is mine," he said handing Richie a carved figure. "It's an African fertility god. I found it in an antique store years ago. It's kind of perverse," he said indicating the figure's oversized erection.

"It's unusual," said Richie. "I guess it's a good thing I measure up."

"Oh, don't get the wrong idea," Anton added quickly. "You're more interesting than just that," and he leaned over and kissed Richie.

In a matter of minutes, both men had shed their clothes and were on the bed making mad, passionate love. Richie had never experienced such intense sex. Most of his other encounters were furtive wham-bam-thank-you-man sessions. Anton took his time. Richie had only previously experienced oral sex and mutual masturbation. Anton showed him a myriad of paths to pleasure. Richie fucked Anton, and was fucked by him. Anton demonstrated something he called rimming, darting his tongue in and out of Richie's ass. He was a patient and tender teacher. When Richie wasn't comfortable with one of the techniques, Anton just moved on to another. They made love for hours, neither of the young men tiring, though their bodies were glistening with sweat.

Finally after three hours of non-stop passion, Anton suggested that they call it a night. He went over to the wall switch and dimmed the lights for the first time. Richie had been so enthralled with their lovemaking he hadn't even noticed that there was a series of spotlights focused on the bed. Thank goodness those windows were covered with drapes, he thought.

What Richie hadn't noticed was the camera perched above the wall of mirrors. In the apartment behind those mirrors, a heavyset man and a slender man had watched all that night's action.

"I think we got some great footage tonight," said the cameraman as he unloaded the film from behind the wall of one-way mirrors.

"I'll get the film from the camera above the bed to you tomorrow," offered the heavy guy. "Between the two cameras, we should have more than enough footage for a 60 minute reel. If not, we can pad it with some stock shots of Anton alone."

"Anton's certainly been a good investment," noted the cameraman. "This is like the fourth guy that he's seduced on film for you."

"Yeah," said his boss. "He's done pretty well. You know, I thought Anton's equipment was pretty massive. But this guy. Wow! We're going to sell a ton of this movie. I'm going to have Anton keep this one around for a while. The fags will love him; he's so big it's almost freakish."

"I could handle being that freakish," the cameraman chuckled as he left.

CHAPTER 55

New York City, Memorial Day

Frankie was in the small courtyard behind their brownstone in the process of firing up the barbecue. It was always a tricky moment for him. This had always been Sonny's specialty. Four years since his best friend had died and he still got choked up. The times at home were always the ones that they both loved best, because it was where they could relax and be themselves. A few months after Sonny's death, Frankie had moved over to Lavinia's side of the house. In public, he still pretended to be married to Rochelle, but at home, they could all stop the charade.

In some ways it was better for everyone, even Rochelle. The kids had grown to realize biology didn't matter, that all through their lives they had had two sets of equally loving parents. Frankie thought of Richie as his son as he always had, just as Francie was his daughter. The kids had always accepted both women as their mothers, despite what they called them. Francie had a little trouble accepting the news at first, but her faith helped her to come to terms with things. She now considered Frankie her father as much as Sonny was. It was a little touchy when Francie first became involved with the church. He and Lavinia and Rochelle were not very devout people. Frankie and Rochelle were Jews, ethnically, yet never observed religious rites. Lavinia was a lapsed Jehovah's Witness. They were concerned that Francie might become some sort of religious fanatic, but if anything; her devotion seemed to bring her a sense of peace.

Richie had withdrawn for a while after Sonny's death. Now that he was in college he'd become a little more outgoing, especially in the past few weeks. When Richie told them that he might not come home for the summer, Frankie assumed that he was having some sort of romance down in Miami. But, two weeks ago, Richie suddenly called and informed him that he had changed his mind. They'd picked him up from the airport last night. His hair bleached to a strawberry blond by the sun, his skin dark enough that you could tell he was Sonny's child. He was friendlier, but still a little preoccupied. Frankie hoped that maybe the family gathering would cheer him up. It had been almost a year since they were all together.

Lavinia came outside carrying a tray with glasses, a cocktail shaker and an ice bucket. She looked terrific, Frankie thought. As beautiful as the day they met at Sonny's record company. She had a great set of legs, and could easily have gotten away with hot pants instead of the Bermuda shorts she preferred.

"Martini?" she asked, not waiting for an answer before she poured one. She brought the drink to him and kissed him on the cheek. He started to respond, but she pushed him away goodheartedly. "Nope, no more until you get that grill going."

"I just can't get the coals to catch," Frankie responded. "Sonny always handled this part. I'm just the cook."

"How 'bout if I try," offered Richie coming out onto the patio.

"My savior!" joked Frankie. "Where's your mother?"

"She's putting the finishing touches on the potato salad," Richie replied, rearranging the coals into a pyramid. "She said to get her martini ready, and she wants . . . ."

". . . double olives," Lavinia and Frankie finished the sentence with him.

"Does she really think that we don't know by now?" Lavinia laughed.

"What time is Francie getting here?" Richie asked. "We've never been separated so long. Then I go away for a few months and she becomes a famous actress."

"She's not famous yet," said Frankie. "The movie won't be on television for a few more months. Let's not swell her head up any more than it is."

"Now, quit," scolded Lavinia, playfully slapping Frankie's arm. Then, turning to Richie, "The book was so long that the movie will take something like 14 hours. They're going to play it in sections, like the old movie serials. They're calling it a mini-series and say it will revolutionize television."

"She said she's going to have a surprise for us," said Frankie. "Maybe she finally learned to cook."

"That'll be the day," joked Richie. "When we were kids and played house, I always had to cook. She claimed that she didn't know how to work the stove."

"Like mother, like daughter," Frankie said. "If it weren't for your mother, we all would have starved years ago."

"Oh, but you would have died happy," added Rochelle, entering from the kitchen with a big bowl of potato salad. Richie took the bowl from her and put it on the picnic table. "Lavinia's martinis are sheer perfection. That's why my food tastes so good to you. So, where's mine?"

Richie started to hand her a glass, "Do you mind if I take a sip?" Seeing their frowns, he responded, "Hey, I'm almost 21, and I don't think the police are watching." As his mother nodded, he took one sip. "Yuck! All these years and the way you all raved about them . . . but this is just as bad as the one I tried at school."

"At school?" Rochelle said. "So this isn't your first?"

"Relax, Rochelle, all kids experiment when they're away at school." laughed Frankie. "That's part of the reason you wanted to go away, isn't it Richie? You wanted to try new things."

Richie started choking. He poured a big glass of lemonade from the pitcher on the picnic table. "Yeah, something like that . . . ."

Just then they heard the front door close as Francie called "Where is everybody?"

Richie bounded out of his seat and ran to meet Francie. He grabbed the large box she was carrying in one arm and lifted her off the ground with the other. "What's this?" he asked handing the box to Frankie, and hugging his sister.

"I told you, it's a surprise. It's for after dinner," she said as she raked her fingers through his hair. "Well, look at you beach boy." She made the rounds kissing everyone.

"Beach boy, huh? You're lucky that the coals are almost ready," Richie joked. "I have to go get the burgers, but when I . . . ."

"No, Honey, tonight it's steaks, not hamburgers," Rochelle said, then seeing the look of surprise on everyone's face, offered. "Tonight is a special occasion."

"What kind of special occasion?" Frankie and Lavinia asked.

"You'll find out soon," Francie answered slyly.

After dinner, the satisfied family was sitting around the picnic table, laughing and joking with each other. Frankie asked Richie what other things he'd tried while away at school.

"Well," said Richie taking a deep breath. "I was waiting for the best time to tell you all this, and I guess that this is as good a time as any. I hope you won't be too upset or disappointed . . ."

"You're not dropping out of school?" asked a horrified Rochelle. "Your father would be so upset. It was his dream for you to . . ."

"Relax, Mom," Richie soothed. "That's not it. I'm, well, this may come as a . . . . I'm gay." The silence at the table was stunning. They all stared at Richie. "Francie, I know that this doesn't agree with your church values, but I want you to know, that I don't feel ashamed or that I'm evil, or anything like that. If you don't . . . ."

"Will you give me a chance to speak, before you start deciding what I think about you?" she barked at him. "I am just so tired of everyone thinking I'm some little goody two shoes just because I go to church. I'll have you know, Richie, that some of the men in the choir are gay, and they're my friends. Anyway, a true Christian doesn't judge others. You're my brother and my love for you is not going to change because you're gay."

He reached over and hugged her. "I was so afraid that you'd hate me. Thank you."

Rochelle stared at him, tears welling up in her eyes. "How could you think we wouldn't love you? You're my son, no matter what."

"Well," Richie explained, "I know that my father didn't feel comfortable about gay people."

"Sonny did have some issues about that. Mostly, he felt that it should be a private thing, something folks didn't discuss. When it came to dealing with people on an individual basis, he always was fine," Rochelle offered. "Don't forget, he was in show business and had met a few gay people in his time. We even went on vacation with Johnny Mathis and his boyfriend once."

"Uncle Johnny is gay?" asked a shocked Francie. Looking at Richie she asked, "Did he ever . . . . ?"

"No, of course not," answered Richie. "Nobody ever . . . . I'm just who I am."
He turned and looked at Frankie and Lavinia, who hadn't said a word the entire
time. Frankie and Lavinia looked back at him, then smiled.

"Thank the lord that you said something," Lavinia said hugging him. "I kind
of guessed about two years ago. I didn't know if I should say anything to you or not.
And, as accepting as I knew your mother would be, I didn't think it was my place
to tell her what I thought."

Frankie hugged the boy, for once grateful that Sonny was gone. He might
have been okay with gay people on an individual basis, but having a gay son was
something else entirely. The kids had had enough turmoil in their lives, they didn't
need to worry about their parents accepting them.

Rochelle broke the tension by rising from the table. "Well, I don't know about
anyone else, but after all that, I could use a piece of chocolate cake."

Lavinia rose with her. "I'll help. By the way Francie, don't think that this gets
you out of sharing your big surprise. As soon as we get dessert and coffee set up,
you're next."

"She's going to have to do something big to top Richie's news, though," Frankie
laughed as he collected the dirty plates from the table. "You two stay put, I'll get
this," he said as he went into the house.

Richie turned to Francie, "Oh, God! Francie, I'm sorry. I hope that I didn't
ruin your surprise, it's just that I've been worrying how to tell everyone and it just
seemed the right time."

Francie took his hand. "Don't apologize. This must have been hard on you.
When did you know?"

"I always knew that I felt different, then, when we found out about our family,
I kind of thought that might be it. But I still felt like I didn't fit in anywhere. I think
I first started to realize what it was when I was about 13. I'd had crushes on some
guys, and when all that gay stuff was in the news, it finally clicked. So, you've got
gay friends, huh?" Richie joked. "Any single ones?"

"They're all too old for you," Francie joked. "So, there's no special boyfriend?"

"I thought there was," said Richie. "I was deep in love, and I thought he was,
too. Then about two weeks ago he stopped calling. I go to school with his sister and,
at first, she told me that he was away on business. Soon she started avoiding me, I
was a little slow on the uptake, but I finally figured out I'd been dumped."

"His loss," offered Francie. "I know how you feel, I wish I could finally meet
someone, but all the good guys are either married or . . . ooops. I was about to say
gay."

Just then their parents returned with dessert and coffee. After they all settled in, Lavinia
said, "All right honey, I think we've waited long enough. What's your surprise?"

"Well, I don't know if I can top Richie's, but I think you'll be happy about this,"
Francie said as she reached into a box filled with magazines. "You don't know how
hard this was for me to keep a secret."

"Yeah, you're usually such a blabber mouth," joked Richie.

Francie handed them each a copy of *Jet*. When they looked at her, confused, she said, "Turn to page 24."

They did, and all cheered at once. There was a full-page picture of Francie and the headline, "Sonny Lewis's Daughter: Making It On Her Own" and a large article about Francie's acting debut and her work with the church choir.

They all hugged and congratulated her. She was beaming with pride, and basking in her family's love. Then she made her pronouncement.

"There's only one thing wrong."

"What could be wrong?" Rochelle asked.

"Your mother and I are so proud of you," offered Frankie.

"The headline is wrong," offered Francie. "I'm not really Sonny Lewis's daughter. I want to change my name. I want to be called Francie Lewis Kaye. I want to tell the world the truth."

They stood looking at her. The gentle breeze teasing the branches of the trees sounded thunderous in their stunned silence. It was a momentous evening in many ways.

CHAPTER 56

Los Angeles

Gina leaned back in the hot tub at Franco's rented house and sighed while he massaged her feet. They'd just returned from San Francisco where Franco was filming some background footage for his documentary. In the past few weeks they had been to more than 20 communities; a pig farm in Alabama, mansions in Beverly Hills, the slums of Detroit and the suburbs outside of Milwaukee. They began to wind up their tour on the West Coast. Their last stop before returning few days ago was a garage in California where a couple of college dropouts were trying to market their invention, a "home computer".

The duo had offered to let them buy stock in the new company. Franco had generously given them a hundred dollars for 100 shares in the company. As they drove away and headed into San Francisco, Franco told Gina that, while he thought the stock in the company was worthless, he admired the kids' gumption. He handed Gina the letter of agreement; he had put the stock in her name. Gina Ferrara was now the proud owner of 100 shares of stock in something called Apple Computers. It was a sweet gesture anyway, thought Gina as she put the letter in her purse.

It was this kind of interaction with people that was helping Franco get the most incredible footage. Gina couldn't think of one aspect of life in America that he had missed. San Francisco had been their favorite, by far. There was something almost mystical about the place.

"Oh Franco, that feels incredible," she moaned. They had become quite close, but never this intimate. "Do you know," she said as a way to break the tension she was feeling, "That someone once said, 'Whenever someone disappears, no matter where in the world, they are eventually spotted in San Francisco.' I can believe it. I think I'm in love with that town."

Franco switched from one foot to the other, "I have heard about a theory that San Francisco is filled with descendants from the lost continent of Atlantis."

"Now you're teasing me," she pouted.

"Never! Legend has it that the tallest building in Atlantis was a pyramid topped with a beacon. What is the tallest building in San Francisco?"

"It's the TransAmerica . . . ." she replied. "Oh my, I think you're right."

"Of course I am," he soothed, as his massaging hands worked their way up her leg. Gina didn't resist; in fact she spread her legs a little. Franco's hands continued to climb as he leaned forward. He kissed her, tenderly at first, then with more passion. She returned his passion with a fervor she had never known. Soon, they were a tangle of hands and limbs tearing at each other's swim suits. He caressed her soft belly and rested his head on her firm breasts as they bobbed in the warm water.

He took Gina onto his lap and began to massage her neck, while kissing it. Gina turned herself around and straddled Franco, taking him deep inside her. She began to buck up and down as he buried his face in her breasts. He reached under her legs and began to fondle her clitoris as she rocked back and forth on his penis. Franco's penis was not large, but it was quite thick and between his penis and the manual stimulation he was adding, Gina came in wave upon wave of orgasm.

When they were both spent. Franco walked over to the bar and poured them each a glass of champagne. On his way back to the hot tub; he bent over and swept up a rubber raft from beside the swimming pool. He insisted Gina lay on the raft in the hot tub. While she relaxed he continued massaging her shoulders and neck until she drifted off. When she awoke, Franco was sitting in a lounge chair next to the hot tub watching her. She suddenly felt very naked and exposed, until he said, "You are the most beautiful woman I have ever seen. Seeing you here, under the moonlight, I am filled with passion again."

This time she went behind him and began massaging his neck. He stopped her by taking her arm and leading her around the chair to face him.

"Gina, you must marry me." he murmured. "Please."

Gina nearly fainted from the shock. They were getting along incredibly and no man had ever made her feel more desirable or valued. She felt great stirrings for Franco, but her experience with Jean had soured her on delving deeper. Gina felt the wall of security she'd erected tremble, much as her legs were doing right then.

"Franco," she stammered, "I'm flattered, but I don't know if I'm ready to make that kind of commitment. Can I think about it a while?"

The handsome Italian smiled up at her, "Of course, cara mia," he whispered as he stroked her arm. "I would wait forever for you." He then pulled her onto his lap and cradled her in his arms.

Gina closed her eyes and leaned her head up to kiss Franco. One part of her thought, "This is what love is like." while a small part of her was waiting for everything to crash around her.

CHAPTER 57

New York City—2 weeks later

Frankie was meeting with his agent, Jack Steiner. Frankie had wanted to take things easy after Sonny's death. Even though Frankie was, in effect, supporting two families, he had invested the money he and Sonny made during the height of their career wisely and didn't need to work. In fact, he could retire and they'd still live well for the rest of their lives. He'd only done a few benefits the past couple of years, but Frankie wasn't the type to take things easy. The fact that Francie was in the business now might have given him the bug again, he wasn't sure. Whatever the cause, he'd asked Jack to look into the possibilities.

Although Jack was pretty busy with Francie's skyrocketing career, he was happy to field some offers for him. People had been clamoring for Frankie's return for some time. Oddly enough, in the years since Sonny's sudden death, the public seemed to forget any issues they had once had with the duo.

"Here's the thing," Jack said unwrapping a piece of gum. "Everybody wants you back. I've had offers from all three networks to develop a series for you."

"Well, that sounds pretty promising," smiled Frankie. Truth be told, he wasn't certain that the public would want to see him without his partner. Dean Martin and Jerry Lewis had been able to go their separate ways pretty successfully, but they were the exception. "What kinds of things are they offering?"

"Forget what they're offering," Jack barked, nearly choking on his gum. "If they want you, we'll make them come to you on your own terms."

"I'd like to at least hear what they're offering, Jack," Frankie replied.

"Okay, Okay! ABC and NBC both want you to host a variety show. They're having big hits with them now. My thought is that there's a glut on the market and the popularity of that kind of show has seen its peak. You don't want to do one."

"That sounds right," Frankie mused. "Besides, I'd just be going back to what I did with Sonny. No matter how good it was, it would always be compared to the first show."

"My thoughts exactly," Jack agreed. "Now, CBS has an original idea. They've proposed a sitcom in which you'd play a bigoted guy in the south. Your daughter marries a Yankee liberal and the series would be about how you and your son-in-law battle over everything."

"I don't know about that," mused Frankie. "I don't really like the idea of playing a bigot. It goes against everything I believe. Besides, it sounds like a rip-off of *All In The Family.*"

"You've got it! But don't reject them outright," counseled Jack. "Remember, they want you; we can tailor the show to what you want. Maybe switch the characters around so that you play the liberal and the son-in-law is a bigot. They have this terrific new actor in mind to play your foil. His name is Steve Martin, he's been a writer for the Smothers' Brothers and Sonny and Cher, and he's been on *Saturday Night Live.* He's going to be a big star. It wouldn't hurt to pair up with him."

"Possibly," offered Frankie. "I like the idea of pairing up with a younger guy; there'd be less comparison with Sonny. I don't want to diminish what we had. Why don't you set up a meeting with this kid and we'll see if there's any chemistry there?"

"Will do," agreed Jack, opening another package of gum. "I'm addicted to this stuff, but I haven't had a cigarette in six weeks. How're things at home?"

"Great! Both kids are in town, though we seldom see Francie. Between *Roots* and her choir practice, she's seldom around. You know she's singing at the Bicentennial Gala?"

"Hey, I'm her agent, I know everything. I made some arrangements for the choir. It's gonna be hot on the 4th, and there isn't much in the way of facilities on Liberty Island, so they're doing a dressing room on a barge."

"Thanks for handling her," Frankie said.

"She's a dream client, I should be thanking you," Jack laughed. "She came in with a contract to negotiate. I usually have to sell these young kids for years before I see payback. I was happy to do the choir stuff as a freebie."

"Has she talked to you about her plans?" asked Frankie. They'd let Jack in on their family secret after Sonny died. "She wants to tell the truth about us."

"That could be tricky," mused Jack. "But, it all depends on how it's presented. It's a different generation than the one in which we grew up. I'll think about how to put the best spin on it."

"I knew that you'd watch out for her," a relieved Frankie replied, knowing that Jack could handle anything. "When Richie finishes school, he'll be looking for an agent. We'll make it a family agency."

Jack took his time unwrapping another piece of gum. Frankie knew Jack well enough to see that there was something he wanted to say, but didn't know how to bring up the subject. "C'mon, Jack," Frankie said, "It can't be that bad. The kid's pretty talented."

"In ways I would never have guessed," Jack said. "I was hoping you'd bring it up."

"What are you talking about?" Frankie queried.

"Then, you don't know?" Jack replied.

"Know what?" a confused Frankie asked. "Is there a problem with Richie? When I left the house, he was working at the piano. He didn't act like anything was wrong."

"Maybe you'd better talk to Richie," Jack responded. "This should come from him."

"Jack, you know everything about us. You're a part of the family. Don't hold back. Tell me what's wrong," Frankie said frantically. "What's going on?"

"Richie made a porno movie," Jack admitted. "It's a gay porno."

"There must be some mistake, Jack," Frankie replied. "Yeah, Richie is gay. He just told us a few weeks ago. Maybe some tabloid reporter found out and fabricated the story."

"No, there's a real porno. I had one of my assistants go out and get it," Jack confided. "He had to go to a dirty book store in Times Square. He had to go to four; actually, the clerk told him he got the only copy they had. They didn't put out too many; it's one of the first porno films for those home video players."

"It can't be Richie," Frankie defended his son. "Maybe it's just someone who looks like him."

"I'm pretty sure it's him," soothed Jack. "He doesn't use his real name, in fact he goes by Peter Biggs, but it's him."

"It can't be," sighed Frankie.

Jack reached into his desk drawer and pulled out a box containing a videocassette. There cover featured a couple of pictures of two guys. They were naked, and there were black bars blocking out their eyes and genitals. "Take a look at the pictures on the box. I'm pretty sure that's Richie. It's the hair that's a dead give-away."

Frankie held the box in his shaking hands. He still prayed that it was all a big mistake, but one look at the picture and all hope dissipated. He began to sob. Jack came around from his desk and put his arm around his friend's shoulder.

"How could he?" wailed Frankie. "Did he really think that we wouldn't find out?"

"Possibly, this thing's getting limited distribution until they see how this video thing goes," answered Jack. "Why don't you take this and go talk to him? I'll contact the distributor and offer to by back all of the copies. If we're lucky he hasn't produced too many."

CHAPTER 58

An hour later

On the cab ride home from Jack's office all Frankie could do was stare at the box he carried. At one point he noticed that the cab driver was watching him in the rear view mirror. He put the box in his briefcase.

"Don't have to hide that on my account," voiced the cabbie. "I get lots of guys carrying that stuff, not just the gay ones, either. Not that it matters to me. Live and let live, I say. Have you seen it?"

"No," stammered Frankie.

"That man is a lucky guy," the driver laughed.

"Lucky?" muttered Frankie

"Jeez, even from the rear view mirror, I could make out the size of his cock! I wish I had one that big," whistled the cabbie. "I ain't never had any complaints from the ladies, mind you, but I guess the gay guys really like 'em big, huh?

"I wouldn't know," said Frankie, paying the guy and getting out of the cab as quickly as possible.

Frankie entered the house quietly. He wanted to avoid having to talk to Lavinia or Rochelle until after he had had a chance to see what Richie had to say. He went into his study and put his briefcase on his desk. Then he went through the house trying to find out who was home. The house was empty. Frankie gazed out an upstairs window and saw Richie sitting on a lawn chair under the elm tree studying. He opened the window. "Richie, can I talk to you, in my study?" he called out. Richie smiled back at him and waved, then rose from his seat and headed toward the house. Frankie flew down the stairs, he wanted to usher Richie into the study and close the door before either Rochelle or Lavinia returned home. Richie was waiting for him in the study. If he was at all worried that his secret would come out, he was cool about hiding it. Frankie shut the door to the study behind him.

"What's the big secret," joked Richie. He assumed that Frankie was planning some sort of surprise for his mother's birthday next week.

"I think you know," answered Frankie, sitting on the couch across from Richie. "When were you going to tell us?"

"I don't know what you're talking about, Dad," he answered, totally confused

Frankie was stunned. How could his son do this? "Maybe I don't know you as well as I thought," said Frankie. "Did you think that we wouldn't find out?"

"What did I do? I thought that you weren't upset with me being gay. Dad, I'm sorry but it's who I am. I tried to be the other way, but I'm not," Richie sobbed, he was beginning to get very upset. He'd thought that things went too easily.

"Son, just because you're gay doesn't mean that you have to do things you know are wrong," Frankie offered. "I have to say I'm very disappointed in you. Did you think you could keep it a secret?"

"I never tried to keep it a secret," said the confused young man. "I told you as soon as I felt I could."

"Your mother and Lavinia will be devastated. When you were doing it, did you ever think of them?" Frankie asked. "Or Francie?"

"Doing what?" Richie finally said in frustration.

Frankie went to his desk, reached into his briefcase, and handed the videocassette to Richie. The young man stared at the box for a few minutes, clearly confused, then paled considerably. Soon a look of intense anger crossed his face.

"That son of a bitch," he spat. "No wonder he stopped calling me. I'll kill him!"

"What are you talking about?" asked Frankie. "Didn't you know about this?"

"Know about this?!?!?!" he gasped. "How could you think that I would knowingly make a porno movie? Do you really think that little of me?"

"No, of course not, Richie," Frankie said. "It's just that seeing this, well I'm sure that you can understand . . . ."

"Dad, I didn't know anything about it," Richie sobbed. "Yes, it's me. But, I didn't know I was being filmed. I thought that I was sharing a private moment with someone I loved."

"You had no idea that this film existed?" queried Frankie.

"No, this other guy is someone I was dating," Richie explained. "His name is Anton Morrison. We went out for a few weeks and then he disappeared. He must have had some kind of hidden cameras at his place. Oh, God! You haven't watched this have you?"

"No, I haven't," Frankie said, taking his son in his arms and comforting him. "I'm sorry to have doubted you, but I'm certain that you can understand why I was upset."

"I'll never be able to leave the house," Richie choked out. "Maybe we can get them to stop making it."

"We might," soothed Frankie.

"What am I going to do? Can I have them arrested? I feel like I've been . . . like a fool," he stammered. "That was supposed to be private. Don't they need my permission or something?"

"Your Uncle Jack is already trying to take care of it," Frankie offered.

"Shit!" cursed Richie. "Ooops, sorry."

"I think that it's okay for you to swear over something like this," Frankie laughed.

"How could I have thought that you'd do something like that when you won't even swear in front of me? Look son, it's done, you can't change that. Did you do anything on this that you're ashamed of?"

"Well not ashamed of," Richie answered. "But it's not something I want shared with the world. I'm so embarrassed!"

"Don't be," Frankie said. "Let's not get too upset. It might not get too much notice, and even if it does, we'll all refuse to comment on it, except to say that you weren't aware that you were being filmed, eventually Peter Biggs and *Biggs Stuff* will fade away."

"I hope so," replied Richie wistfully. "I don't suppose there's any way to keep this from Mom and Aunt Lavinia?"

"We can try, but I wouldn't count on keeping it from them for more than a few days," answered Frankie. "Besides, we've known about your "gift" since you were a baby. We've all changed your diapers, remember."

"Come on, stop it," said an embarrassed Richie. "This is difficult enough."

Frankie smiled. "You know, I shared many a dressing room with your father, and I saw him naked. All I can say, is . . ." he said pointing to the black bar on the box photo, sticking out like a two by four from his crotch, "That must come from your mother's side of the family."

CHAPTER 59

Malibu

Cilla lit another cigarette and took a sip of the tea with honey. She hadn't performed live in about three months. After she met Tim she'd worked with him on his documentary. He'd asked her to narrate the film and she'd happily done so. It gave her something to do, and she and Tim had clicked immediately. Almost everyone thought he was gay, but Cilla knew better. He swung both ways. While Cilla didn't go in for group activities, Tim was a great lover, and since it made him happy, she'd complied a few times. His taste in boys was nearly the same as hers, slim, toned and smooth, so it wasn't that big a deal. It was usually a pain to get them out of their "Oh, my God, I'm with Cilla Best" diva worshiping, but once they were over that, it was usually fun.

That was how she met her current musical director, Bobby. They were at a reception honoring one of Broadway's top composers, when the composer's widow introduced Cilla and Bobby. Bobby was helping the widow catalog all of the composer's sheet music. Although he was thrilled to meet Cilla, after a few minutes of chat, it became very clear that he was attracted to Tim.

In the aftermath of some great sex, the three of them had retired to the living room for drinks. They'd been sitting around and Bobby mentioned that he once played in the orchestra for Rosie. Then, like in a scene from one of her mother's movies, they suddenly found themselves around the piano, Bobby playing and Cilla singing better than she had in years. He'd become Cilla's best friend and accompanist almost immediately after that first night.

They all agreed that the sexual aspect of the relationship had to end. Tim was excellent about separating sex from relationships, so that was no big deal. Instead, Bobby had become her vocal coach, teaching her tricks to compensate for her limited range. She had a powerful voice; she could hold a note almost as long as Mama could. Now, with Bobby's help, she was trying to expand her limited vocal range.

Bobby entered the room, and gave Cilla a hug. He'd looked as if he was no more than 19 years old. In fact he was nearly 30, and had even accompanied her mother during her rehearsals in London. He was filled with energy, and today was no exception.

"Okay, Girl, let's do some warm-ups," Bobby chirped as he sat at the piano. Cilla hated warming up, but she knew it was the right thing to do, so she complied.

After about 20 minutes, Bobby stopped. "All right, have you made a decision about what you're going to sing at the Bicentennial gala?"

"Not a clue," Cilla responded, as she mopped her brow. "All the patriotic songs are so hackneyed. But, if I do one of my hits, it will look so self indulgent."

"Your fans will be disappointed if you don't," he offered. Then he brightened up, "How about singing one of your mother's songs?"

"Never!" said Cilla adamantly. "Long ago I vowed that I wouldn't. It's too weird."

"Look, how about your doing it as a tribute, a one-time thing. Your mother was known as America's Sweetheart, so what could be more appropriate?" he cajoled her. "It's been seven years since she died. Her fans will love it and your fans will need to be peeled from the rafters. It's perfect."

"What would I sing?" she wondered. "I won't do *Will I Ever See You Again?*".

"You'll have to," Bobby said. "But, you won't have to do the entire number. I can work up a medley, and we could include a bit of it."

"I don't know," Cilla explained. "It's the first song we performed together professionally. I don't think I could get past it."

"I'll put it in as the finale then, and just a few bars," he offered. "Oh! I just thought of how it will start: you'll do an intro to set it up, then go into *I Love This Country*. It's the perfect song, and it's from your mother's first movie, *"All American Girl."*

"That's not bad," Cilla offered, picking up a dark chocolate from the candy dish. "That was always one of my favorite movies of hers. I think because that's the one where she met my father. Oh shit! I'm going to have to check with him to see if he minds."

"I'm sure he won't," Bobby said eagerly. "It's all coming to me, we can segue from *This Is My Country* into *Now's the Time* and then all I have to do is find a way to transition into *Will I Ever See You Again?'.*"

"How about adding a few bars of *Time to Go*?" asked Cilla. "That was always my father's favorite song."

"That's perfect," Bobby gushed. "Let me work on this for a few minutes."

"Take your time," Cilla said as she crossed the room to the phone. She picked it up and dialed long distance. It was the middle of the afternoon in New York. "Hi, Daddy . . ." Cilla began.

CHAPTER 60

Washington D.C.

J en sat in Bruce's office and looked over the papers in front of her. This was the last project he had worked on, legislation guaranteeing that all government files, except those pertaining to national security, be made available to the public. This was the reason he had run for office in the first place. All she had to do was sign it, and the proposal would be on its way becoming law.

"Mrs. Goodman, is there a problem?" asked the secretary standing on the other side of the desk waiting for the document.

"No, it looks fine," Jen answered. She reached for a pen, and the secretary put one in her hand. Donna Wienold was certainly efficient; Bruce had said that she scared him sometimes, with her ability to anticipate his every need. She had been just as efficient for Jen and, in fact, had helped her through the past few months. Donna gave practical and tactical advice, shepherding Jen through every step of her inauguration and her first days in office. "Thank you Donna—I've asked you to call me Jen."

"I'm sorry Mrs. Goodman, I don't think that it is appropriate," the petite redhead explained.

"Okay, how about when it's just the two of us alone?" Jen compromised. "It would really make me feel more comfortable."

"All right, Mrs . . . Jen," she smiled. "Now, if you could sign the document where I've flagged it, we can get it over to the House in time for registration before the recess." Jen started to sign, but her hand was shaking so much that she had to stop. "I'm sorry, I didn't realize that it would be so emotional for me," she explained as she took a deep breath.

"It is for all of us, Jen," said the secretary as she came around the desk. "This is what your husband considered his main ambition." She rested her hand on Jen's shoulder, which comforted her considerably. As soon as Jenny signed the document, it was whisked out of her hands and Donna left the office. Jen leaned back in her chair and closed her eyes. The intercom buzzed.

"Yes," said Jen as she lifted the receiver.

"Mrs. Goodman," said Donna from the outer office. "Please hold for the President." There was a moment of silence on the line. Jen found herself sitting up straighter and patting back her hair.

"Mrs. Goodman," President Ford intoned from the White House. "I'm very pleased to see that your husband's proposed legislation is moving forward. I know this has been a difficult time for you and I appreciate the speed with which you helped expedite this matter."

"Thank you, Mr. President," Jen responded. "I appreciate the courtesies you have shown me."

"I was wondering, Mrs. Goodman, if you could do me a favor," continued the President.

Payback time thought Jen. That's what Washington runs on. "Of course," she responded.

"Would you please join us at the Bicentennial gala and make a speech?" he invited.

"Yes, of course. Thank you," she responded automatically.

"Fine, our offices will set it up. Goodbye."

"Goodbye," said a stunned Jen as she buzzed for Donna.

"I've already arranged for a driver to pick you up at your New York apartment on the 4th. I assume you'll want to stay in your apartment," said the secretary entering the room with a note pad. "He'll take you to the special ferry being used for the gala participants. Your speech is to be 4 minutes long. What topics would you like the speech writer to cover?"

Jen was agog. In Washington everything seemed to move at a snail's pace, each step in a process had to be carefully planned. This was moving at lightning speed.

"But how . . ." she sputtered.

"This has been in the works for weeks," Donna informed her. "I didn't want to say anything until it was official."

"So, you knew about this before I did?" asked Jen.

"Assistants always know everything before their bosses do," she replied efficiently. "It's part of the job description. Now, about the subject of the speech."

CHAPTER 61

Malibu

Jon was working at his desk, trying to compose a sentence that didn't seem hackneyed. His new book was proving to be a difficult one, he had never written about something quite so intimate. Even his book about his father and mother was easier. Perhaps it was because they were both dead and he didn't need to worry about what they thought. But every time he tried to write a sentence about the special bond he and Keiko shared, he froze up. Perhaps his agent was right; this wasn't such a good idea after all.

His agent wanted him to do a book about baseball. But, Jon had no desire to look back at that part of his life. As much as he had enjoyed it, it wasn't important. Relationships were important, culture was important. Baseball may be America's pastime, but it's not mine, he thought. Not any longer. He was so bereft of ideas, that he actually welcomed the phone call interrupting him. 'Yes,'" Jon said as he doodled on his note pad.

"Mr. Mason," the voice began. "My name is Sharon Martin; I'm coordinating the events for the bicentennial celebration."

"Yes," Jon answered warily.

"I was just wondering if you have decided which of your poems you'll be reading," she continued.

"I'm sorry," he responded. "I haven't found anything I think is appropriate. I'm trying to write a piece especially for the occasion."

"You've been slated for six minutes. Is this going to be a problem?" she snapped. "If it is, I need to know right away so I can make alternative arrangements."

"No, I guess not," answered Jon. Augh! Those East Coast bureaucrats were so officious. "I'm certain that I'll have something by the 4th."

"No! That won't do! You have the text to me by next Friday," she continued. "I need it at least a week before the event, so that it can be approved and given to the sign language interpreters."

"Approved?" Jon asked.

"Well, of course. We have to make certain that there's nothing inappropriate. Orlando Letelier, the Chilean ambassador will be President Ford's guest, and with all the trouble in Mexico and South America, we need to be especially careful. I'm certain that you understand. As soon as you have it ready send it to me at . . . ."

Jon didn't hear the rest of the information, although he wrote it down. He was already composing the poem in his head.

CHAPTER 62

Independence Day—Liberty Island, 8:00 A.M.

As the zero hour for the Bicentennial celebration neared, Liberty Island began to resemble an al fresco Carnegie Hall. The tech crews had been on the island for the past week, installing the riggings for the sound system, erecting a stage, and lining up rows of bleachers for the invited guests who didn't rate the padded chairs in the VIP section. Now, with the seats extending from the stage, and the lights and sound system being installed, everything was coming together.

Until a few days ago, many on the crew thought that they would also have to install a huge tent to dome the entire area, but the storm that had threatened the East Coast suddenly changed direction and veered out to sea. Additional workers readied the trailers that would serve as dressing rooms for the performers. The decision was made to focus on stage and music stars since so many recent movies had been critical of the U.S. and didn't seem appropriate for the event. The Bicentennial event's producer, Danny Kopelson, had had to turn down both Robert Redford and Dustin Hoffman. Although the mega-stars would have garnered a lot of publicity, the fact that they were starring in *All the President's Men* would have brought up too many memories of the Nixon administration, and seemed an insult to President Ford.

The president wasn't going to appear on stage, he was in the middle of a campaign for reelection and having him speak would entitle the Democrats to equal airtime. Although the intent was to keep the show patriotic, yet non-political, the fact that the president was in attendance, and was bringing the ambassador from Chile as his guest, made that difficult.

The focus on stage actors made Kopelson's life easier. Broadway stars may have egos to equal those of Hollywood stars, but they aren't accustomed to being pampered. Not one of the performers involved in tonight's event had complained about their accommodations. Only the representative for the gospel group had made a demand of any kind, and it was quite reasonable. He requested an air-conditioned barge for his group. Though Kopelson thought it an extravagance, he agreed, especially since the gospel group got the production company for *Roots* to underwrite the costs involved. The barge proved a wise idea; the fifty-member chorus would have had to stand around in the hundred-degree heat otherwise.

With Neil Simon, Tammy Grimes, Lynn Redgrave and Cilla Best to tend to, he was spinning enough plates. He was glad that he didn't need to worry about choir members dropping from heat prostration. In fact, Cilla Best was due to arrive in a couple of hours to do a tech run through, and his crew hadn't finished installing the lights and sound.

"Hey, Danny," one of the Teamsters called, "You'd better come see this." The man gestured towards a small portable television one of the guys had plopped down next to the sound board.

Danny, who had had enough trouble getting the Teamsters hustle after a dispute over some immigrant nationals working with them, was not amused They had already started an unofficial work slowdown and now they were watching television, on *overtime*.

"I haven't got time Joe," Danny called back. "How about if we watch *Match Game 76* after we get these lights installed?"

"Okay, wise guy," Joe mumbled as he headed back to work, "But don't say I didn't warn you."

If Danny had taken a peek at the screen he would have seen Francie Lewis being interviewed on The Today Show by Barbara Walters.

CHAPTER 63

New York City—Rockefeller Center—8:15 A.M.

Francie's palms were sweating as Barbara Walters began her introduction. Francie must have done one hundred interviews in the past few weeks. *Roots* wasn't scheduled to air for months, but the press blitz had already begun. Francie would be singing with the choir and had a solo at the opening of the Bicentennial gala. You couldn't open a newspaper or magazine without seeing her picture.

Francie thought that she was ready for all the attention but, even though she had experienced the glare of the spotlight second hand, from the sidelines, she hadn't realized that it would be quite so intimidating when it was suddenly focused on her. She sneaked a quick look over at Rochelle, Richie, and her mother and father standing just behind one of the cameras. Frankie gave her a thumbs up, she was still scared to death. After today, she knew that her life would never be the same. The poised brunette reporter finished her introduction as the advance footage from *Roots* played out on the screen. Then the light on the camera in front of them turned red. Francie took a deep breath and smiled.

"That was some very impressive acting," Walters smiled. "And, is it true that this is your first role?"

"Well, yes, I suppose," Francie stammered. "I did some workshops in school and, of course, I've studied acting for a number of years, but, yes, this is my first professional acting job. The role of Kintana is a dream come true. She's such a strong and proud woman. I've been blessed."

"You were discovered on our show, actually," Barbara said, offering Francie a chance to elaborate.

"Yes, Mr. Haley happened to be watching your show when my church choir performed just before Christmas," Francie said, trying to make the story sound fresh, after she had already told it to dozens of other reporters, dozens of other times, "He remembered me when they were looking for someone to play the gospel singer in the show."

"Do you think that the producers approached you because of your family connections?" Barbara asked.

"Oh, no. In fact, they were surprised when I told them," Francie responded, awaiting the comment that inevitably followed.

"For the few people who don't know, we should explain that your father was the legendary singer, Sonny Lewis," Barbara added.

"No, I'm afraid that's wrong," Francie said as she stole a look past the cameras.

"I beg your pardon," asked the surprised newscaster, looking at her note cards. Francie took a deep breath and plowed ahead. "That's what most people think, but it's not true."

"Oh," Walters said, raising an eyebrow. She knew that if she just let the silence hang there, her subject would nervously spill all, and she sensed there was a major story about to happen.

"Yes, my mother *is* Lavinia Lewis, and she was married to Sonny. He loved me like a daughter, but he wasn't my biological father. People just assumed that I was his daughter, and we never bothered to correct them."

"Are you in contact with your real father?" the reporter asked.

"Yes, although I want to make it clear that Sonny was also my real father, in every other sense of the word. He loved and treated me as if I was his own flesh and blood. Even I didn't know otherwise until a few years ago. I grew up with a loving extended family, who, thank Jesus, have been very supportive of me, and of my decision to be open about this." Francie took a deep breath. It was now or never. "My real father is Frankie Kaye."

"Your father's partner?" asked an incredulous Walters. The interview had already gone past the allotted time, but she didn't care. She didn't want to stop now. The broadcaster knew that if they took even a brief break, the young woman would be hesitant to continue. She ignored the director's frantic gesturing and continued. "Frankie Kaye, the comedian, is your real father?"

Francie glanced over at her family and they were all smiling. She sensed that they too felt a great weight drop from their shoulders.

"Yes," she said. "I was raised by both my father and his wife and my mother and Sonny. I've always felt as if I had two full sets of parents. To me it didn't matter who my biological parents were, I loved everybody equally, and felt that love in return."

"But, why the pretense?" asked the interviewer, knowing full well the answer she would get.

"My parents felt that most people weren't ready to accept interracial couples, much less the children of such a union."

"And you think America is ready now," Walters smiled.

"No, I don't," Francie replied. "Frankly, I don't really care. I just didn't want to continue living a lie. I am a devout Christian, and lying is a sin. When I was younger, I never had to lie; I truly thought that Sonny Lewis was my father. I still think of him that way. But, now that I'm getting so much attention because of my role in *Roots*, people are crediting my singing ability to Sonny Lewis, so I had to set the record straight."

"I have to say that I admire your honesty," Walters replied. She knew it was time to wrap things up; she could only string the interview along so much before a commercial break had to occur. "With your career just taking off, aren't you afraid of negative repercussions?"

"No," said Francie matter of factly. "Because my performance in *Roots* will be my first and last acting job. I think the Lord has other plans for me. I'm going back to work for my church and spread the word of God."

"Thank you," was all the stunned reporter could think of to say in response.

"Bless you," said Francie as she looked over at her family. They were all smiling at her.

CHAPTER 64

The green room at NBC Studios in Rockefeller Center, 8:45 a.m.

Francie hugged her father, her real father. He could feel her trembling in his arms. For all her bravado a few minutes ago, she was still a frightened young lady. He looked over at Lavinia and Rochelle, who gazed back at him and Francie. The feeling of love and respect was palpable. Only Richie, sitting on a threadbare couch on the other side of the room, didn't seem to share their . . . what was the feeling? An odd mixture of relief, fear and joy. He was still stewing over the porno, wondering how much publicity it would get. He was worried that he would shame his family and wondered how the other family members would react when they found out.

Francie walked across the room and sat next to her brother, taking his hand and stroking it. "Richie, relax, everything will be okay," she soothed.

"You don't understand," he said, a catch in his voice choking off all other communication.

"Yes, I do," she said putting her arm around his shoulders. She turned to her parents, "Can you all wait outside for a minute? I want to talk with Richie in private." After they left, she pulled a chair over to face Richie. "Don't you think I know what's worrying you?" she asked.

He looked up at her with tears in his eyes, "No, you don't. I'm not worried about what you just said. I'm glad it's out in the open. It's just that . . ." he stammered, not knowing how to tell his devoutly religious sister about his shameful experience.

"I know about the movie," she said calmly.

He stared up at her, his jaw moving up and down, but no words emanating from his lips. Finally he choked out, "Oh no! Have you seen it?"

"No! Of course not," she replied. Then she smiled, "Like I want to see my brother doing that! I know the whole story, Dad told me."

"I'm so ashamed," he said.

"You shouldn't be," she answered. "You didn't do anything wrong. Sure, you're embarrassed, who wouldn't be? But you don't have to worry about it anymore."

"What are you talking about?" he asked incredulously. "When the press hears about this . . ."

"They won't," she reassured them. "Uncle Jack has seen to that. He's a very powerful agent you know. He has incredible connections."

"But how?"

"Since the company was trying out that new, what's it called? Betamax? Well, they had only distributed a copy or two to a few stores in New York. Most of those have been taken care of. There are one or two still circulating, that we couldn't track down, but I wouldn't worry too much."

"But what if the press finds out? It will embarrass the family," he worried.

"I think the press is going to be pretty busy with the bombshell I just dropped," she smiled. "Even if they do discover the film, it will be swept aside by the news we just let loose."

"We?' Richie asked.

"The idea of how to tell the family story was Uncle Jack's," she explained. "He made deals with the few members of the press who knew about the video. Dad and I each agreed to give some exclusive interviews, and in return, they promised to forget about the movie.

"But, this could kill your career," Richie said. "I can't let you do that. Even if you don't want to act, you still won't be able to sing if this becomes news."

"Who says I can't?" Francie replied. "All of the stuff with *Roots* helped me realize that. I've decided I don't want to have all the attention and lack of privacy that comes with fame. I will be perfectly happy to just sing in the choir and do church work. You can go and become the famous musician in the family." She smiled at him, "After all, it's in your genes."

He didn't know what to say, so he just hugged her. There was a knock on the door and Frankie poked in his head. "I hate to interrupt, but we do have to get Francie to the Liberty Island. They want to do a sound check at 10:30."

Francie and Richie stood up together, holding hands.

"So, everything's okay?" Frankie asked. When they both nodded, he put an arm around each of them and they headed towards the door.

CHAPTER 65

A pair of adjoining suites in the Plaza Hotel—10:00 a.m.

The kids sat on Jen's lap as she read them a story. Although she loved being an aunt, she felt a slight stab of regret that she and Bruce hadn't gotten a chance to have kids of their own. She smiled at the idea, thinking about the hellions they'd be if they took after either Bruce or her.

Jon came in from his suite and looked at his sister. She looked so domestic; no one would ever guess that she was becoming one of the most influential political figures of her generation. "Okay kids, Mommy has got your bath ready. Go see her, 'cause we've got to get going soon."

The kids gave their aunt a hug and dashed off. Jen looked after them wistfully. Jon smiled at her. "Your kids would have been incredible."

"Hey, it's not like I'm too old to have them yet," she mock pouted. "Don't put me out to pasture."

"I know you," he replied sitting next to her. "You wouldn't have kids unless you could be the best mother ever. I just don't see you staying at home and baking cookies. You like to get in the middle of things too much."

"I still miss Bruce so much," Jen sighed and leaned against her brother's shoulder. Just being next to Jon gave her a feeling of peace. It was as if there was part of her missing when she wasn't with him. They remained like that for a few minutes, until they heard Ani enter. Then they turned their heads in unison.

"You two look exactly the way you did the first day I met you," she smiled. "I remember your father taking me to your room. You were standing side by side, playing with a dollhouse. When your father and I entered, you both turned simultaneously and smiled identical smiles."

"I remember," laughed Jen. "Jon, do you remember that?"

Jon recalled. "I do remember. I thought that the pretty lady looked so nice."

Ani gazed at them and smiled. "I wish your mother and father had lived long enough to see you two honored like this. They would both have been so proud."

They were silent for a moment before Jon spoke. "Ani, I need to tell you something, something I haven't talked about with anyone except Keiko and Jen. I need to tell you, because I'm going to write about it in my next book."

Ani and Jen sat on the sofa; Jon sat on the coffee table across from them and held both their hands in his.

"Jon," Jen started, "If this is what I think it is, whatever you decide, I'll support you and be proud to be your sister."

Jon breathed a sigh of relief and turned toward Ani. "Ani, I don't know how to explain this to you. It's not something I'm ashamed of, but it is . . . rather unusual," he stammered. "I want you to know that if you have a problem with it, I won't write the book. I'll just forget it."

"What is it?" Ani asked. "I can't imagine anything that you could do to make me want to stop you from writing what you want to write."

Jon took a deep breath and plowed right into his revelation. "I like to dress up in women's clothes," he explained. "Not out in public or anything. It's something I do in private," he looked at her, searching for a clue in her eyes.

Ani exhaled deeply. "Oh, is that all?" she giggled. "Jon, I've known about that since you were a teenager. Frankly, I could care less. If it makes you happy and it doesn't hurt anyone. I assume that Keiko is all right with it?"

"Yes," responded a befuddled Jon.

"Then whose business is it?" she smiled. "If you want to write about it, I'm certain that you'll do it tastefully. I'm with Jen. Whatever you decide, I love you and support you. Don't worry about it another second. Now, can I go help Keiko get those lovely grandchildren of mine ready?"

Jon and Jen turned to each other and wide smiles broke out across their faces.

CHAPTER 66

The Dakota—noon

Cilla removed the sleep mask from her eyes and crawled out of bed. Mornings had always been the worst for her. Like mother, like daughter, in that respect. The difference was that Cilla knew it was merely a case of low blood sugar that caused her to feel as if she had been dragged behind a truck. Rosie had always assumed it was the result of her sleeping pills and would pop a bunch of Benzedrine pills. Cilla knew that a cup of coffee and some fruit would do the trick just as well.

She slipped on her robe and made her way for the breakfast nook where Marguerite, her Dominican assistant, would have a carafe of coffee, a chocolate chip scone, and copies of *Daily Variety* and *The New York Times* waiting.

If Rosie had been irresponsible when it came to money matters, Cilla more than compensated with her financial savvy. She had invested her earnings well, mostly in real estate, and was quite secure. Her only risky investment had been going into partnership with a friend who wanted to open a store on Sunset Boulevard. Cilla's financial advisor had warned her against the venture, but she had faith in her friend's concept. A store that sold cookies, not just any cookies, but his own secret chocolate chip recipe. Since the total investment was only $10,000, and she lived well within her means, Cilla could afford it. Her investment in Famous Amos Cookies proved to be a smart move.

Years of taking care of Rosie had served Cilla well. She kept a tight rein on her life. She never wanted to be homeless, as her mother had been in her later years. Oh, Rosie was never out on the street, but going from hotel to hotel was no way to ground yourself. A person needed a place to call home. Cilla had two places, a small beach house in Malibu, and this two-bedroom co-op overlooking Central Park, where she spent most of her time, both of which were paid for. The trust fund she had established could easily handle all the expenses related to the two homes for at least 50 years. She limited her staff to Marguerite, who traveled with her, and a housekeeper for each home; all three trustworthy people who understood her need for privacy.

Even during her wild years with Allen, there was never any gossip in the press about her. Well, there was some gossip, most of it hinting that Cilla was blind to the fact that both the men in her life had been gay, and somehow, that was related to a father fixation. She chose to ignore the armchair psychiatrists and, since she didn't comment on it, the talk soon died down and the press moved on to someone who made bigger headlines. The worst she had ever read about herself was that she was a workaholic and a perfectionist. That kind of reputation, she did not mind one bit.

Cilla sipped her coffee and looked out over the trees lining the perimeter of Central Park. She could tell that it was a scorcher by the way the people dragged through the streets and the homeless people took refuge in the shade of the trees. She hoped it would cool down in time for tonight's performance. She glanced at the clock, it was nearly one and Bobby was due in about half an hour for a final run through of the medley she'd be performing.

"Marguerite," she called as she headed toward the small office off the kitchen. "Is everything all set for today?" The handsome woman stuck her head around the doorway and arched an eyebrow at her employer. Marguerite was probably the most efficient woman Cilla had ever known. She was asking, more to reassure herself than to check up on the woman. "I'm certain that it is, but would you run through everything for me, please?"

Marguerite carried her note pad as she entered the room. At nearly six feet tall, she dwarfed Cilla as she joined her at the breakfast nook. She sat across the table from her, pulled a pencil from her tightly coiled bun, and checked off each item as she recited it to Cilla.

"Mister Bobby will be here shortly. You are scheduled to rehearse with him until three. You are expected at the performance site for your sound check and tech run-through at five-thirty. You are not needed again until seven. I have arranged for a car to pick you up after your rehearsal here and take you to the dock where the ferry will be waiting. I will have everything ready in your trailer behind the stage. I have your clothes for tonight ready and hanging in your closet," she looked over her pad at Cilla who was about to speak. "I have already installed the heavy duty perspiration shields in the dress, and will bring both the dress and its duplicate to your dressing room at the site."

Cilla's perspiration problem was the bane of her existence. The least amount of physical exertion would cause buckets of sweat to pour out of her body. The trait became apparent when she first appeared on Broadway with her mother. Cilla remembered going through a particularly demanding rehearsal that her mother had sailed through, looking fresh as a daisy. Cilla, on the other hand, was dripping puddles onto the floor.

Cilla had stared at her mother in awe and asked, "How do you do all this work without breaking a sweat?"

"Darling, don't say sweat," Rosie gently chided her. "Horses sweat, gentlemen perspire, ladies glow."

"Well," Cilla responded, "I'm glowing like a pig."

After a number of visits to some of the city's top doctors, all anyone could figure out was that she had an incredibly active metabolism, and once she got it revved up, there was nothing to do but let it work its way out. Many of the doctors had suggested some drugs, but Cilla refused. She'd rather sweat than rely on drugs, a method Rosie could not comprehend.

Over the years, Cilla's fans began to view it as an endearing trait. They felt that it was evidence that she was really going all out for them. Some of them even brought towels to her performances and held them up for her use. Cilla couldn't imagine why someone would want a towel infused with her sweat, but she long ago learned to accept it as a compliment. When performing at concerts she tried to have the temperature in the room set as cold as possible, but at an outdoor event she had to take her chances. Luckily she was only doing a ten-minute set at the end of the show, so she could perform, then duck into her dressing room before her "motor" kicked in too much. She would have plenty of time to change out her sopping wet outfit, shower and put on the dry copy of it during the fireworks display before she returned for the show's finale. With her trademark pixie cut, she didn't even have to worry about styling her hair. She could return to the stage looking fresh and exit before she started to perspire again.

"I have checked and they already have the air-conditioner running in your dressing room. It will be cooled to 65 degrees by the time you arrive." Marguerite confirmed.

Cilla smiled at the woman, "Marguerite darling, what would I do without you?" For the first time the Dominican's stern face cracked wide with a smile, revealing two rows of large, white teeth. As professional as she tried to be, Marguerite felt protective of her employer. As in control as Cilla always seemed to be, Marguerite knew that the star also needed someone to take care of her, someone with whom she could let down her guard. Marguerite had never said anything to Cilla, but she knew what it was like to live with an alcoholic parent. Marguerite had practically raised her younger sister and brother while their mother drank herself to death. Miss Cilla had been very generous, not only by paying Marguerite a substantial salary, but also by putting her sister and brother through college. Marguerite was devoted to Cilla.

"Miss Cilla," she offered as she rose to return to her office, "I'm sure that your mother would be very proud of you today."

"Thank you, Marguerite," Cilla sputtered, wondering how she knew that Cilla had been thinking of her mother at that very moment. The woman was uncanny. "By the way . . ." Cilla began.

"There's a fresh bottle of your special antiperspirant shampoo in your bathroom," she answered Cilla's question before it was even completed. "I had the pharmacist make it extra strong for tonight."

Cilla simply shook her head and smiled.

CHAPTER 67

Liberty Island 2:00 p.m.

G ina and Franco huddled together in the press tent looking over the various proof sheets for the photos she had shot so far. They had been up most of the night, screening the footage Franco had accumulated for his documentary and were a little bleary-eyed. Tonight's show was going to be their last chance to get shots they needed. They were particularly interested in the experimental program that paired established Teamsters with recent immigrants. It tied in perfectly with the theme celebrating the concept of America as a melting pot. It was to be the theme for the book and film.

Franco noticed a group of workers gathered near the stage and suggested that Gina get a few still shots while his cameraman shot some footage.

"I'd like to get a close-up of that muscular dark skinned man and the tall fair-skinned guy working together," Gina suggested. "Maybe even just their hands." As they neared the men, Gina noticed that even the fair-skinned guy was speaking Spanish. Neither of the workers appeared to be Teamsters. So, so much for the working together idea. One of the workers was peering under the stage as Gina and Franco approached. Upon hearing them, both men stood upright quickly, turning their attention to Gina.

Latin chivalry, Gina thought. Spanish or Italian, it didn't matter; the attitude toward women was the same. She didn't speak much Spanish, but Franco was fairly fluent. She hoped he would be able to explain what they wanted. After a few attempts at conversation, the men shook their heads and dispersed. Franco just looked at her and shrugged.

"I don't know what the problem is," Franco explained.

"Couldn't you understand each other?"

"They speak a South American dialect, but, no, comprehension wasn't the problem," Franco mused. "They just didn't want to be photographed."

Gina looked around and saw three workers hoisting a giant flagpole. She was thinking that maybe the men working on that project would be more receptive. Suddenly, a thought occurred to Gina. "Oh, my God," she muttered. "I can't believe it."

Franco put his arm around her, "Gina, what is it? Is something wrong?"

"No," she responded. "But looking at the men over there, I suddenly realized something. Franco, when we were screening all the raw footage last night, did you have a gnawing feeling that something was missing?"

"What means this gnawing?" he responded. His English was almost perfect, but he sometimes didn't get the idioms of the language.

"A feeling that keeps bothering you, but you can't figure out why," she explained.

"Yes!" he exclaimed. "That is exactly how I felt, that is why I kept looking at everything again and again."

"I've figured it out," Gina offered. "We don't have one picture of the American flag in any of your footage, or any of my photos!"

"How could we forget such a thing?" he gasped.

"Sometimes the most obvious omissions are the hardest to catch," she answered. "Luckily we'll have plenty of chances to include shots of the flag tonight."

"But, won't it seem strange to go the entire movie without one shot of the flag? I know that in my country the flag is the most important symbol of our government."

"Well," offered Gina, "We could stage some shots in the next few days, I suppose."

"I was hoping that we would be finished shooting tonight so that I could complete editing the picture before we got married," Franco moaned. "I don't know if I can wait, but I suppose I'll have to."

"Unless," Gina said thoughtfully.

"I love it when you get that look on your face," Franco smiled. "I see your genius at work."

"We could use a shot of the flag in the last frames of your film and on the last page of my book," she offered. "It would make it seem as if we held off with the expected on purpose."

"Of course," Franco shouted. "It will also help tie the book and the film together, give them a sense of continuity. Gina, Darling, you are brilliant!"

"Necessity is the mother of invention," she responded modestly.

"Speaking of which," Franco offered, "When you stopped talking so suddenly, I thought for a minute that you were going to tell me that you were pregnant," he laughed.

"Well, now that you mention it . . . ." Gina smiled slyly.

Franco stood stunned for a minute, then grabbed her in his arms and swung her around the small tent in which they were working. Gina was surprised that, until he lifted her, she hadn't thought about the eventual weight gain, and what's more, she didn't care.

CHAPTER 68

Greenwich Village 2:45 p.m.

Richie was in his room setting out his clothes for the celebration. Rochelle knocked on the door and poked her head in. "Frankie says that we need to leave in about half an hour. Will you be ready by then?"

"Yeah, no problem," Richie responded with a sigh. As much as he loved his sister Francie, he dreaded going out in public, especially to such a high profile event. Despite the reassurances he'd received, he was certain that someone in the press would say something.

"Honey, you seem so depressed lately. Is there anything I can do to help?" Rochelle asked as she sat on the edge of her son's bed, taking his hand. "You know that there's nothing that you can't tell me."

"Don't be so certain of that," Richie mumbled. He didn't know what made him feel worse, the fact that the porno movie was out there or waiting for the news to hit. He looked down at his mother. She looked so worried; he couldn't begin to imagine the pain he was causing her. Maybe she would not need to know what a fool he had been, but if the story ever got out, he'd feel awful if he didn't tell her first. Finally, he took a deep breath and began his story. "Mom, I did something I'm not very proud of . . . ."

Afterwards, his mother held him in her arms and stroked his hair. He should have known that she would have taken it all right. She'd never shown him anything but love and acceptance. He felt better for having told her. He wanted to stay where he was right now. He felt safe and protected. There was a knock at the door, then Frankie peeked in. One look and he knew exactly what had transpired.

"Sorry to bother you two and this isn't the best timing, I know," he apologized. "But Francie needs our help."

"What's wrong?" Richie asked jumping to his feet, practically knocking his mother over in the process.

"She just called from the island. The accompanist for the choir just came down with food poisoning," Frankie explained. "She wants to know if you can fill in for him."

Richie glanced at his watch, he had just five hours to get to the site of the celebration, rehearse with the choir and with Francie for her solo, and get dressed. "Of course I can. I only need to shower, shave and get dressed. Tell her I can be there in an hour."

"Tell her 45 minutes," offered Rochelle. "Honey you get showered and head over to the island. I'll press your tux and bring it over when I come by later. That will save you a little time."

"I'll call for a cab," Frankie said as he raced down to the phone to tell his daughter the news. He smiled. Perhaps this crisis would keep Richie's mind off of his problems.

CHAPTER 69

Liberty Island 4:00 p.m.

The ferry bringing the VIPs across from Manhattan docked at the pier. Jen was sitting inside the cabin area going over her speech with her assistant, Donna, when one of the Secret Service men assigned to protect her caught her attention.

"Yes," Jen snapped impatiently, then feeling guilty apologized. "I'm sorry; I guess I'm a little nervous about tonight."

"No need to apologize, Ma'am," the clone in the dark suit and glasses responded.

"I just wanted to let you know that we're ready to transport you to the holding area."

"Transport me to the holding area?" Jen chuckled. "You make me sound like a box of cargo."

The agent tried, but failed, to hide his smile. "I'm sorry Congressman, I mean, Mrs. Goodman," he corrected himself quickly knowing that Jen preferred not to be called by her official title. "I guess it did sound like that. We're just concerned about getting you to a safe area as quickly as possible. Perhaps I should have said that we're ready to take you to your dressing room."

"Don't worry about it," laughed Jen. She rose as Donna gathered all of the papers in her usually efficient manner. She reached for the small case containing her make-up and a change of clothes. Donna tried to protest. "Donna, I'm perfectly capable of carrying this." Jen had had a hard time adjusting to the fact that as a public official, she couldn't be seen struggling with a briefcase, purse, and whatever else she needed to conduct business. She was aware of how important it was for her to look calm and collected whenever she was in public, but in more private moments she preferred to carry her own things. Her father had stressed in her that just because they were famous and well off was no reason to treat other people like servants.

Jen thought about her father a lot recently. She would have liked for him to live to see this, his radical daughter asked by a Republican president to speak at such a patriotic event. Jen was certain that asking her to speak was a ploy by the Republicans to look good. Asking the widow of the left wing radical Congressman made them appear open-minded.

A widow. Every once in a while she managed to let herself forget that Bruce was dead, that they weren't a couple of upstart kids trying to bring about change in the Establishment. She didn't feel any different now than she had in her youth.

Sometimes when she looked in the mirror, she was shocked to discover that a mature woman looked back at her.

Donna came over from a group of people with whom she had been conferring. She walked silently next to Jen as they waited outside the trailer that would serve as Jen's office, dressing room and, Jen chuckled, her holding area. A second Secret Service agent exited the trailer and nodded to the first. Only then did they allow Jen to enter. As soon as they were both inside, Jen turned to her assistant and asked, "What's with all the security? I don't usually rate two agents."

"They're just taking extra precautions because the president will be here, and he'll have the Chilean ambassador with him. There have been some protests at his other appearances," she explained.

"I guess that makes sense," said Jen hanging up the garment bag she'd been carrying. She looked at the paper Donna was holding, "What's that?"

"They've revised the schedule a little bit," her assistant explained, barely glancing at the sheet. Jen was certain that Donna had memorized all the changes within seconds of receiving it. "They want to move your speech back about twenty minutes. Then, after you've finished speaking they want you to introduce to next performer. I told them that I would check with you before giving them an answer."

It sounds fine with me, why would it matter?" Jen asked as she laid out the contents from her make-up case on the table before her.

"Mrs. Goodman, you are a Congresswoman. There is a level of protocol," she answered as she stared at Jen's make-up. "You needn't bother with laying out your things; I can take care of that for you."

"Donna, please relax, I don't mind doing this, in fact I find it rather soothing," Jen reassured the woman. "Is there really that big a problem with me speaking a few minutes later?"

"No, not really," Donna responded. "I do think, however, that it's inappropriate for a woman of your standing to introduce a singer."

Jen knew that there were times when Donna's political instincts were sharp. And, while Jen would even happily introduce a performing seal act, there were times, she now knew, she had to say no. "All right," she sighed in resignation. "Tell them that I don't mind speaking later in the program, but that they're going to need to get someone else to do the introduction."

Donna picked up the phone from the table and dialed the number listed for the show's coordinator. "Please tell Mr. Kopelson that Representative Goodman agrees to deliver her speech at the later time, but will not be able to introduce Ms. Best."

"Hold it a minute," Jen interrupted. "They want me to introduce Cilla Best?" Donna nodded to her. "Tell them I will be happy to do it."

Donna relayed the information, hung up the phone and looked at her boss quizzically.

"Cilla was my camp counselor when I was a kid," Jen explained. "I haven't seen her in nearly 20 years. Of course I'll introduce her. What a kick!"

CHAPTER 70

Liberty Island 5:15 p.m.

Cilla got off the ferry and headed straight for her air-conditioned trailer. Marguerite had arrived an hour earlier and had made certain that the thermostat was set at 65°; Cilla breathed a sigh of relief as she entered the trailer's welcoming coolness. It would be hours before the sun set, the humidity was incredibly high and it was at least 90° in the shade, or would be. Actually there was no shade on Liberty Island. Cilla cursed the weather and took the towel Marguerite handed her as she began stripping out of her already soaked clothes. She then wrapped a light cotton robe around her and collapsed into a chair. "Marguerite, can't we make it any cooler in here?" she pleaded.

"Now Miss Cilla, you'll be fine in a few minutes. Just take a few deep breaths. That will help your metabolism slow down," she calmed her employer as she handed Cilla a tall glass of iced herbal tea.

Cilla unwrapped a piece of chocolate and settled back in her chair. She found that the most relaxing thing in the world for her was to pop a piece of rich dark chocolate into her mouth and focus on feeling it dissolve. Within five minutes she was composed and ready to focus on the night ahead. Thank God for chocolate, she thought. The confection was her drug of choice, and one pleasant side effect of her over active metabolism was that she could eat as much as she wanted and not gain an ounce. She absentmindedly unwrapped a second piece as she reviewed the lyrics for the medley she was performing.

Gina and Franco were prowling around the island. Their backstage passes allowed them unlimited access. As they scouted for the best locations for their cameraman, Gina kept an eye out for that one perfect shot that she could use for the conclusion of her book. She and the show's producer were also reviewing the audience seat assignments. Gina was particularly interested in where the president was sitting. Although she was not a huge fan of President Ford, she felt his wife Betty was an incredible woman. Her own feelings aside, she wanted to get a candid photograph of the two of them sometime during the evening. As the director pointed out their seats, she felt her heart rise. If she could get the right angle, she'd have a shot of them with the Statue of Liberty in the background. She thanked the director and walked over to where Franco was conferring with his crew.

"I think I have the spot picked out for my shot of President and Mrs. Ford,"
she offered. Gina pointed to the general area of their seats. "If I can get low enough,
I can have a terrific shot. I'm going to go scout out the area near the front of the
stage."

"Be careful," Franco urged. "I don't want anything to happen to our little
package," he said as he patted her stomach.

"It's a little early for that," she laughed as she bounded down the stairs and
scooted around to the front of the stage. She found that if she knelt down low
enough, and laid on her stomach with her legs half under the stage she could almost
get the shot. As she practiced, the shorter of the two men she had seen earlier came
running over.

"Senora! No, No!" he said as he attempted to pull her to her feet. He kept
jabbering on in Spanish, although Gina could only make out a few words.

Suddenly a voice behind her said, "Perhaps I can help, I speak Spanish. You're
Ms. Ferrara, aren't you? I'm Miss Best's assistant, Marguerite. She's mentioned you
often."

"You are a lifesaver, Marguerite," replied Gina. "Would you please explain to
this man that all I want to do is slide under here a little, so that I can see if it will
get me a good shot of the president later?"

Marguerite and the man discussed the matter for a few minutes; the normally
collected Marguerite getting a little worked up in her discussion with him. Finally,
she turned toward Gina and said, "I'm sorry Miss Ferrara, he insists that it is not
possible. He says that there are too many wires connected below the stage and you
might disconnect one."

"It didn't seem like there was much under there," said Gina as she tried to lift
the skirt of the stage to get a better look.

The man grabbed her hand and barked something at her.

"He says . . . ." Marguerite began.

"I'm sorry I couldn't be of more assistance," the woman offered. "I don't think
Miss Cilla knows that you are here. I know she'd love to see you."

Gina saw Franco approaching; she waved him over and introduced him to
Marguerite. After chatting for a few moments Marguerite excused herself. "Well, I
must get these papers to the show's director for Miss Cilla. She's in the third trailer
from the left."

Franco and Gina headed towards the trailer. Suddenly, Gina stopped. She turned
to Franco and said, "I should warn you, it's probably going to be very cold in Cilla's
trailer," and she went on to explain everything to Franco as they walked up the steps
of the trailer and she knocked at the door.

Cilla opened the door a crack and the hot air quivered as it met the cold front emanating from the trailer. Cilla popped her head out, saw Gina, and gave out a screech. She dragged them inside and within minutes it was if the two childhood friends had never been apart.

CHAPTER 71

A barge off Liberty Island 6:30 p.m.

R ichie had just finished doing a final run through with the choir. Luckily, he had always been a quick study and the group's regular accompanist had marked his charts clearly. It only took a couple of tries before he got the number down. The choir's second song was an a cappella number, so all that was left for him to do was practice with Francie. Since they had performed together all of their lives, he didn't anticipate any problems.

"Francie, you look tired, why don't you rest a bit and then we'll run through your number in about half an hour, okay?" he offered.

Francie looked relieved. Although she tried to act blase about it, he knew her well enough to know how rattled she got before any performance, much less on national television and in front of the President and First Lady. "Thanks, Richie," she whispered, saving her voice for later that night. "I need to go check on my dress anyway." She headed towards the women's dressing area.

Richie decided to take a walk around the island. He liked the warm air and needed to clear his head. His folks would be arriving shortly with his tuxedo, and after he changed, he'd need to stay on the barge until it was time to perform. He didn't like to feel confined.

As he walked around the perimeter of the island he thought about the discussion he had had with his mother earlier. He didn't know many gay folks, but he knew enough to know that he was really lucky to have such an accepting family. He was so lost in thought that he was startled when he came upon two guys standing behind a bush.

He must have startled them as much as they startled him, for all three of them jumped. Richie saw that they were sharing a cigarette and guessed that it was a joint. He didn't need to be around that, especially with all the government agents on the island. Richie just smiled at the duo, excused himself and continued walking. It was not until he was a few yards away, and one called after him in a thick accent, that it even registered that the guys had been speaking Spanish.

"Excuse me," the taller of the two called after him. "My friend and I were wondering what you are doing in the show."

He sounded suspicious of Richie, but Richie figured security was tight. He hadn't had a chance to be briefed on all the rules, maybe he was somewhere off limits. "Oh,

I play the piano," Richie offered, looking at the two men. The shorter of the two had an incredible body. Compact, yet well muscled. He wore a white tank top and a pair of tight jeans, which left little to the imagination. "I'm sorry if I'm not supposed to be here. I just needed a little air. I'll head back to the stage."

The muscular man noticed Richie's glance and rubbed his hand across his crotch suggestively. The two men exchanged a few words in Spanish, then the taller of the two again spoke, "My friend says he thought you were a movie star. You are very handsome."

Richie smiled at the man, "Thank you. I must be going," he said as he turned to leave. Richie was still a little wary about men who offered compliments. He waved as he began walking away.

"Please wait," the tall one said. "My friend would like to talk to you some more." The short man came alongside Richie and began stroking his arm. He said something to the tall man, who turned to Richie and asked, "Do you speak any Spanish?"

"No, I'm sorry, not a word," Richie answered. He began to feel very uneasy. Maybe these guys were doing something wrong. He looked around and did not see anyone. It was then that he noticed something metallic near the bushes where the men had been before Richie disturbed them. Richie averted his eyes.

He did not really care if they had a bong, or a hash pipe. He had plenty of trouble on his own, and didn't need more. He tried to act nonchalant as he left. He heard one of the men say the word "Maricon". Richie didn't speak Spanish but he knew that whatever it meant, it was not a compliment.

He continued walking, looking over his shoulder to see if he was being followed. He didn't feel safe until he could see the ramp leading to the choir's barge.

CHAPTER 72

Liberty Island, backstage 7:55

Jon and Keiko sat on the sofa in Jen's trailer. Ani was reading a story to the kids while Jen poured them all a drink.

"This is it, Kid," she said handing Jon a glass of champagne. "After today your life won't be the same."

"Thanks," Jon replied. He looked at Keiko lovingly. "Are you certain that you're all right with this?"

"Jon, whatever makes you happy, makes me happy," his wife answered. "It is going to be a little rough. It's not like you're just anybody. You and Jen are the ones with the well known faces, you're the one who's going to need to answer the tough questions," she looked at Jen. "I can walk down the street and nobody knows who I am. After a few weeks, it will all fade away and our lives will go on as they always have."

"Jen, this could be the end of your career in politics, are you really ready for that?" Jon asked.

"I've thought about that," Jen replied. "I even talked about it with Donna," she said nodding toward her assistant, and her closest confidant. "She pointed out that the folks who will have a problem with this, who might not vote for me when I run for office, wouldn't have voted for me anyhow. When I asked Bella Abzug for her advice, she agreed. I'm fine with it professionally. Personally, I just want to say that you're my brother and anything you want to do, I'm there for you."

Ani got the kids busy with a project and joined the conversation, "Jon, you know we all love you and support you. I can't say I understand why you feel you need to tell the world about this, but if you do it, I know you'll do it with dignity."

Keiko stood up and raised her glass, "I'd like to offer a toast to my husband. To the sweetest, strongest and most honorable man in the world."

They clinked glasses, finished their champagne silently, and then prepared to head out of the trailer to take their seats. Ani, Keiko, and the kids would be sitting in the audience. Jen and Jon were in the "green room", the backstage holding area, awaiting their assigned times on stage.

Donna left Jen's side for a moment and walked over to Jon just before he was set to go on stage. She shook his hand, leaned close and whispered, "I gave the sign language interpreter copies of both of your poems. He's a friend of mine and he'll be ready to interpret whichever poem you decide to go with." Jon was taken aback for a second, then looked at Donna's smiling face, "I'd do anything for your sister. All she wants is for you to be happy." Then she straightened his lapel, and scooted him onto the stairs for the stage. "I believe they want you in the wings now."

CHAPTER 73

Liberty Island, on stage 8:22

W hen the lights came up on the stage the choir was already in place. They looked regal, their new purple choir robes adorned with strips of African fabric on each lapel. As Richie played the opening chord and vamped, the choir began to sway and chant softly. Miss Peaches stepped forward. She positively beamed as she spoke to the assembled crowd and to the millions of people watching on television. "When I was a little girl growing up in Alabama, my biggest wish was to one day meet the president. I thank the Lord that He gave me the opportunity to not only meet you, Sir, but to share with you the gift that I have been given," she indicated the choir. "The gift we have all been given. We salute you, and this great nation on the occasion of the Bicentennial." Miss Peaches turned to face the choir and indicated to Richie that he should begin the melody.

The choir's voices rose as one and began to sing *The Battle Hymn of the Republic*. Richie and Francie stole a glance at each other. Francie was smiling broader than she had ever done in her life. Richie could tell that, for her, being one of the joined voices gave her the greatest pleasure. When she sang her solos, she was tense. She enjoyed singing, no matter what, but she was happiest to be out of the glare of the spotlight. Richie wondered if his parents could see Francie from where they were sitting. As he played, he scanned the audience, hoping to be able to spot his family.

They were in the last row of the first section, right on the aisle. Frankie's and Francie's celebrity status made certain they weren't relegated to the bleachers. They were all beaming, his Mom, Frankie and Lavinia. Tears of joy were streaming down Lavinia's face as she held Frankie's hand. He leaned over and kissed her on the cheek, the first time he had done so in public. Richie looked back at Francie, who was so caught up in the rapture of her singing, that she did not even see the moment. They were nearing the end of the song and soon Miss Peaches would introduce Francie's solo. Richie glanced to the side of the stage to make certain that her mic was set.

That's when Richie saw the Latino man who had wanted to speak with him earlier. He was standing there off to the side of the stage, just staring at Richie. Richie looked back at the sheet music. The notes appeared to swim about on the page. Only his years of training kept him from screwing up his performance. He looked over to see if the man was still there and he could swear that the guy winked at him and licked his lips.

Richie broke out in a cold sweat. What was the guy going to do? Had he followed him? He was wearing the standard coveralls that all the technicians wore. He even had on what appeared to be an official stagehand's ID. He had not been wearing any of those earlier today, Richie was certain of that. He remembered noticing his huge muscles in the tight t-shirt. Richie took the choir to their rousing finish, but he barely heard Miss Peaches introducing Francie. He looked back to see what the man was doing and he was gone. Richie glanced around the stage area and could not spot him. Maybe he had imagined it.

Miss Peaches was just wrapping up her introduction, "Yes, indeed, she will certainly make a name for herself with her appearance in *Roots*. We all saw her grow up on Sonny Lewis' television show. Ladies and Gentlemen, Francie Lewis Kaye."

Francie stepped up to the microphone; "I'd like to dedicate this song to my parents, Lavinia and Frankie Kaye, my Aunt Rochelle and my brother Richie." She then looked heavenward and added, "This one's for you, Dad."

The applause was thunderous. There was no doubt that many of the folks there had seen or heard of her appearance that morning on *The Today Show*. If the family had any doubts about Francie's decision to tell the family story, they were dissipated by the show of support they received that night.

CHAPTER 74

Liberty Island, on stage 9:10

Jon strode onto the stage as Neil Simon was introducing him. Neil and his father had done a couple of plays together, so he understood the producer's reasoning in his choice, but Jon had never met the man until he shook hands with him on stage. In fact, most of the introduction had centered on Neil's recollections of his father, and how it made him feel like an old man to be introducing the son of one of his contemporaries as the nation's poet laureate.

Jon felt a little sheepish and made some lame comment as he took the microphone. It was a pun about Neil Simon and his father being an odd couple. As soon as the words came out of his mouth he forgot them, but they must have been humorous, for the audience chuckled good-naturedly. That eased Jon's discomfort somewhat.

"Contrary to popular myth, poets do not sit around in coffee houses composing lines of verse. When asked to read a piece of my work to commemorate our country's Bicentennial, I looked through my files and just couldn't find anything I liked that spoke about our country. As many of you may know, I lived in Japan for a number of years. I love Japan and have written a great deal about my life there; the people, the culture, my beautiful wife, even my children. But I have written little about what I value most in America, my home.

He took a deep breath and began speaking the words that would change his life. "What I most value in America is the belief in personal freedom. The belief that the rights of the individual hold as much importance as the rights of society. Maintaining that balance has not always been an easy task, and there are many that are threatened by what they do not know, by what seems strange to them. However that is what makes America strong, resilient and unique.

"Our citizens come from all over the globe, with customs and beliefs that may, at first, appear foreign to us, but with time, those customs are adopted as accepted practices, not just for the immigrants who brought those practices with them, but for all of us. Each culture adds a piece to the mosaic that is America. That's what makes our country great. The fact is we are all a little strange in our own way. I may not understand the way that you practice your religion, but I will fight for your right to do so. You may not agree with what I believe, but I have no doubt that true Americans will fight for the right of their neighbors to express their beliefs, practice their religion, preach their politics, to live their lives in a way that brings them peace and joy."

Jon looked out at the crowd and he saw Keiko, the kids and Ani in their seats and suddenly everything seemed clear to him. As he continued the sign language interpreter kept right with him, "I thought about that and how our founding fathers had made certain to address the need for personal freedom in terms so strong and poetic that it would be presumptuous of me to try to top them. Who could do better than 'All men are created equal, endowed with certain unalienable rights and among these are life, liberty, and the pursuit of happiness.'?"

The audience applauded enthusiastically, as Jon turned to exit he saw Jen standing in the wings with tears in her eyes. Her assistant Donna handed her a tissue, she blotted her eyes and strode onto the stage to join her twin brother. She took his arm and brought him with her to the podium.

"Well, who'd have ever thought that the two of us, Hollywood's wild ones would be here?" The audience chuckled and Jen continued. "Let's give my brother a hand. I am so proud of him." Jon stepped aside from the podium and gave a little bow; some of the habits he picked up in Japan were hard to break. He walked to the stage exit and heaved a sigh of relief as soon as he was backstage. Cilla Best stood there waiting to make her entrance.

"That was great, Kid," she said.

Jon stood there for a minute waiting for Jen to finish her introduction. She was telling a story about the time that they had gone to summer camp and Cilla had been one of their counselors. He looked over at Cilla. She had shut out the world and was gearing up for her performance. It was as if she had a dimmer switch installed inside her and someone was slowly turning the lights up. The change was breathtaking. Then she flew on stage as Jen passed by her.

Jen hugged Jon as she stepped off stage, "That was great. You know, in all these years I don't think I've ever heard you read one of your own poems."

"I don't usually," Jon responded. "It's very painful for me. Was I okay out there?"

"You were fine," she responded. "So you decided against telling everyone, or did it just frighten you? Either way, I think you did a great job."

Jon looked at his sister, "You know when it came to the moment of truth, I suddenly realized that I had already told everyone that mattered, so what was to be gained? I don't even think I'm going to write the book of poetry about it. I think that instead I'm going to write the bio of Dad that my publisher's been pushing for. That is, if you don't mind."

"I think it would be a great idea. How about if we go get your wife and kids and Ani and grab some dinner after the finale? I'm starved!" She put her arm around his waist and they walked toward their trailer. They spotted Gina heading around the side of the stage.

"That woman with the camera looks familiar," said Jon indicating Gina.

"That's Gina Ferrara," replied Jen. "Gina Ferrara?" Jon was puzzled. The name meant nothing to him.

"Yeah, she was a counselor at summer camp. She and Cilla were best friends. Remember her father was the one with that silly puppet?"

"That's Angelina Ferrara? She used to be such a stick. She's incredibly voluptuous. Wow! She looks great now, and I love that outfit."

"You would notice that," laughed Jen. "She's got her camera. No doubt she's heading toward the front of the stage to get some shots of Cilla."

"Are they still friends?" asked Jon.

"I don't know, but Gina is some sort of hot shot photographer now," Jen chuckled. She almost tripped as two of the tech crew went running past her.

CHAPTER 75

Liberty Island on stage 9:30

Cilla was on stage selling it like there was no tomorrow. Her hair was plastered to her scalp; the sweat was pouring down her back. Richie had managed to hang around back stage waiting to catch a glimpse of her close up. He didn't know what it was that made him such a fan. He knew that she was not really that great of a singer. If she had a range of much more than an octave, that would be pushing it.

She also had sloppy enunciation. Part of him cringed every time she said any word with the letter s. She always pronounced it "sh" and she had chosen to sing one of her mother's songs littered with the s sound, "I know you're shcared, caush you weren't prepared to fashe sho many people, but they're all your friendsh."

If you went strictly by technique, she wasn't even close to good, but she had a magical charisma. And, she was just working so damn hard, you had to love her. He chuckled to himself; he should have known he was gay when he put a poster of her on his bedroom wall when he was nine years old.

"Young man, I'm afraid that I'm going to have to ask you to move," Marguerite ordered as she came up behind Richie. "Miss Best will be making an exit from here and she needs the space clear. She's got a quick change to make and needs to be back on stage as soon as the fireworks are over."

"Of course, Ma'am," Richie responded. He turned to exit down the stairs, when he spotted the Latino who had been hanging around. He was with the other guy he had been with earlier in the day. Richie stepped back into the shadows. Something about the duo rubbed him the wrong way. He looked around. He was the only one in the area behind the stage. The tech crew were all in the wings or at control panels. With Cilla Best at the end of her performance, everyone was enthralled. Even if someone could hear him above the applause, most of the guards were up front keeping an eye on the President and First Lady. If these two tried something, Richie would be on his own, and now that the fireworks were starting, any cry for help would be drowned out.

He heard a noise behind him and saw Cilla and her assistant coming down the stairs. The Latinos heard them, too. They said something to each other in Spanish. Although he didn't understand them, something in their tone told him that he was in trouble. He turned to warn Cilla and her assistant to head back onto the stage when one of the guys grabbed him and pulled him down the short flight of stairs that he'd been standing on.

"I knew you'd be trouble," the one who spoke English muttered to Richie. The muscular one had Richie in a chokehold. The English-speaking slender one had a grip on Cilla and her assistant, his hands encircling their arms. The man who had Richie pulled out a gun with his free hand.

"I'm due on stage as soon as the fireworks are finished," Cilla said trying to shrug him off. "If I'm not ready someone will come looking for us."

"All of you keep quiet," he ordered as he tightened his grip on Cilla. He then barked something in Spanish to his accomplice.

Marguerite stiffened when she heard the man speak. The two men herded them into a corner while the short one held a gun on them. Marguerite whispered, "They've got a bomb planted under the front of the stage. They were waiting for everyone to be preoccupied watching the fireworks before they set it off. They're trying to kill the Chilean ambassador."

The muscular one looked at Richie with hatred in his eyes. "Maricon," he said as he spat at him.

Cilla stiffened at the epithet. She looked him in the eye and said, "That's enough! I'm calling security," and she took a step forward.

The tall one aimed the nozzle of the gun at Cilla and started to pull the trigger. Without thinking, Richie reached forward and knocked his arm. The gun went off and Cilla spun around before falling to the ground. There was a period of a few seconds where everyone stood still. They all looked at Cilla in shock.

"Hey, what's going on?" called one of the Secret Service men who were guarding Jen's trailer a few hundred feet away.

The two Latino men turned to flee, and Richie went after them.

"They've got a bomb set at the front of the stage," Marguerite called, as one Secret Service agent headed for the President's detail, while the second joined Richie in the chase. Marguerite knelt next to Cilla and began to apply pressure to the wound on Cilla's arm where the bullet had hit.

Richie was a lot taller than his muscled former captor and caught up to his muscle-bound prey in a few seconds. Richie reached out one of his long arms and grabbed the man by his hair. One tug and the terrorist fell backwards. His head crashed into the pavement and Richie was on him in a second, beating him senseless.

The Secret Service men pursued the taller man around the side of the stage. As the Latino neared the front of the stage, he ducked underneath it. One of the Secret Service men yelled, "He's got a bomb!"

The men on detail guarding the President and First lady had already gathered around them and the ambassador and ushered them out of the audience. The Secret Service men in pursuit split up and one went under the stage, while the other went around to the front.

During all of this Gina had been kneeling in front of the stage waiting to get a shot of the President with the fireworks and flag behind him. She was in an awkward position and couldn't get up immediately. As she started to stand and turn to run away, she saw the small skirt surrounding the stage move. She stopped momentarily and watched a head peek out from below the stage. Instinctively she pulled her camera out of harm's way, then raised it up and smacked the guy on the head. She wasn't sure if the sound she heard was the camera lens or his head cracking. The man collapsed at her feet.

Within seconds, a Secret Service agent had the culprit in handcuffs and was leading him away.

CHAPTER 76

Liberty Island backstage area 10:30 p.m.

The paramedics patched up Cilla's arm and suggested that she accompany them to the hospital.

"Am I in any immediate danger?" Cilla asked.

"No not really," responded one of them. "But you should have a doctor take a look at that. It may be only a flesh wound, but it could get infected."

"I promise I'll have my doctor take a look at it tomorrow," she charmed them. Marguerite began to usher them away.

"One last thing, Miss Best," asked one. "I hate to bother you at such a time, but could I have your autograph?"

Cilla stared at the embarrassed man, then burst out laughing. "Of course, Darling, but I really can't write very well now. He shot my writing arm. Marguerite, please get their addresses and I'll mail them something later." As Marguerite ushered the men out, Cilla sat on the steps next to Richie. "I think that I owe you my life, young man. Thank you."

Richie blushed. "You were so brave stepping forward like that."

"Not brave, stupid," Cilla admitted. "But, when I heard him call you a faggot, it just got me so angry, I acted without thinking."

"Is that what he said?"

"You mean I defended your honor, without you even knowing that you were being insulted?" Cilla began laughing uncontrollably.

Richie's family was being ushered backstage by the guards and entered just as Cilla started laughing. They were relieved that Richie was all right, but confused by Cilla's laughter. Francie knelt down next to her brother and held him tightly.

"You're a hero," Francie exclaimed. "There are a ton of press people out front waiting to talk to you."

"I didn't do anything, really" Richie protested.

"You saved my life," Cilla interrupted. "That son-of-a-bitch was going to shoot me and you just knocked the gun out of his hand."

"I did?" Richie asked. "I thought I just made him miss his shot."

"Why do you think that they ran?" Cilla asked. "They didn't have any power over us anymore."

Marguerite returned and helped Cilla stand up, "You need to go to your trailer and rest," she ordered.

"By the way," called Cilla as she walked away, "I liked your performance on stage, too. Give me a call. I'd love to work with you."

Richie looked up and beamed from ear to ear. "All this would almost be worth it if I got to work with Cilla Best."

Rochelle put her arms around Richie. Frankie and Lavinia sat on the steps. "I don't want to talk to the news people," Richie said. "I just want to go home."

"Your Uncle Jack is out front talking to them now," Frankie said. "I'll have him tell them we'll make a statement tomorrow. I guess you will be getting press coverage after all, Richie."

"Just a lot more positive than we expected," laughed Francie.

As Cilla walked up the steps of her trailer, she passed Jen as she walked with Ani, Jon, and his family. "Are you all right?" Jen asked Cilla.

"Yeah, the bullet just grazed me. It's no worse than some of the scrapes we got at Camp Ori-Pahs," Cilla joked. "It's a good thing that your Secret Service agents were around, though."

"Yeah," said Jen. "I've always thought that it was a waste of time to have them guard me. But, I guess you never know." Jen took her brother's hand. They had both changed from their dress clothes to jeans and work shirts. The Mason clan was all together as they headed for the ferry that would take them back to Manhattan.

"Thanks, again," Cilla offered. Marguerite shooed her inside the trailer and insisted that she rest.

Gina and Franco were waiting inside on the sofa, Gina was unwrapping a piece of chocolate from the bowl Cilla always kept handy. She popped it in her mouth and offered one to Cilla.

Her childhood friend took it, plopped down next to her and said, "What a night! All we need to make this a true reunion is for Koko the Clown to walk in."

"With his needle dick!" Gina offered. The two of them burst into laughter.